SOUTH BEACH *Cartel*
PART TWO

Melodrama Publishing
www.MelodramaPublishing.com

FOLLOW
NISA SANTIAGO

FACEBOOK.COM/NISASANTIAGO

INSTAGRAM.COM/NISA_SANTIAGO

TWITTER.COM/NISA_SANTIAGO

Order online at
bn.com, amazon.com, and
MelodramaPublishing.com

www.melodramapublishing.com

Library of Congress Control Number: 2018957341
ISBN-13: 978-1620780985

First Edition: December 2018

Printed in Canada

SOUTH BEACH *Cartel*
PART TWO

NISA SANTIAGO

PROLOGUE

September 2017

I'm ready," Apple said to a familiar ally on a burner phone. "We both knew that bitch was always living on borrowed time."

"You can't let this shit go, huh?"

"She wanted a war, so let's bring it to her fuckin' front door."

Cartier sighed. "We waited too long—allowed her operation to expand. I heard her and her brother Cane are dropping bodies all over the east coast. You really wanna fuck wit' that?"

Apple sighed and rolled her eyes. A lot had happened since Miami, but none of it changed the way she felt about exacting revenge. Citi was always at the forefront of her mind. That bitch had violated them in the worst way by stealing from them. She'd stolen everything they had while the Gonzales Cartel was on their asses—looking to kill each and every last one of them. Apple ended up broke and was forced to go on the run. She had to hide, and she hated to hide. She ended up in Maryland, had met Twin, and the rest was history.

"We've gone up against cartels, Cartier. You can't be fuckin' serious right now! I'm from Harlem and you're from Brooklyn. This bitch is from *Queens*." Apple's voice escalated when she said, "Queens," indicating it was the weakest borough.

She continued to clown Citi. "Queens bitches are soft like butter! You know that shit, Cartier, and don't act like you don't."

Cartier chuckled. "You know there are a couple of screws loose in that bitch's head, Apple. She's always been a little off—a young bitch lost. She murdered her moms and was fuckin' her stepdad. That bitch got issues."

Apple couldn't believe what she was hearing. Something was up. Cartier was one of the deadliest bitches she knew. She'd murdered her childhood friend off a simple hunch that turned out to be wrong. So everything she was saying was suspect to Apple.

"Bitch, stop playin'. You know you 'bout that life, so what's really good?"

Cartier sighed heavily, and said, "A'ight, to keep it one hundred wit' you, Head is coming home this year, and I want to travel back to the east coast from Seattle to see where we stand. I fucked up and lost him once. I don't wanna make that mistake again. I can't properly put this pussy down on him if I'm shooting my gun and dodging fuckin' bullets."

First Kola and now Cartier, Apple thought. Both bitches wanted to become housewives. She wasn't thrilled, but she understood. Being a wife just wasn't for her.

"You wanna pass up a chance at revenge to be boo'd up for the winter?" Apple mocked. "Yeah, bitch, it's cuffing season. I get it. Get your dick and forget about Bad Apple out here goin' to war alone. If something happens to me, then it's your fault. I always had your back. I was hoping that you would have mine."

Cartier's mood shifted into seriousness. "Apple, don't fuckin' play me like that. We've both seen too much death, and we've both been spared more times than we can count. How about you sit this one out?"

"It was a damn joke, Cartier," Apple countered. "Ain't shit gonna happen by that weak bitch's hands. If Citi was a real thorough bitch, she would have murdered us back in Miami when she was planning to take our fuckin' money. Instead, she leaves us alive to get at her. Citi is just a slut who only knows how to suck dick and take from muthafuckas. She's a dumb fuckin' ho, and dumb hoes become dead hoes."

"Don't underestimate her, Apple. Citi and Cane won't be easy to kill."

"Watch me!" Apple replied before she abruptly ended their call.

1

B e there in ten minutes." Apple hung up with her sister Kola feeling like she was going to throw up. She didn't like where things were going. Everything had changed. Kola wasn't the same hardcore bitch who didn't take shit from anyone. Kola sounded happy, but she had become domesticated. Apple would have never thought that her twin sister would become this docile fuckin' housewife, not to mention Kola and her man were babysitting and raising Eduardo's kids. It was sickening.

Eduardo apparently wasn't going to send his goons to murder Kola and Kamel as long as they took care of his Colombian children. It was a fair exchange, but the couple was still cautious. Eduardo was a murderous lunatic who was obsessed with Kola. They both knew that any day Eduardo wanted to have them killed, he wouldn't hesitate to give the order. It was a hell of a way to live, but they didn't have a choice.

After their wedding, Kola and Kamel moved into a beautiful home in an affluent neighborhood in Westchester County. The home was 5000 square feet of luxury, with a wrought iron fence, an in-ground pool, marble flooring, and sprawling manicured lawns. Of course, Kola was used to more, but this home was compliments of Eduardo.

What Apple didn't like was that Kamel had become Eduardo's bitch. He had accepted servitude to a drug kingpin instead of going out like a man. Apple felt that Kola deserved better. How could a man like Kamel live in the home his wife's ex-man bought for them?

Apple didn't give a fuck that Eduardo was in a foreign jail. In her eyes, Kamel had gotten lazy. He didn't want to hustle to earn a living for her sister and those kids. Apple had lost respect for the nigga. She felt his twin brother had more heart than he did.

But the main thing Apple cared about was her daughter. She finally allowed Kola to raise Peaches full time. Kola was the stable one with the home, the family, and the kids. Though Apple somewhat despised Kola's transformation into a housewife, it was useful when it came to giving Peaches a proper home and putting her in the best schools. Kola would keep Peaches during the school year, and Apple would take her for the summer to spend some quality time with her daughter. The arrangement they had would give Apple just enough time to track Citi down, overthrow the bitch's throne, and reign over her empire.

Kola might have thrown in the towel, but this wasn't the end for Apple—no way. Apple felt she was just getting started.

*** *** ***

It was a pretty fall day with a slight breeze that touched the leaves and made them dance on their branches. It was a comforting breeze on a warm fall day with the sun peeking through the clouds. Apple came to a stop in front of her sister's home on the attractive tree-lined block. It was a quiet neighborhood and the complete opposite of where they'd grown up in the mean streets of Harlem. Apple wondered if they'd been born and raised in a neighborhood like this, would her little sister Nichols still be alive today? There wasn't a day that Apple didn't think about her—and her tragic death. It was so long ago, yet it still felt like it all happened yesterday.

Apple sat in the car quietly, lost in her thoughts. She then turned around and she gazed at her daughter seated in the backseat. Apple smiled. Peaches was growing up to become a lovely young girl with her long, soft, black hair, beautiful brown eyes, and rich brown skin. She didn't look like Apple. Apple had no idea who was father was. Peaches was conceived in Mexico, by one of the many men who raped her when she was held captive in a grungy brothel. But no matter how her daughter was conceived, Apple still loved her unconditionally.

It was the day after Labor Day, and Apple was dropping her daughter off at her sister's for the school year.

"You okay, baby girl?" Apple asked Peaches.

"I'm fine, Mommy."

"You know Mommy loves you, right?"

Peaches smiled. "I know, Mommy."

"And I would do anything for you—anything."

"I know, Mommy."

"I will always have your back."

"And I have your back too, Mommy."

Apple smiled at her most prized possession. Her little queen was so smart and beautiful. Her personality was endearing. Peaches had an extremely bright future ahead of her. She had a chance at a good life, something that Apple felt she and her sisters never had while growing up in Harlem.

Apple climbed out of her cream Lexus and escorted her daughter to the front door.

"How do you like living with Auntie Kola and her husband?" she asked Peaches.

"I love it, Mommy."

It was what Apple wanted to hear. She rang the doorbell and stood there patiently on the front steps, holding her daughter's hand.

The front door opened and Apple immediately frowned. Kamel was standing there wearing an apron, and she could smell something cooking in the kitchen. The mere sight of him thrust her into a foul mood. She didn't bother with pleasantries or small talk. She immediately pushed past him with her daughter's hand in hers.

Kamel spun around and grimaced at his sister-in-law's rudeness toward him in his own home.

Apple crouched to hug her daughter goodbye, and then Peaches ran upstairs to find her Auntie Kola, Eduardo Jr., and Sophia. It left Apple alone downstairs with Kamel, a big mistake. Neither he nor Kola hustled anymore. Kola would receive money each month from Eduardo's goons and everyone was happy-go-lucky. Apple felt it made them lazy and worthless, and she never was one to hold her tongue.

She glared at Kamel in his cooking apron and growled, "How you up in here living in the house that my sister had to suck dick for? Your brother would never go for some shit like that."

Kamel barked, "What the fuck is you talkin' 'bout!"

He was tired of Apple's slick mouth. He hated the bitch with a passion, and it was a sad thing that she looked exactly like his wife.

"You fuckin' heard me, you bitch-ass nigga!" Apple rebuked. "You in here baking cakes, cookies, croissants, and shit, doing fuckin' daddy daycare runs for the whole neighborhood. Nigga, look at you—you look fuckin' weak right now! You allowed yourself to become emasculated, nigga. Eduardo got ya fuckin' balls in his hands."

The scowl that grew on Kamel's face would probably scare the devil himself. He tightened his fist and exclaimed through clenched teeth, "Yo, Apple, you better watch ya fuckin' mouth! Who the fuck you think you talkin' to like that?"

"Or what, bitch?" Apple continued to challenge him. "Your bitch ass wasn't barking on Eduardo. I heard you were damn near in tears begging and pleading for your life. You sucked his dick too? And now you wanna yell at me like you a tough guy? Nigga, please!"

The remark hurt. And it sent Kamel flying off the edge with rage. The only person who knew about his face-to-face with Eduardo was Kola, and apparently she had told her evil twin.

Kamel rammed his fist through the wall, creating a gaping hole in the living room. He then angrily marched closer to Apple.

Apple continued to challenge him. She didn't care about his feelings or his manhood.

On the second floor of the home, as Kola was hugging and loving on her niece who'd just returned home, she could hear Apple and her husband shouting and screaming at each other. Most likely, the entire neighborhood heard too. They both were loud and obnoxious.

Kola scowled. It was always one thing or another between the two of them. She hated when they fought and argued with the kids in the house. Hearing enough of their bickering, she told the kids to stay in the room. She stormed out of the room, closing the door behind her, and marched her way downstairs. But the kids didn't listen. They hurried out of the bedroom on her heels, all three curious to the drama downstairs.

Apple and Kamel continued to exchange insults.

"You miserable cokehead fuckin' cunt! I don't know how my brother ever fucked your contaminated *uno peso* pussy without putting on at least ten fuckin' condoms! You're a miserable fuckin' bitch, Apple, and nobody fuckin' likes you. Not even your own fuckin' kid! She loves us more than you and I know you hate that shit!"

"At least I got a fuckin' kid, you fuckin' faggot! Your weak dick must be shooting blanks—and speaking of worn-out pussies, you must be talkin' 'bout your own fuckin' wife, you stupid nigga!"

Kola screamed, "Apple!"

Apple turned and narrowed her eyes at her twin sister. "Nah, fuck that shit! Your faggot-ass husband is on some foul shit!"

Kola's presence wasn't a deterrent for Apple. She had no limits.

"Get the fuck out my house and go look for your baby daddy at the Home Depot parking lot," Kamel scolded.

"Kamel!" Kola screamed. Noticing that the kids had disobeyed her orders and were standing behind her, Kola pivoted and shouted, "Y'all kids go upstairs! Now!"

They immediately ran back upstairs.

Apple stepped closer to Kamel, invading his space. "Say something slick about my child again, nigga!"

Kamel inched closer to her, not backing down. "Or what, bitch! You supposed to scare me? You ain't shit but a worthless whore and a lousy fuckin' mother."

And just like that, they drew their guns on each other. Apple thrust a 9mm at Kamel's head, and Kamel responded with a .45 aimed at her face. The hateful words had transitioned into a physical threat.

Immediately, Kola placed herself between them. "Stop it!" she screamed at the top of her lungs. Then she suddenly collapsed on the floor, crying out hysterically. She was losing it. "I'm so tired of all this fuckin violence!"

Both Apple and Kamel quickly lowered their guns. They had never seen Kola like this. Kola was always the one who had her shit together, being in charge and that bad bitch in the hood. But now, she looked completely vulnerable and exhausted.

Kamel tried to wrap his arms around his wife for comfort, but Apple pushed him aside and shouted, "Nigga, I got this. She's my fuckin' sister!"

Kamel frowned. How dare that bitch put her hands on him? He cursed her back and was ready to punch her in her face. They started to argue over who should comfort Kola. It was a mess.

Finally, Apple allowed Kamel to carry her sister upstairs to the master bedroom, while she went to calm the kids. She walked into the kids' bedroom and saw them nestled together on the bed. They were upset.

Apple crouched and extended her arms out. "C'mere, y'all. I need a hug."

They all jumped off the bed and ran into Apple's open arms.

"Look, I apologize that y'all had to hear that mess downstairs. I'm so sorry. I am. It was just two grown-ups arguing with each other and using foul language. It's foul language that I do not want any one of y'all to repeat. Y'all understand me?"

They nodded.

"But once again, I'm so sorry that y'all had to hear all that. Do y'all forgive me?" Apple asked.

They nodded their heads and uttered, "Yes!"

And once again, Apple gave them all a big hug and a kiss.

With the kids settled in and taken care of in the bedroom, Apple went into the master bedroom where Kola was lying down with Kamel seated next to her. They exchanged looks, and both of them thought it was best not to fuss any more for the day—for Kola's benefit.

Kamel stood up and said, "I'll go take the kids downstairs and make them something to eat."

He left the bedroom in silence. Apple stepped farther into the bedroom and took a seat near Kola.

"You okay, sis?" she asked.

"I'm fine," Kola replied lowly.

Apple wanted to know why her sister had a mental breakdown. She was concerned.

"You're not losing your mind. Right, Kola?"

"No, Apple, I'm not losing my mind. I'm okay."

"Okay. Because that shit downstairs wasn't like you. You've always been the strong one in the family," said Apple.

"Things have just changed with me. I just want something different, sis . . . I want some normalcy in my life, that's all. I want this family and I want this marriage with Kamel to work. I want a new beginning."

Apple nodded.

Kola locked eyes with her sister. "And I guess I've become so emotional lately because I'm pregnant."

Apple sat there wide-eyed. "You're what?"

"I'm pregnant, Apple."

"Oh shit!" Apple searched for the right words, but this came out, "I thought you had an STD that fucked up your tubes and the doctors said you'd never be a mom?"

"Facts! So you can understand how this miracle baby is a gift and I can't begin my pregnancy stressing over you and Kamel's soap opera drama. It's just too much, Apple. And to keep it one-hundred, you're the instigator."

Apple pursed her lips tightly together to keep from squeezing out something slick. She bit her tongue and then replied with, "Whatever I can do to help, I'll do. But what's Kamel doin' for you?"

"I had planned on telling Kamel today, but you ruined that moment for me."

Apple shrugged. "Tell him tomorrow."

Kola rolled her eyes. "I guess I'll tell him tomorrow, then."

Apple didn't like her sister's tone, but it was expected under the circumstances.

"I'm out, Kola. And congrats on the baby. I'm really happy for you, sis."

Before leaving, Apple stopped to check in on Peaches and couldn't resist shooting a nasty look at Kamel on her way out the front door.

2

Citi leaned closer to the glass coffee table, scooped the white powder out of the little baggy, and cut it into lines with a credit card. She placed the thin, short straw into her right nostril and snorted a line of coke that was hardly stepped on. The hit was exhilarating—like an abrupt orgasm. She quickly did another line and felt that extreme high attacking her nerve endings. She pinched her nostrils, closed her eyes, and sank into the plush seating as she allowed the potent cocaine to take effect on her. The coke felt like it was hitting the back of her throat, and then she got that drip. Her buzz lasted for about fifteen minutes. She was ready to do a third line.

Citi was in her three-bedroom condo in Astoria, Queens. She had become a recreational user of cocaine but was always a firm believer in the saying, *you never get high off your own supply*. But today, she needed the pick-me-up to get her mind off of her problems, even if the relief was temporary. One of their stash houses had gotten raided by the local police department. It was a significant blow to their operation.

Apparently, the raid on their stash house happened on a humble. A detective was fucking some young bitch on the block, and one night he'd noticed Wise, one of Citi's soldiers, exiting the stash house down the block with a gun tucked in his waistband and then leaning into a vehicle to retrieve a few small boxes. Instead of arresting Wise on the spot for weapon possession, the detective decided to observe the house. For weeks he sat parked outside the location and snapped incriminating pictures of the operation and took down license plate numbers. All this surveillance led to him being granted a search warrant for the place.

In the early morning, with a tactical unit poised on the block, the detective and several officers kicked in the front and back doors and swarmed the place. They made several arrests and seized money and drugs. The early morning raid was all over the evening news.

All that shit Citi could live with. It was part of the game—police raids, losses, and arrests. But what Citi felt like she couldn't live without was her side dick—the nigga who had her infatuated. Pacho was a sneak fuck, and he was going to be arraigned today.

From her seat, she heard the shower running and then stopping. Soon afterward, Scar walked into the room from taking a shower and saw Citi zoned out and high, sitting in the plush hunter green chair wearing nothing but a black thong. He eyed the cocaine on the table and shifted his eyes toward Citi, who still had her eyes closed.

"You stressin' for nuthin', yo," he uttered. "All them dudes know to keep their fuckin' mouths shut. We know where their family lives and you know I won't hesitate to start droppin' bodies should anyone start snitchin'."

Slowly, Citi opened her eyes to look at him. Scar stood in front of her with a white towel wrapped around his waist. His cold black eyes were set on her deadpan. He was a scary lookin' dude with heavy gang tattoos and war wounds covering about sixty percent of his body. He had gashes, knife injuries, burns, and bullet wounds across his flesh. It wasn't a pretty sight. He had a Fetty Wap looking eye, wore a low Mohawk, and was bow-legged with huge hands. His dick was average, but it wasn't why Citi was with Scar. She fucked him for protection. And one thing Scar was good at was protecting her. His fierce reputation on the streets preceded him, and she needed him around.

When Citi had stolen the money from Cartier and Apple, she needed a thorough dude by her side until she was able to locate her brother. She'd met Scar in a Brooklyn nightclub, where he was surrounded by his dangerous goons. Scar immediately took a liking to Citi, with her pretty eyes, long hair, and flawless skin. Scar was a stone-cold killer, and because of that, she fucked him.

Scar didn't have a ferocious sexual appetite like most men his age. Making money was his bitch. Hustling was what turned Scar on. He could fuck with it every day. In fact, they rarely had sex, and when they did, Scar was on some freak shit. Early on, he introduced a dildo into their sex life. The kicker was, it wasn't for her. Scar loved a thick dildo shoved deeply into his asshole. Citi didn't mind. *To each his own,* she thought. But when he wanted to ram both his dick and the dildo into her booty hole, she quickly shut him down and let him know that she wasn't down for that type of party.

Citi sat in silence and allowed the cocaine to stimulate her entire body. She kept her eyes closed because she was thinking about Pacho and his big dick and how she was going to ride it as soon as they let him out on bail. Then Scar had to come into the room and ruin it for her.

He dropped his towel and started to lotion his tattooed and worn-torn body right there in front of her. Citi remained silent. Scar was quick-tempered, and it was something that truly irked her.

"Yo, get ya ass up!" he roughly said. "We got fuckin' moves to make. I gotta go meet up wit' this nigga Cane and make the exchange wit' those Bronx niggas. We down a lot of fuckin' paper and product from that bust and some connects got spooked and want to lay low until this shit blows over. Between bail and lawyers"—he whistled—"this gonna fuckin' cost me like two hundred large."

He went to put on his boxers and repeated to Citi, "Yo, get ya ass up! I need you to take them stacks to this list of lawyers and the bail bondsmen."

Citi stared at him. She would be remiss if she didn't state the obvious. "You mean it's gonna cost *us*—and when I say *us*, I mean it's costing *me*—two-hundred large. Let's not forget who built this shit!"

Citi rolled her eyes, stood up, and tried to walk past Scar to get into the shower herself. But Scar had other plans. He wasn't having any of her slick mouth. His violent backhand came like lightning striking, and it smashed across Citi's face and sent her crashing to the floor. He stood over her and snarled. "You don't ever fuckin' learn, do you!"

She gazed up at Scar and suddenly burst into tears. She jumped up and ran into the bathroom to lock herself inside. Scar gave quick chase, but he was too late. He banged his fist on the door and yelled at her, "Look at what you fuckin' made me do! You gonna fuckin' learn today, though!"

Citi kept herself locked in the bathroom for over an hour. Scar was crazy and she'd never seen anything like him before. He was almost demonic.

She finally heard silence on the other side of the door and assumed he was gone. She slowly opened the bathroom door and discovered she was right. Scar had left the apartment.

"Good fuckin' riddance," she said to herself.

She hurriedly got dressed and grabbed her Prada duffel bag with her money inside and left the apartment to get her real boo out of jail.

3

artier pulled the blinds open to let some sunlight into the bedroom. The problem was that there wasn't any sunlight. It was gray and rainy out—a depressed looking day—and it had been that way for almost a week now. It was early morning and the weather in Seattle, Washington was a mild 65 degrees on a gloomy September day.

Cartier sighed at the weather and shook her head. "Fuckin' suicidal," she uttered to herself.

She stretched and yawned by the window. She needed to prepare herself for another work day. For a moment, she stared out the window and observed a few of her neighbors making their way to work in the light rain. Where she stayed was quiet, nice, and peaceful—and a bit expensive too. The makeup of Seattle was completely different from the east coast and from other cities. It was a city surrounded by water, mountains, and evergreen forests, and it contained thousands of acres of parkland, making it a great place for outdoor activities like hiking, kayaking, camping, fishing, and skiing. The culture had a little bit of everything, but the city was proud of its blue collar roots, and lots of folks worked hard to keep those intact. The people were mostly aloof where Cartier stayed. They weren't unfriendly, but most folks just kept to themselves.

Cartier glanced at the clock on the dresser. It was 7:05. Her job at Starbucks was a downer, but at the moment, it somewhat helped with the bills. She worked as a barista and she was barely making ends meet. It was a stark contrast to her old life in New York, California, and Miami. Some days, Cartier would look at herself in the mirror and not recognize the woman she'd become—a bitch with a regular-ass job who was living with a roommate she occasionally had sex with. She shared the apartment with a man named Edward for her convenience.

Edward worked as a software developer at a tech startup. The two had met at a local lounge a few months back. Cartier was there with a few of her coworkers, enjoying the scenery and music. She and her coworkers were dancing seductively on the floor and she caught Edward's attention. He wasn't her type and vice-versa. In fact, Edward couldn't even play in her league. But Cartier was a bitch who always saw an opportunity in everyone—and sizing Edward up, she knew he was someone she could take advantage of. He had a good job and, most importantly, his own place.

The two talked and Cartier openly flirted with him. After striking out with every white girl in the place, Edward felt he had hit a homerun with Cartier. That night, he brought her back to his place. It was a one-bedroom apartment with rent costing him $3000 a month, and that was without utilities. It was a quaint place, just less than 700 square feet with a small terrace that overlooked the iconic Space Needle. Edward had a thing for cleanliness and order. Everything had to be in its place. He didn't like clutter, and his place was an indication of that.

She fucked him that night—and fucked him good. Cartier put her pussy down on Edward so good he looked like a drug addict who couldn't get enough. He wanted perpetual repeats. For Cartier, having sex with Edward was business—but the dude was open. After sex, he was the one who initiated the pillow talk, but Cartier refused to tell him anything about herself. When he asked about her accent, she simply told him that she was from the east coast—New York City.

"I never met a girl from New York City before," he'd said.

He couldn't handle Cartier, and she knew what type of fool he was. Cartier was exotic and intriguing to him—something different than his typical. The fool was down with the white girls, the blonde-haired and blue-eyed Beckys of Seattle. She and Edward would never be a couple. Cartier was too hood to introduce to his friends, and she didn't have any friends of her own, only coworkers she occasionally hung out with.

After a week of throwing down with Edward in his bedroom, sucking his thin dick and giving him some of the best pussy he'd ever had, she mentioned her job at Starbucks and her long commute each morning.

He was listening.

It took her nearly two hours to get to work in the morning from where she lived on the outskirts of the city, where the rent was cheaper. Edward came up with a viable solution.

"I could use a roommate," he'd said, "so why not move in with me?"

It was music to her ears. Cartier's smile was wide and she figured the suggestion to move in with him was perfect. In her mind, it seemed like a freebie. She would give him some pussy from time to time, and staying there would shorten her long commute. But Edward quickly set the record straight. She would pay half the bills in the place. Cartier's wide smile had quickly faded. She'd griped about what she was and what she wasn't used to, but Edward was adamant—take it or leave it.

She was paying $1,400 a month for her larger one-bedroom apartment outside the city, and what she would save in public transportation each month could be added to her share with him. And all the hours she would save in commuting made sense.

She took him up on his offer.

Cartier had a plan, and Edward was a mere footnote. Though they were now roommates, she saw him as an Uncle Tom. She knew about his relationship with his coworker named Jill—his Becky. Edward and Jill were in a tricky situation. Jill's father was a state senator and her mother was a doctor, and they were very wealthy folks. They also had a vision for their daughter, and that vision didn't include her shacking up with a black man unless his name was Barack Obama—and not Barack Obama-ish. Edward regularly kept pressing his girlfriend to meet her parents, but she would always become evasive. Although Jill gave the best blowjobs, in bed she was as vanilla as they came. She would lie there in the missionary position, wanting Edward to do all the work and come quickly.

However, Cartier had pussy that blew him away, and she was a freak in the bedroom. But that was it. Edward enjoyed the sex, but he was attracted to white women—blondes to be more precise. Cartier's newly dyed blonde hair didn't sway his heart. He felt she was uncouth, most times too ghetto, and too secretive. Yet, she had her share of the rent money each month and his rental savings allowed him to splurge on Jill.

Cartier didn't care about Edward and Jill's silly dilemma. Her agenda was to save money and do her—and get her man back. Her fall from the throne was painful. She had lost everything and was now on the west coast trying to rebuild her life. It was a slow and gradual process. It was taking time to save money, but she was managing. As soon as she had $5,000 saved, she planned to leave the vampire city and head back east to reclaim her life. She wasn't made to become someone's lackey inside a small apartment, where he wanted her to cook, clean, pay half the rent, and give him sex.

The man she was in love with would be home soon. Head had about four months left on his sentence, and she wanted to be back in New York when he got out and touched down in Brooklyn. She told herself, "Fuck the authorities, fuck my enemies. No more hiding." Cartier was determined to be by her man's side, no matter what.

Dressed for work, she walked out of the apartment carrying her 10-speed bike and took the stairs to the first floor. Outside, she straddled the bike and traveled several blocks to her job. The Starbucks where she worked was one of the busier ones in the city. The entire morning and afternoon, Cartier stayed on her feet, back and forth behind the counter, serving people who were far different from her. They came from a different world than her—privileged and prejudiced, she felt—enjoying their smart looking coffees or espressos and flavorsome snacks while they busied themselves on their laptops or chitchatted about current events or some tech issue. The customers she served wouldn't survive one night in Brooklyn. Shit, they probably wouldn't be able to find Brooklyn on a map.

Cartier had to serve them with a bright smile. This wasn't her, a server to these people. Every day she felt fraudulent, but she was in hiding and had to start a new life. It felt like she was in the witness protection program, but she wasn't a snitch.

Her shift at Starbucks dragged like a snail on concrete, and it was tedious work, but she got through it. By late afternoon her shift ended and it was time for her to go home.

Like routine, she straddled her 10-speed and rode off, stopping at Burger King to get a bite to eat and picking up her mail from her work friend. A letter from Head came, and she couldn't wait to rip into it and read what her boo had to say. She'd been writing him for almost a year now, but with no reply. She had given him her coworker's address, and now it looked like he had finally given in to her many pleas for forgiveness.

As soon as Cartier got home, she stood in the kitchen and tore into the letter. Her hand slightly trembled as she opened the envelope. As she read his letter, she found herself stuck on stupid. His words threw her for a loop. The things he was saying were downright disrespectful and unpleasant. He called her all types of trifling, conniving, cum-guzzling bitches. Head stressed that she was not to be trusted and to stay the fuck away from him when he got paroled. The handwritten letter was three pages long and every word was bitch, cunt, whore, fuck you. She got the hint. But she was hurt. Was what she did to Head unconscionable? As far as she was concerned, that was the past. She was young and immature back then and she wasn't ready for the type of commitment he was looking for at the time. She agreed, previously, she had been a grimy bitch. But cum-guzzling? That was taking insults way too far.

Cartier went into her bedroom with her bag of Burger King and penned her reply to him.

My dearest Head:

Look, nigga, I fucked up. But how many letters can I pen telling you the obvious? When you came to South Beach, to be honest, a bitch was feeling herself. I was with one of the top players in the drug game and I let that shit go to my head. I hurt you because I was hurting over the murder of my family. And hurt people hurt people and I took our love for granted. After what happened between us in South Beach, I can only apologize to you and hope that we can move on from the past. I never loved Hector. I thought I did until he was murdered and I felt nothing cuz you had my heart. You've always had it. You know we were made for each other, so stop acting hard to get back. And if you want me to guzzle your cum e'ry day, I will. If you want me to beg you to come back to me, I will. You will always be my baby. No other bitch can have you, so get that out your stubborn mind. If I see you with a bitch, I'm fuckin' her up. If I hear a new bitch's name, I'm fuckin' her up. So please don't get a new bitch fucked up, cuz you know I will fuck a bitch up. You don't have to write me back, but just know that when you come home, I'll be tapping on ya shoulder. Act like you know!

Love you, my nigga.
Your bae,
Cartier xoxoxo

Right after she sealed her letter with a kiss, she received a text message from Edward.

WORKING LATE. DON'T WAIT UP.

She rolled her eyes and sighed, tossing her phone on the bed. "Nigga, do I ever?"

4

Apple was back in New York City—back in the trendy neighborhood of SoHo in the late evening with the sun gradually setting behind the horizon. The trip from Westchester had taken her a little over an hour. She climbed out of the car and stood in front of the attractive brownstone in lower Manhattan. She was renting a two-bedroom duplex apartment, and it was costly, but for Apple, it was well worth it. There was no way she was going to move to the Midwest or the west coast like Cartier had—and hide. This city was her home and no one was going to force her out of it.

SoHo was different from Harlem, and any other place she'd lived. The area was truly a melting pot with various races, young professionals, and all the cool kids. People walked the streets all hours of the night, hopping in and out of cabs, Ubers, or Lyfts. It was a neighborhood of lofts, art galleries, and a variety of shops ranging from trendy upscale boutiques to chain outlets. The area was also known for the multitude of cast-iron facades and cobblestone streets. Apple's block was like a scene from *Sex and the City*.

The moment Apple arrived at her front door, her cell phone rang. Her caller ID said it was Nick calling. Her heart smiled, somewhat. She answered with a halfhearted, "Hey baby."

She walked into the building chatting with Nick.

Apple loved men who were thorough and street, but she also loved men she could control. She had to be the boss bitch at all times. She'd vowed to never allow herself to stoop low again for any nigga. Between Supreme, Chico, Guy Tony, and Jamel, she had made a lot of mistakes and the best way to guard her heart was to never fully give it to a man again.

Nicholas Davis was a powerhouse not to be fucked with, but Apple knew she could most likely manipulate him. He was much older than Apple, being forty years old with a respected resume in the streets, while she was in her mid-twenties.

Nick's father was Corey Davis, a man who ran with Nicky Barnes, Bumpy Johnson, and Guy Fisher in the sixties and seventies. Corey had gotten locked up in 1977 on conspiracy and murder charges and received a life sentence. Corey named Nick after Nicky Barnes, and Nick was only a couple of months old when his father was locked up for life. Nick had to learn to be a man on his own, and he learned from the streets, so it was inevitable that he would choose his father's gangster profession.

By the time he was fourteen, Nick caught his first body when he stabbed a rival drug dealer named Malik Noland in a Harlem alley. A young girl named Stephanie Hawkins saw the whole thing and was ready to testify for the prosecution. Nick was looking at a life sentence in a state prison and becoming even more like his father.

Nick's best friend and partner in crime, Amir, wasn't about to let that happen. Amir tracked the young girl down, and late one night, he climbed through her first floor tenement building window and shot her in the head while she slept in her bedroom. She died instantly.

The prosecution tried to charge Nick as an adult for the murder of Malik Noland, and then they tried to add charges for the death of Stephanie Hawkins, but their case quickly fell apart and the D.A. had to cut him loose. Nick dodged a serious bullet, thanks to Amir. But there is no statute of limitation for murder, and his case had been dismissed without prejudice, meaning it could be reopened.

Nick and Amir were extremely loyal to one another, and together, they wreaked havoc for decades, getting fast money and taking lives until Amir got knocked by state police for riding dirty with five kilos in the trunk of his car. He received a lengthy prison sentence and left behind a five-year-old son named Abraham.

That was twenty years ago, and Amir's incarceration left Nick on the streets without a right-hand man. But Nick made it his business to visit Amir at least once a month. It was a coincidence that Amir was in the same prison as Nick's father, and he would visit them separately. Nick also made sure that both his father and best friend were well taken care of inside prison by keeping money on their books.

***

Apple was laying on the king size bed watching Netflix when Nick walked in with a wide smile, a bottle of champagne, and a small, black duffel bag from the scene of his latest and final crime. He had just gotten back from North Carolina and left behind two bullet-riddled bodies in the trunk of an old car.

Seeing Apple looking delicious in her panties and bra only added to his good mood. He had missed his young thang.

"This is it for me, baby," he said.

"I take it you came off in North Carolina."

His smile continued and he tossed the small duffel bag on the bed near Apple's feet. Curious of the contents, she reached for the bag and opened it, seeing the cash inside. She reckoned it to be nearly sixty thousand dollars, which wasn't shit in her eyes. Apple was used to being around millions of dollars.

"I'm done, baby," Nick repeated. He picked up the duffel bag and dumped the cash all over the bed.

Apple looked at him deadpan. He had been preaching about retiring from the game since the day she'd met him. Nick had made a promise to himself, his father, and his best friend that he would get out of the game if or when he reached his fortieth birthday. He stood there in the bedroom looking proud, rugged, and handsome. He was six feet tall with a lean and fit body. He was dark-skinned and had intense black eyes that could rouse fear in any man. He had a thick, black beard that he always kept trimmed and shaped-up. He was clad in all black—a hoodie, jeans, and Timbs.

Nick popped the champagne open to celebrate with his lady. Together, they drank and ate Chinese food that Apple had ordered earlier. Nick was excited about Apple—he was open—maybe in love with her. She was the prettiest thing he'd seen in a long while. She was smart, intriguing, and somebody not to be messed with. Her assertive attitude was a turn-on for him. Nick didn't like weak women.

"Where's Peaches?" he asked as he poured more champagne for them.

"I dropped her off at her aunt's place," she said.

"Damn, I was hoping to see her before she left. You know she's my little princess," he said.

She smiled. "I know."

Nick loved the little girl like she was his own daughter, but they'd agreed that now wasn't the right time for Apple and him to raise her.

"I can't stop thinkin' about that bitch," Apple announced.

Nick already knew she was talking about Citi. It was a common subject inside her home. The contempt for Citi oozed from Apple's pores. She wore her hate and vengeance for the girl like her own skin.

Apple, knowing her man was a cold-blooded killer, continued to tell him about her lingering beef and unresolved issues with the girl. "You know how much she took from us!" she exclaimed.

She wanted to go in, torture and kill the bitch, and keep her life moving. Apple wasn't going to be satisfied until she executed street justice on Citi and took back what was owed to her.

However, Nick was reluctant to participate in the street justice Apple yearned for. He was thinking about his retirement from the game. He had put in a lot of work on the streets and racked up bodies and lots of cash. Nick felt his luck was going to run out if he continued in that direction. After seeing his father sentenced to life in prison and then Amir getting caught up, Nick figured that it was time to change up his MO. He stopped hustling and began robbing and killing drug dealers. It had netted him a pretty penny. He had spent a lot of his blood money on the finer things in life, but he also had managed to stash away a healthy nest egg for himself, over a million dollars to be exact. It was enough money to retire on, he felt.

It took nearly two decades and a lot of dead dealers to accomplish the feat, but to Nick, murdering niggas was light work. He worked alone. He didn't have an organization with goons, runners, and triggermen. He didn't have to cook coke, cut it up, or distribute it. He had no partners or underlings to snitch on him, and it was one of the reasons he'd lasted so long doing what he did.

Nick would take his time to hunt and study his prey. He was a very patient man, knowing that impatience and carelessness got men captured or killed. He would attack his victims when they were most vulnerable, take what he needed, execute them, and then disappear into the night. He wasn't on anyone's radar, because to them he didn't exist. He had no connections to his victims. He worked his own hours, took long vacations to exotic locations, and he had little overhead.

Apple continued to talk about Citi. She made it clear to Nick that she needed his help in getting her revenge. It was a lot more difficult for her to carry out her plan on her own.

"I told you, Apple, I'm done. North Carolina was my last job."

"There's a lot involved here, baby."

"I told you before, I just want to take my million plus and invest in my bar and a few other businesses and just watch my money grow."

Nick needed to prove to himself and his father that he was more than a killer—that he was smart too.

"So just like that, you're retiring from this shit—from who you are?"

"What you think? I made it this far by being smart, Apple, not stupid."

"Not even for me, baby?"

"Look, I know you hate that bitch with a passion, but this some shit I need to fall back on," he said.

"But I'm asking you for your help on this. You're my man—I fuck and suck your dick good every night, and I expect for you to have my back."

"And I do have your back, baby. But I told you that I'm retiring!"

Apple became irritated that he couldn't make an exception for her, even after she told him what Citi had done to her and Cartier.

Apple allowed Nick to table the discussion—for now. Tonight he won the battle, but the war was hers to conquer.

Nick began kicking off his boots and unbuttoning his jeans. He had hoped that Apple would have done it for him, but he could clearly see that she had an attitude, and now he had one too.

"So we not gonna watch Netflix and chill?"

Apple smirked and then rolled her eyes. "No shade, but I got shit to do in the morning." She was highly irritated but didn't want to argue and ruin Nick's high. She could tell that her man was caught up kissing his own ass from his latest and last lick.

Nick exhaled his frustration. It had been a long day. All he wanted to do was make it back alive, retire from the game, and make love to Apple. And from the sour look on her face he knew he wasn't getting any pussy.

What a fucking day.

"You need to really think about this beef you got wit' this bitch. My pops always said when seeking revenge, remember to dig two graves."

"I'll fuckin' dig ten if I have to, and I promise it won't be me in one." Apple always was hardheaded, and she hated being told what she couldn't do. She walked to her mirrored hutch, pulled on a T-shirt, and began wrapping up her long hair. She was making a statement. She glared at Nick as she placed each bobby pin in.

The ambiance and mood was over.

"Let this shit go, ma. Take the L and stop lookin' in your rearview." Nick knew that he had to school Apple on the game. "I have a code, bae. I don't act off emotions and ego 'cause I'll end up in a box or in a cell. My pops and Amir wanted to make names for themselves—wanted their names echoing off city streets and tumbling out niggas' and bitches' mouths—and look where that got them."

"You and I got two different playbooks. You think 'cause you ain't do jail time or trap that makes you special? You lookin' down on me because I won't walk away and you took the easy way out?"

"Easy?" Nick was about to lose his cool. Her stubbornness was getting under his skin. "You think it was easy to not set up trap houses and feed the streets and do what's in my blood? I was born into the drug game at the highest level. No, ma, it was hard as hell and took great discipline to slowly build my stash. It took sacrifice, forethought, and patience. I could have made a million decades ago had I stayed in the game. But I wouldn't have been able to spend that bread. I would have never met you or had the opportunity to go legit. Think, baby, think. This bitch got ya mind."

"No, that bitch got my muthafuckin' money and I want it back!"

Nick shook his head. She wasn't hearing him. "You fueled by failure."

Apple swung around. "And you fueled by—"

Bingo! Apple didn't finish her sentence. She knew the one thing that got Nick's trigger finger twitching, and she would use it to her advantage. She redirected with, "You know what baby? Let's not fight. I'm beat and tomorrow's a new day."

Apple climbed in bed looking unsexy and cold.

"So no pussy tonight?"

"I'm on my period."

5

Citi's long brown hair with blonde highlights flowed gracefully down her back as she stepped out of her custom baby blue Range Rover five blocks from her destination. It felt like today was going to be a good day for her—and her pussy. Pacho's bail had been posted with the bondsman and his attorney fees had been paid.

It was a breezy and chilly day, and Citi was dressed for Pacho in tight jeans, an expensive silk Gucci tank that accentuated her tits, and a short Burberry trench coat. She bit her lip as she paced up and down the sidewalk on the side of Pacho's apartment building, her heels working the cement in anticipation. The only thing she could think about was wrapping her arms around Pacho, hugging him, kissing him, and most important, having great sex with him.

But Citi had to be extremely careful about Scar being in the area too. To him, she hardly had a reason to be at Pacho's place. So she was on alert the entire time.

Finally, a yellow cab pulled to the curb in front of the building, and Citi watched with glee from a short distance as Pacho climbed out. She hurried toward him. Pacho pivoted to his left and was shocked to see Citi coming his way. She was all smiles.

"Hey baby!" she cried out.

The sight of her put a bright smile on Pacho's face. Citi jumped into his arms and they hugged each other tightly. It felt so good to have him in her arms, Citi wanted to come out her clothes right there and give him some, but she had to be patient.

"I missed you, baby," she said.

"I missed you too," he said.

They shared a passionate kiss and then Pacho noticed the bruises on her face. "He did this to you?"

Citi didn't want to talk about it. She was with Pacho right now and that's all that mattered to her. She said, "Can we take this inside?"

He nodded. Pacho ushered her into the building and they soon stepped inside his sparsely furnished apartment with the 50" television mounted on the living room wall and the leather sofa—the ultimate bachelor's pad. For a brief moment they stared at each other. She was slightly trembling from the weather outside, so Pacho wrapped his arms around her, shaping his hold into a tight and sentimental hug, and the two passionately kissed.

Their romantic moment soon transitioned to the bathroom, where they peeled away their clothing and took a hot shower together. Pacho's hard dick drilled deep inside her dripping wet pussy as he fucked her from behind with her hands against the shower wall. She cooed from the repetitive motion behind her, feeling all of him intensely like her body was super sensitive.

"Ooh, I missed you," she moaned. "Oh, you feel so good in me, baby."

She maneuvered to face him, the shower water still cascading against their naked flesh and making rivulets down their bodies. With the sound of water splashing against the tile, Pacho hoisted his woman into his arms with her legs straddling him and slammed his dick into her with her back against the slippery wall. They kissed strongly and she moaned while feeling his hands explore her naked flesh. He nuzzled her neck and continued his upward thrust inside of her.

"Ooooh . . . ummm, I missed you, baby," she cooed.

After a lasting moment of passionate sex, Citi found herself exploding from an orgasm while still in Pacho's grasp. Her legs trembled against him and the cries of pleasure echoed from the shower.

Once clothed and in the living room, Citi only wanted to enjoy Pacho. But Pacho, seeing her bruises, couldn't keep quiet about their situation any longer. "I can't take this sneaking around shit any longer, baby. I'm tired of it."

"I don't have a choice."

"What you mean you don't have a choice? I'm your choice. And if you help me murder this nigga Scar, then we can be together without this hiding shit," he said with conviction.

It was tempting and Citi had weighed her options. She had a large stable of enemies out there. Pacho was a killer, but Scar was something else—something a lot more menacing. Scar commanded respect and knew how to keep his thugs in line. He was born a body snatcher and enjoyed being one. Citi didn't know if Pacho was built for life as the head enforcer.

Citi had double crossed two thoroughbred bitches in the game— Apple and Cartier. These women had gone up against one of the deadliest cartels around and lived to tell about it. The fact they were still out there somewhere spooked Citi. Apple was a bloodthirsty bitch with no fear, and Cartier was smart and ruthless. If shit got thick again on the streets, Citi knew that Scar would become a killing machine for her.

Sure, she had her brother Cane, who was equally intimidating, but she didn't want to see anything happen to him. Citi had already lost too much with her other brother Chris doing hard jail time and both her parents dead. If she lost Cane, she would feel like an orphan again. She would be alone, and she didn't want to be alone.

Pacho noticed her hesitation. "You fuckin' love that nigga!"

She was taken aback by the remark. "What? No! Hell no! I love you, baby," she said wholeheartedly.

Pacho didn't know what to believe, but Citi continued to try and convince him, saying that Scar was creepy and made her skin crawl.

"Then why not set him up—get rid of this nigga for good, Citi?"

"Because I need him right now, Pacho. Now is not the time to lose him when my organization has just taken a huge hit," she argued.

"Look what he did to your fuckin' face," he griped.

"I'm a big girl, Pacho. I can handle it. Besides, too many of my men now have open drug cases and some might bitch out and take plea deals. I can't afford to lose anyone else."

They continued to argue. Pacho was being hardheaded. Why couldn't he understand her point of view? Why couldn't he see that she was only using Scar? She didn't love him, but Pacho had a tendency of only seeing shit from his perspective.

As they fussed about Scar, several hard, rapid knocks on the door caught their immediate attention.

Pacho went toward the door and shouted, "Who is it?"

"Yo, open the fuckin' door, nigga. It's Scar."

Hearing his voice caught both of them by surprise. They stared at each other nervously. *Shit!* Why was he there? Citi wondered if she had been followed. Did he hear them arguing inside? So many thoughts and worries flooded them both.

"Go hide in the bedroom," Pacho told her.

Citi hurried into the bedroom and hid in the closet while Pacho threw on some jeans and a T-shirt. He closed his bedroom door, reached for his .45 and tucked it into his waistband, and went to open the door.

Scar stood in front of him with a deadpan gaze. He hadn't come alone. A goon named Damon was with him. Scar and Damon marched into Pacho's place without an invitation.

Closing the door after they entered his place, Pacho turned toward them and said, "What's good, Scar? Why the sudden appearance?"

"What, nigga, you ain't happy to see a nigga? Huh, muthafucka? I'm sayin', you just got bailed out. I came to check on you, nigga."

Pacho's eyes darted back and forth. The apprehension he felt was thicker than a brick wall. Scar was a psychopath. He was sure that both men were there to murder him. Pacho stood still and kept his eyes fixed on Scar as he leisurely walked around his apartment like he owned the place.

Scar grinned at Pacho and said, "Nigga, you been fuckin' already? Damn, it smells like pussy up in here."

Pacho ignored the statement. "What's good, Scar? Is there a problem?"

"Yeah, there is a problem, in fact," Scar replied nonchalantly.

"So talk to me."

Scar fleetingly looked at Damon, Damon smirked, and then Scar turned his attention back to Pacho. "Look, we gotta fuck some nigga up."

"Who?"

"Wise," said Scar.

"Wise?"

"He needs to be taken care of for exposing our organization. You already know I can't let that shit go. He gotta pay for his fuckin' incompetence."

Pacho knew he didn't have a choice. Once Scar said to do something, you had better do it.

"A'ight, let's go see this nigga."

"My nigga," replied Scar.

As they were about to leave the apartment, Scar pivoted toward Pacho and abruptly asked, "Who you up in here wit', nigga?"

Pacho remained cool and replied, "I ain't got nobody in here."

"But I swear I heard you arguing wit' some bitch before I knocked."

"You must have heard the TV," Pacho said.

"The TV, huh."

"Yeah, the TV."

Scar started to walk toward the bedroom door and said, "What bitch you got hiding from me? Cuz you lookin' mad shook right now, nigga. Lemme find out you got that bitch Monique wit' the big titties up in here. That bitch definitely knows how to deep throat some dick, nigga. You feel me?"

Pacho maneuvered himself close to Scar, nearly blocking his path to the door. "You invading my space, nigga. I thought you came here so we can handle our business."

Scar stopped short of opening the bedroom door. A sudden smile appeared on his face. "I'm just fuckin' wit' you nigga. Calm down."

Scar laughed. But Pacho didn't find his humor amusing.

6

Apple couldn't get Citi out of her head, no matter how hard she tried. The agonizing thought haunted her that a young bitch like Citi had gotten the best of her—taken everything from her, embarrassed her. There was no way she was going to allow that to slide. Without Cartier having her back and Kola playing house, she was alone. She needed Nick to get with the program. She needed his skills, and she was willing to do whatever it took to get her man on her side and stop him from talking about this retirement. She wanted things to happen her way, no matter what.

She sighed heavily. She had grown into her own, long ago shedding that dependent-on-a-man attitude. Supreme had made her into the bitch she was today, and though what happened with her little sister was a tragedy, it seemed like a blessing in disguise for her.

While staring at herself in the bathroom mirror, Apple slowly peeled away every piece of clothing she had on. Nick was lying in the bedroom watching TV and smoking a blunt. After a couple days she had finally forgiven him. It had been a quiet evening for them. They had been drinking champagne and chilling, but Apple was tired of chilling. She was tired of lying around and not doing anything about her situation. She couldn't just chill every day and go into retirement with Nick. She was a restless spirit, and she figured that all Nick needed was a little convincing to see things her way.

She coolly walked out the bathroom naked and smiled flirtatiously at Nick. He couldn't help but to take in her nakedness. It was a beautiful thing to see and it never got old to him.

"Damn, baby . . ."

"I take it you like what you see?" she said.

"You know I do." He took a long drag from the blunt and doused it in the ashtray near him on the nightstand. He'd found something else to enjoy for the evening.

Apple walked toward him with a look in her eyes that would frighten the average man. Nick propped himself against the headboard, knowing the next hour or so was going to blow his mind. Apple was that type of bitch who knew how to keep her nigga happy.

She joined him on the bed and freed his dick from the slit in his boxer shorts and leaned closer to his erection. Nick fell back as Apple sensually kissed the tip and then took him into her mouth and drew him deeper into her throat.

"Oh shit . . ." he moaned.

Her head bobbed up and down as she took him as far as she could into her mouth, holding his giant erection tight and moving her mouth slowly. Apple dragged the flat of her tongue down Nick's length, all the way to his balls. He continued to groan and squirm a little. This was Apple's show, and Nick had a front row seat. The moaning continued, as he caressed her face and shoulders and said, "You gonna fuckin' make me come, baby."

As she sucked his dick, sometimes fast and sometimes slow, Nick continued to groan, feeling his muscles tense as her mouth became a powerful vacuum that was trying to milk the come from his balls. Apple had no time to stop or come up for air. She was focused on pleasing her man. Her lips repetitively sucked from the root of his stiff dick, the spit from her mouth becoming a lubricant. She could feel his pre-come leaking on her tongue. It was a treat for her, knowing the best was yet to come.

"Ooooh . . . oh shit…. Ooooh shit, baby . . . damn it!"

His moans echoed throughout the bedroom and intensified when Apple took his balls into her mouth, sucking and licking them, and bouncing them around on her tongue. Nick didn't know what to do with himself. This young girl was putting a hurting on his genitals, but in a good way. He felt her lips stretch around his hard dick and she started to hum. She could feel his dick throbbing repeatedly in her mouth, like the sneakers of an experienced runner hitting the park trail.

This intense oral action went on for several minutes with Nick looking like he was about to explode from every suck and lick. When Apple finally stopped with her oral blessings, Nick was so hard and so ready to fuck that he looked like a crack fiend who'd just copped a rock. Apple's pussy was a thumping river. She pushed him back on the bed and straddled his body. She took his hard length into her grip and gently slid him inside of her, feeling the dick fill her walls.

"Fuck me," she cried out.

The sensation of the young girl's pussy was always phenomenal for the forty-year-old gangster. He easily found his rhythm inside of her, his big dick stretching her to new limits. Apple felt him going in and out of her, each thrust pounding her walls like a jack-hammer breaking up concrete. It was how she liked it—rough and taking no prisoners with the pussy.

"*Ooooh*, just like that, nigga! Fuck me!" she cried out.

Nick erupted like a volcano, but not before giving Apple a few orgasms of her own.

Nick lay beside Apple looking deflated. He was happy with her. She gave him everything he needed—sex, comfort, and conversation. It was good to come home to something so sweet after being in the streets. He held Apple in his arms, the softness of her body and her curves a blissful feeling to him.

Apple said, "That was nice."

"It always is."

For a moment, they shared some pillow talk. Apple said, "I believe in you, baby, and your bar, but a bar is going to take a lot of capital to start and to upkeep. A million dollars is hardly enough money to retire off nowadays."

Nick remained silent, choosing to listen to the young girl rather than get defensive.

She continued with, "What if we make this worth it for you? This is easy money, baby—no different than any other lick you hit. We go in quick, rob that bitch's trap houses, and kill that ho. That way we both get what we want. I'm telling you, baby, there's too much money in this to pass up. If you wanna retire, then retire with a few million instead of just one."

Nick knew that he was being seduced. "How many millions are you talking about?"

"I don't know, but I heard she flipped our money and she's now doing bigger things wit' it. She got a whole fuckin' drug crew—underlings, trap houses, and all that. She might be holding over fifty million—maybe more—to be running that kind of operation. We can snatch a small taste of that in one night," she proclaimed.

It wasn't a figure Nick was expecting to hear—fifty million or more. He could open a franchise with that kind of money in his reach. He started salivating as Apple continued to tell him about Citi's operation and her riches. Apple had done her homework. Shit, it took him decades to save a cool million, and there was a chance he could double that in one night. Maybe retirement needed to be put on hold.

Apple continued to give Nick the details she'd gathered, and Nick said that he would start to do his own investigation. Thing is, he believed Apple, but he also believed to never trust any information but your own. If he did decide to get on board, he reasoned this would be the one and only stick-up for him, one murder for her, and then he would be out of the game for real this time. With the kind of money Apple was talking about, he would be set for life.

"I have one request, though," she said.

"Oh, you do?"

"What we take from that bitch, we split it three ways."

Nick was baffled by her request. "Three ways?"

"I have a friend, Cartier, and she deserves her share too," she said.

"No!" he flat out told her. "We're taking all the risk here and you want to split it with some bitch that I don't know? It's not happening."

He was sweet on Apple, but he wasn't a fool.

Reluctantly, she agreed it'd be just the two of them. Besides, Apple had given Cartier a chance to be down, but she would rather stay out west and play it safe.

7

Dusk settled over the Brooklyn neighborhood of Bushwick on a cool and quiet night in the infamous hood. Scar took a few pulls from the blunt as he sat in the backseat of the dark green GMC. Damon was the driver and Pacho sat shotgun. Scar took one last pull of weed and leaned forward to hand the blunt to Damon. Pacho slightly flinched.

Scar laughed and asked, "Nigga, you good?"

"Yeah, I'm good, Scar," said Pacho.

"Fuck you actin' nervous for then, nigga?"

"I got a lot on my mind."

"I bet you do." Scar laughed.

Damon took a few strong pulls from the blunt and then shared it with Pacho. Pacho needed the high right now, but at the same time he felt like he needed to stay sober. *Fuck it.* He took a few hits from the blunt, not wanting to make Scar suspicious.

Pacho knew he was in a daunting predicament. Scar was seated directly behind him, and he had no idea what he had planned. Scar could easily put a bullet or a knife into the back of his head, and Pacho would have no way to defend himself.

Damn, would Scar really kill me over some pussy? He really liked Citi and she liked him. The sex was great and she was good peoples. Pacho knew she was only using Scar for his murderous reputation, but it started to have an effect on him.

Pacho took in the potent strain of weed and it slightly rumbled inside of him. He exhaled. *I did nothing wrong*, he said to himself. But at the same time, he tried to have eyes in the back of his head.

"So, was that bitch's pussy and throat good at ya crib, nigga?" Scar asked Pacho out of the blue.

"What? What you mean?" Pacho unwillingly responded.

"You lookin' spaced out right now, nigga. I figure you got pussy on ya mind. That bitch's sex game must got you trippin' and shit, nigga." Scar laughed.

"Nah, I'm just focused and ready to handle some business, ya know what I'm sayin'?" he replied.

"Yeah, I know what ya sayin'."

Pacho passed the burning blunt back to Scar. He was a killer and Scar was a killer, so if Scar did try to make a move on him, Pacho knew he needed to be ready. They were like two wolves in the wild, eyes glaring and slightly snarling at each other over the female.

Finally, they spotted who they'd come there for. Wise was exiting his building and he was alone.

"There that nigga go right there," said Damon.

"Yeah, yeah, roll up on that nigga, Damon," Scar said.

Damon slowly moved the vehicle parallel to the sidewalk with all eyes on Wise walking alone. Scar rolled his window down and hollered, "Yo, Wise! C'mere, nigga. Come take a ride wit' us."

Wise spun around to see Scar calling his name from the backseat of the GMC. The look on Wise's face said it all—*Oh shit!* He appeared to be nervous and hesitant.

Scar kept his eyes fixed on Wise, knowing the nigga didn't have a choice. "Yo, what the fuck you standing there for, nigga? Get in the fuckin' truck and let's go," Scar shouted. "What the fuck? Nigga lookin' all retarded and shit."

"I got some shit to do, Scar. It's important," Wise replied.

Wise was testing his patience. "*We* important, nigga!"

"I'm sayin', Scar . . ."

Scar and Damon quickly exited the truck and approached Wise with a bully's stance and surrounded him. Scar said, "I'm gonna have to insist that you go for a ride wit' us, nigga."

Damon hastily lifted Wise's shirt and removed the gun Wise had tucked in his waistband. Wise found himself in a fucked-up situation. They weren't giving him a choice—not even a chance to react and defend himself. Pacho sat and watched it unfold from the front seat, reluctant to get involved.

"Yo, y'all gonna do me like this?" Wise exclaimed.

"Nigga, just get in the fuckin' truck so we can go for a ride and talk. That's all, nigga. We just gotta make a fuckin' run. Why you wanna make shit difficult?"

Wise stared silently their way. He nodded and apprehensively climbed into the backseat of the truck with Scar. He knew it was a lie, but he didn't have a choice. Scar was a crazy muthafucka who didn't take no for an answer. Even the most hardcore killers feared him.

The four men drove off. Immediately, Wise started to run his mouth, trying his best to talk his way out of the inevitable.

"Yo Scar, that shit ain't my fault. I got knocked on a humble, you know what I'm sayin'? And I ain't say shit to nobody. Shit, nigga, you know I got a family to support—a little girl, and she's all I got," Wise proclaimed.

"Nigga, why you talkin' so much? I'm sayin', you talkin' like you nervous 'bout sumthin', nigga. You nervous, Wise?"

"Do I need to be nervous?" Wise replied.

Scar laughed. "Wise, you my nigga, fo' sure. Ain't shit gonna happen to you," Scar said in what sounded like a sincere tone.

"I'm just sayin', Scar . . . we good, right? Y'all my niggas and I know I fucked up gettin' knocked, but I'm gonna be more careful. And I'm gonna pay back all y'all losses. Whatever is owed take that shit out my cut each week. Just don't do me this way. I gotta look out fo' my little girl, you know what I'm sayin'?"

Wise was trying to say all kind of things to tug on their heart strings, but they remained silent.

Damon navigated the vehicle through the city and rode through the Holland tunnel. The duration of the long ride from Brooklyn to New Jersey gave Wise and Pacho a lot to think about—or worry about. Why were they in New Jersey? Where were they going? Scar was saying nothing to them at all, but he wanted everyone to be cool.

They traveled south on the New Jersey Turnpike and ended up in a thickly wooded area called Wharton State Forest. It was a few miles north of Atlantic City.

Damon maneuvered the vehicle off the main road and onto a narrow dirt road that seemed to close in on them with towering trees that seemed limitless. The area was dark and thick and consumed by absolute silence except for the humming of the engine, and there was nothing around for miles. They traveled a mile into no-man's land and finally came to a stop at a small open area. It seemed like they'd been swallowed up by the forest.

Damon killed the engine and Scar ordered everyone to get out the truck. Wise looked hesitant. In a secluded area like this, it seemed his death was inevitable.

Scar noticed his hesitance. "Nigga, you deaf? I said get the fuck out!" He wasn't asking.

Wise and Pacho slowly climbed out of the vehicle and saw Scar grab a shovel from the back. Unarmed and in the middle of nowhere, they both knew that they had little chance of surviving this. It seemed like Scar wanted to take out two birds with one stone.

It got real when Damon pulled out his Glock and pointed the weapon directly at Wise's head. Wise's eyes instantly grew wide in fear and panic, and he stammered, "C'mon . . . c'mon, what the fuck, Scar? Yo, yo, you don't need to do this."

"Don't tell me what I don't need to do, muthafucka," Scar scolded.

"I ain't do nothin'," Wise shouted.

"Yeah, well, I'll be the judge of that. Walk, nigga. We got someplace to be," Scar instructed.

Damon stepped treacherously closer to Wise with the gun aimed directly at his face. Wise wasn't in a position to object, so he started to march toward his looming grave while being held at gunpoint.

Pacho followed in silence, wondering about his fate too.

"Please, Scar—don't do this, man. Yo, whatever you want me to do, I'll do it," Wise pleaded.

They ignored him. It felt like every step they took was a dramatic one, shit moving in slow motion. It was dark, so Scar had the flashlight to get them through the woods. The strangest thing Pacho noticed was that Damon and Scar seemed too familiar with the area—like they'd done this before. Pacho couldn't help but to wonder how many niggas they'd brought to their fate this way. He felt like he was in a nightmare with two serial killers.

"Scar, I don't wanna die, man. Please, let's work this out, you and me. I fucked up and I'll make it up to you. I promise, man. How far we go back? You know I'm a real nigga, Scar. I got a daughter, man. She needs me," Wise continued to cry and plead for his life.

But all that begging and crying fell on deaf ears. In fact, it irritated Scar to the point where he turned around and shouted, "Nigga, shut the fuck up! Man up! Shit, you already know how I do! This life we live, it's fuckin' gangster, muthafucka. So go out like a fuckin' gangster and not no bitch-ass nigga beggin' fo' his fuckin' life! Stop fuckin' cryin', nigga."

But Wise couldn't stop crying. He didn't want to die. Damon pushed him forcefully. Wise staggered and nearly fell down, but quickly caught his footing.

"Keep walking," Damon growled at him.

They made it to an area creepy enough to scare Jason from *Friday the 13th*—completely dark and isolated. Wise shivered when he saw what would become his impromptu grave. No! No! He couldn't go out like this—not here! Not where his family wouldn't know what happened to him. He knew his body would never be found if they killed him out there.

Wise dropped to his knees in front of Scar. His face was awash with tears and he continued to beg for mercy. Even if he ran away to try to escape his fate, his chances of making it out of the area alive without freezing or starving to death were slim to none. The forest was too massive.

Scar shook his head in disgust at Wise. He nodded to Damon and Damon put the gun into Scar's hand. He wanted to do the dirty work.

Wise dropped to his knees in defeat. His cries turned into a soft whimper. It was already written. Wise drank in the scenery; the trees and the vegetation. He looked up at the dark blue sky and the bright crescent moon and exhaled. Thoughts of his daughter flooded his heart and he said a silent prayer that she would have a father figure to help navigate her through the tough times in life. He looked into the faces of the men he once thought of as his brothers. Brothers he loved and thought loved him. Brothers who now looked at him with disgust and hatred. Brothers who had decided he could no longer live.

Wise had one last request. "Scar, I don't want to die out here and no one know I'm dead. What's the point in living then? You owe me a funeral and a fuckin' headstone. A place where my daughter can come check on me! I need a DOB and DOD, nigga! I'm pleading, don't do me like this!"

Scar gazed at Wise with complete apathy, raised the gun to his head, and fired without an ounce of hesitation—*Bac!* Wise's body fell over on its side. Scar fired three more shots into his head, guaranteeing the nigga was dead.

"I don't owe you shit but those hot slugs. Bitch-ass nigga!"

Pacho stood there in absolute silence. He wasn't shocked. He'd seen niggas killed before, even killed niggas himself. What he was concerned about was, would there be one grave tonight or two?

Scar tossed him the shovel and said, "Start digging, nigga."

Pacho did just that. It took him a while to dig a deep enough grave to place Wise's body in. He assumed that he was digging his own grave too, but they tossed Wise's body into the unmarked grave, covered him up, and left Wise's body to rot in the ground. Pacho sighed with relief. Tonight wouldn't be his night to die.

During the ride back to New York, Scar started to crack jokes on Pacho, saying to him, "Nigga, you shoulda seen your fuckin' face back there. You looked like a scared bitch. What, nigga? You thought you were gonna get bodied too?"

"It's the life we live, right?" Pacho muttered. "You never know in this game."

Scar laughed. "Nigga, I saw the bitch come out of you when I shot that nigga."

Pacho tried to laugh it off, but he knew it was true. He thought there were going to be two bodies left behind instead of one. With Scar, you never knew what to expect.

8

A light of the Newport and then a few drags kept him stabilized for the moment. It was a comforting habit for Nick as he sat inside the nondescript vehicle on the Brooklyn corner and observed the comings and goings from a certain stash house. Next to him was Apple, his partner in crime. They were like two hawks perched on a towering tree, ready to swoop down on their prey.

It was a cool evening with a full moon above. Although Nick was used to working alone, he and Apple decided to stake out Citi, Cane, and her entire organization together. He figured two heads were better than one, for now. Apple had brought him the intel, and she wasn't the type of bitch to sit back and let everyone else do her dirty work for her. Nick knew Apple was more thorough and vicious than most niggas he knew. Her eyes could get just as cold as his—sometimes colder. When they first met, he did his homework on her. Her name did ring out, and he was impressed by her.

For a month, they watched everything in the shadows. It was just the two of them, sitting back and plotting. It was something like the perfect date for two twisted and heartless individuals. Watching Citi's organization from a distance, they saw that everyone was either heavily guarded, lived in high security buildings, or they were so low on the totem pole that they didn't have access to any real money.

"She runs a tight ship," Nick said.

"That cunt is fuckin' stupid," Apple cursed. She didn't want to hear her man praise that bitch.

"I'm saying, we've been watching this bitch and her crew for a month and they leave little to no openings."

"That bitch got a crack somewhere, and I'm gonna find it and shove my fuckin' gun down it, torture that fuckin' bitch, and blow her fuckin' brains out," Apple said with a snarl.

Nick stared at her. She was obsessed with revenge, and he saw that as a problem. He knew firsthand that being thirsty to execute revenge could cause fuck-ups and fatal mistakes because you weren't thinking straight.

"I need for you to have a clear head on this, Apple. We're in this together, and the last thing I need is for you to make a mistake."

"I don't make mistakes," she replied.

"If you think like that, then you will make a mistake."

Apple cut her eyes. She wasn't in the mood to hear a lecture from him.

"I've been doing this shit for a long time, Apple. Trust me, relax, and think this plan all the way through. You don't need to do this shit while running off your emotions. You make this shit personal, get emotional, and you won't see that shit coming. That detail you missed—that fuck-up will get us killed," he said.

Apple frowned. "Nigga, I've been doin' this a long time too, and I know how to survive. I don't need you holding my fuckin' hand, Nick. You're fuckin' me, but you don't need to babysit me."

Nick simply looked at her. She could be stubborn, but he had to trust his judgment. She had the intel, and this was her baby, not his. She'd convinced him that this was going to be a huge payday for him, and once again, he reminded himself that this was going to be his last job.

Another hour went by, and both of them were patient inside the car, smoking cigarettes and talking. Their heads were on a constant swivel, watching and observing everything in the area—and not just the stash house, but neighbors coming and going, cars passing by, pedestrians, and bike riders. In Nick's mind, you couldn't trust anyone. Even the unassuming individual could be a hidden threat. He kept his Glock poised on his lap, and the doors were locked with the windows cracked open just a little. His line of sight was perfect—not too many blind spots for someone to sneak up on them.

"So, tell me about your twin sister," said Nick.

"Why?"

"Is she as crazy and dangerous as you?" he asked.

Apple looked at him. He had no idea. "Where do you think I get it from? Now she's living this different life, though, tryin' to be some fool's housewife and have babies. I remember a time when Kola was something fierce in Harlem. I even looked up to her at one point," she said.

Nick was listening. Apple rarely talked about her past with her family, especially her sister. She intrigued him, and though he'd never met Kola, he could tell that Apple and Kola together was a force to be reckoned with.

"We had our ups and downs," Apple continued. "But real talk, she did teach me a lot. I was a different person a long time ago—naive, foolish, and reckless. I was a square-ass bitch that got down wit' someone dangerous and it cost me someone very close to me."

It was hard to imagine Apple as a square bitch. Nick laughed to himself. He'd assumed she was born with a gun in her hand.

They continued to talk and observed the block. Apple felt she couldn't stomach another month of nothing happening. Watching the bitch's crew was tedious work, but they had to do it. There were times when she wanted to suck Nick's dick in the front seat of the car just to pass some time. But the pleasurable distraction would only hinder their stakeout, not help it.

Another cigarette was lit, and the night was growing late. From their position, things were quiet—maybe too quiet for Apple's comfort. They hadn't seen any activity in over two hours. But that soon changed.

A BMW i8 loomed onto the block and parked directly in front of the house they were watching. The car was black and sleek—eye-candy in such a poverty-stricken area. The driver's door opened vertically, and a long-legged, dark-skinned beauty gracefully climbed out of the expensive vehicle. Nick and Apple fixed their eyes on the stunning woman, who was from Ethiopia and was model-tall, slim, and very pretty. She was fashionably dressed in a black tailored business suit that accentuated her curves, a black trench coat, and red bottoms.

"Who the fuck is that?" Nick asked, almost in awe at the dark beauty.

The two thought she was someone famous. The way she dressed and moved, she had this air about her that exuded sophistication. She looked like a young Iman. Apple perked up in her seat and didn't blink once.

Right away, Cane exited the house and greeted the woman with a tight hug and an affectionate kiss. Cane shared a brief conversation with the woman, handed her a black vegan leather duffel bag, and then the woman turned around and walked in the opposite direction of where she'd parked and climbed into a white Mercedes Benz C300. They were switching cars for some reason.

"We need to follow that bitch," said Apple.

"Why her?" Nick asked.

"I just got this feeling we onto something wit' that bitch."

They watched Cane go back into the stash house, and the Benz pulled out of the parking space. Once the Benz drove past them, Nick quickly maneuvered out of the parking spot they were in, swung the car into an abrupt U-turn, and followed the driver. Where they were headed, Apple could only imagine. But she knew if the lady was important enough to meet with Cane at their stash house, then she was important enough to follow. Apple assumed that Cane handed her some money in that duffel bag, but it was strange for her not to have any security following her if it was money that she was transporting.

Nick carefully followed the car from Brooklyn onto the BQE and into Long Island. Forty-five minutes later, they found themselves in the exclusive neighborhood of Glen Cove—an affluent city with homes costing half-a-million or more, and where the streets became more deserted.

"Fall back a little. We don't want to spook her," she told Nick.

He did so. Apple noticed that the woman had begun riding her brakes and making one right turn after another, like she felt like she was being followed. So, when the C300 made a right at the intersection, Apple told Nick to make a left. He did, against his wishes.

***

Takenya repeatedly looked through her rearview mirror to see if that same car was still following her. But the moment she made a right turn at the intersection, she saw that the gray Accord had made a left. Maybe she was just being paranoid.

She'd started to suspect she was being followed once she got off the Long Island Expressway and was nearing her home. She had already reached for her pistol in her handbag and kept it close, but sighed with relief that she didn't have to use it when she saw the Accord turn the opposite direction. As an extra precaution, she rode around in circles for a few moments before heading to her picturesque home nearby.

She turned into her driveway and parked inside the one-car garage, with the garage door closing behind her. Finally feeling safe, she climbed out of the Benz with the bag in hand, and then popped the trunk. Inside were two duffel bags containing $250,000 each. The small duffel was a diversion containing $20,000 just in case anyone was watching her. The real prize was what was inside the trunk of the Benz. Takenya was skillful at laundering money, and in a few days the half-million would be transferred to various bank accounts overseas for her man, Cane. They had a good thing going.

The duffel bags were heavy, and she had some difficulty removing them from the trunk, but eventually she did. She went and shut off the alarm to her home and then placed both bags inside a hidden space in the wall in the garage.

It had been a long day for her. She just wanted to draw herself a nice bubble bath and unwind with some white wine and soothing R&B music. Tomorrow, she planned on taking care of business.

***

Apple and Nick circled around the block just in time to see Takenya's white Benz circling the area and make a left on the next block. Apple smiled. It was fate. They crept slowly down the block and saw the Benz turn into a short driveway and disappear inside the one-car garage.

"Bingo!" Apple uttered with glee.

They were on it. Their plan was coming together like a puzzle. The home was nice with a sprawling front lawn, small porch, bay windows, and a beautiful flower garden in the front yard. The bitch was living comfortably in the suburbs, probably feeling safe and protected away from the harsh and cruel Brooklyn streets. Apple knew she was of some importance to Cane, and she couldn't wait to find out the details.

Nick, being the old school professional he was at breaking into homes and robbing muthafuckas, had a knack for moving in the shadows and entering places that wanted to keep him out. The first thing he noticed was the motion lights placed around the home. But he didn't see any surveillance cameras. The rooms were dark, but there was a light on in the back—maybe it was the bedroom. He deduced that this wasn't another stash house. Still, every movement they made toward the place had to be careful and calculated. There was no telling what they would be facing once inside. Maybe she was alone, maybe she wasn't.

Parked nearby and trying to remain unassuming, the two geared up with black latex gloves and pistols. Nick fixed his eyes on the neighboring homes nearby. He saw no lights on, no shades drawn to the side, and no people moving about. He figured that everyone was sleeping with the time being so late.

Nick started the car, kept the lights off, moved closer to the home, and boldly parked right in front. He and Apple exited the vehicle with a sense of urgency and maneuvered toward the backyard, keeping an eye out for anyone or anything. To their benefit, the homeowner desired their privacy, meaning there was a high wooden fence shielding them from neighbors' eyes in case someone was peeking out their windows. They remained crouched and moved in the shadows to the backdoor. It was a single door, no screen door, and no distractions around, meaning no barking dogs and no blinding flood lights.

Nick looked at Apple and said with his eyes, *You ready to do this?*
Apple nodded. *Of course.*

It had to be quick, as subtle as possible, and violent. Their guns were drawn, and Nick did the honors. He lifted his knee vertically in the air to give himself some momentum and propelled his foot forward against the door with brute force, kicking it nearly off the hinges. It created a disturbance, and their adrenaline started to pump like whitewater rapids. Immediately, they charged into the home and Nick knew where to go—to that light he saw glimmering in the backroom.

Takenya heard the disturbance inside her home and she jumped out of her bubble bath. Something was wrong, and she wasn't about to get caught slipping. With no time to reach for a towel, she scurried naked from the bathroom into the hallway and saw that her worst nightmare had come true. There were two strangers inside her home, and they weren't there to play nice. Panic rapidly consumed Takenya, and she ran for the bedroom to get her gun.

Nick and Apple gave chase, and when Takenya abruptly pivoted in a desperate attempt to slam the bedroom door behind her, Nick was there to aggressively push it open. Takenya stumbled backwards and turned to get her gun from the dresser, but Nick grabbed her from behind and slammed the butt of the gun against the back of her head and she collapsed.

"Bitch, stay your ass down and don't do anything stupid," he warned.

Takenya was dazed and confused. The blow to the back of her head was thumping. She lay there naked on the carpeted floor scared out of her mind. Nick and Apple stood over her, scowling.

"Don't make this shit difficult, bitch," scolded Apple.

"Please, don't kill me!" she begged.

"You fuckin' scream, and I'm gonna have my nigga slice you up into tiny pieces," Apple threatened through clenched teeth.

Nick manhandled her into the nearest chair, where they tied her up and placed duct tape over her mouth. Takenya's eyes were wide with panic written all over her face.

Nick looked at Apple. "Go check outside. See if we have company."

Apple left the bedroom to see. Their entrance through the backdoor could have stirred up some unwanted attention from a neighbor, and there was no telling if someone had called 911 or not. Apple went into the living room and drew back the curtains slightly and gazed outside. The block was quiet. There were no lights on in anyone's home as far as she could tell. She went from window to window, carefully gazing out each one, and it was all the same. But yet, it was too early to tell.

Takenya was shaking like a leaf on a windy day. This wasn't supposed to happen. She couldn't take her eyes off Nick. The nigga looked as threatening as they came. Occasionally, they would lock eyes and his look brought about a deep chill down her spine. He was no amateur at this.

Ten minutes later, Apple came back into the room and assured Nick that everything was okay. She didn't see any problems outside—no cops, no neighbors, no goons coming for a late-night visit. She figured the bitch lived alone, but it wasn't guaranteed. But now it was time to get down to business—to get what they'd come there for.

Apple shoved her gun in the girl's face and threatened to blow her brains out if she didn't cooperate with them. Surprisingly, they didn't have to do much threatening. Takenya wasn't about that life. She didn't want to die, so she gave everything up so easily.

"The money is in the garage," she spewed.

"In the garage, huh?" Apple said.

She nodded. "Yes. I'm just their bank, that's all. I only launder their money. But I promise that I can be a better asset to you alive and do the same for you two."

They didn't care for her offer. They were there for only one thing, and they were determined to get it.

"Where at in the garage?" Apple asked her.

"Behind a hollow wall," she said.

"I'll go check it out," said Nick.

Apple thrust the gun into Takenya's face and exclaimed, "Bitch, you better not be lying."

"I'm not."

Takenya honestly never saw this coming. She felt she'd done everything right. She was always careful. No one knew where she lived, not even Cane. When they had sex, it was always at his place. Her relationship with Cane was meant to be business, but then it turned personal, and the money she made from their organization was good—really good. Now these two intruders were inside her home and she didn't know if she was going to live or die.

It didn't take long for Nick to find the three duffel bags of money. He brought them into the bedroom and showed Apple. Her eyes widened at the amount.

"Shit!" she uttered.

"Yeah, I love it," Nick announced.

"See? I wasn't lying," Takenya chided.

"There's gotta be more where that came from," said Nick.

"No, there is no more . . . only half a million, plus the twenty thousand," she said.

"I don't' fuckin' believe you," Nick growled at her.

"I promise you, that's it. That's everything in the house."

Nick stepped closer to her in a threatening manner. Takenya was trembling and terrified. What more did they want from her? She'd given them everything.

Nick fixed a frosty stare on her with the gun in his hand. "Where the rest at, bitch?"

"There is no more!" she cried out.

"You lying bitch! I will tear this fuckin' place apart, but if you don't save me the trouble, I'll kill you right now," he threatened.

Takenya was in full-blown tears. The look in Nick's eyes was just about satanic. Takenya swore she saw hell hiding behind his dark pupils.

He put the barrel of the gun to her temple and once again asked, "Where that money at?"

Crying and becoming hysterical, she started to beg and plead for her life. She had nothing else to give him.

"Please, don't kill me, there is no more money. That's all there is. I just help them launder it, that's all!"

Bac!

Just like that, Nick parked a bullet into her temple. Her body slumped in the chair. *Such a waste*, Nick thought. She was a pretty and smart woman—nice body too.

Apple didn't flinch. It needed to be done. Nick looked her way and said, "We need to find the rest of that cash."

Apple wondered if there was any more cash in the house. They already had over a half-million dollars, but Apple saw the greed settling into his eyes. When he saw all that cash, he felt there was more.

He started in the bedroom, ripping open walls, tearing down the ceiling, rifling through the dead woman's things. He wanted more, and he wasn't going to stop looking until he was satisfied that Takenya had told the truth.

Apple felt that she'd created a monster. Nick was hungry for more money like he was the Cookie Monster. She became irritated. He was being greedy and risking both their lives. What if Cane was coming or what if he'd sent a kill squad to his bitch's place?

It was around 4 a.m. when Takenya's cell phone started to ring. Apple picked up the phone and the caller ID said, "Daddy Cane."

Apple showed Nick the name and they both shared a quick laugh while a dead Takenya continued to lay slumped in the chair.

"We need to go," she said to him.

Finally, he agreed. Nick had torn the entire house apart. They'd spent hours looking for more money that wasn't there. She was telling the truth.

Nick was incredibly hyped and in a great mood. It had taken him nearly two decades to save one million, and tonight he had made half that off of one lick. Listening to Apple's instincts and following the girl was a smart move, and Nick was proud of his bitch. She was street and smart. She was a survivor and knew how to get money.

With the mood feeling so right, it was inevitable that they went back to Apple's place and fucked hard and long. The thrill of money and murder turned them both on.

Nick's dick was harder than it had been for some time now and Apple loved it. He fucked her from the back while reaching around to squeeze her tits, taking possession of her body while feeling her love muscles contracting around his erection. Apple submitted to him with her profound groans, as her hands gripped the sheets to hold her position. Nick was in pure beast mode, and they were having some of the best sex of their lives. For Apple, stealing half a million dollars from Citi was about to make for an intense orgasm.

9

The stream of piss that poured into the toilet was a never-ending golden waterfall, but Cane really had to go. The Hennessy had him pissing like a race horse, and last night was almost a blur to him. He did know that he'd had a good time with the young beauty lying in the master bedroom. He remembered her young, tight pussy and busting a couple of nuts—and her head game was through the roof. All they did last night was get drunk and fuck, which made it the perfect night for Cane. Shaking his dick and making sure every drop hit the toilet, he bothered not to flush and turned to leave the bathroom butt-naked.

He went into the kitchen, removed some orange juice from the fridge, and started to drink from the carton. He guzzled a good portion of the orange liquid like he had just run the NYC marathon, burped loud, and scratched his ass. It was early afternoon and Cane wanted to get his day started. He had plans. He took another swig from the carton, looked around the quiet kitchen, and then it dawned on him that it had been several days since he had heard from Takenya.

He'd called her the night of the exchange, but she didn't pick up. He was sure everything was okay. Takenya knew how to move and be careful, but it was still unlike her to go days without reaching out to him. She left the stash house with half a million dollars in the trunk of the Benz, and that wasn't an amount to be taken lightly.

Lately Cane had been caught up in sex, booze, and having a good time, but still handling his business. His sister ran the show, and her nigga, Scar—well real recognized real, and Cane knew Scar was a stone cold killing muthafucka. But Cane wasn't intimidated by Scar, because he could equally match his craziness. They had mutual respect in some twisted kind of way, and they stayed out of each other's way.

Cane decided to give Takenya a call. Though they'd done the cash exchange nearly two dozen times and she was always successful at laundering their money, this time something felt different for some reason. Cane went to get his cell phone and dialed her number. Her phone rang several times and then it went to her voicemail. He dialed her again and got the same results. He dialed a third, fourth, and a fifth time, and each time it was the same. She wasn't answering her phone.

"Shit!" he cursed.

Something was wrong. He felt it. He'd fucked up. This time he hadn't kept tabs on his bitch and the money, and he let too much time go by without contacting her. He had gotten used to shit moving smoothly. Takenya would contact him to let him know that everything had gone well and the cash was transferred to overseas accounts or into various shell companies and it would come back clean to the state's bank accounts for profit. She would give Cane the account numbers and proof of transactions to reassure him that she'd done her job.

Irritated that he couldn't get in contact with Takenya, Cane marched into the bedroom and started to rudely stir the girl awake. She was a young and dim-witted bitch with easy and good pussy, just how he liked them.

"Bitch, get the fuck up!" Cane yelled, turning the TV on full blast.

Stacy complained about the rude awakening. She was still hung over from last night. "Baby, I'm tired. I just wanna stay and sleep for a moment. Can I just chill and suck your dick later on?"

"Fuck that. You need to fuckin' go. I got business to take care of."

He had moves to make, and he wasn't about to allow any bitch to stay in his place alone. Even if he had to drag the bitch out of bed and toss her out of his place butt naked, he was willing to do it. He was giving Stacy fair warning.

She sighed. Cane was being an asshole.

"Stacy, get the fuck out now before I throw your ass outside naked!" he shouted.

Stacy finally caught the hint. She leaped from the bed with a serious attitude. Glaring at Cane, she cursed, "Muthafucka, fuck you! Why I gotta fuckin' leave, Cane? You can't even let a bitch sleep after we done fucked all night? See if you get this good pussy again, nigga! Fo' real, nigga!"

"Just shut the fuck up and get the fuck out!"

She stormed around the bedroom collecting her things and got dressed. She felt used and rushed. She was upset, but Cane didn't care. He stared at her with no regard for her feelings.

When Stacy was finally gone, Cane got down to business. He called Takenya's cell phone and got her voicemail yet again. It was time to take action. He needed to find her and his money.

He went into the bathroom to pick at the small, curly afro he had growing. He could hear the TV blaring from the bedroom, and as he was picking out his hair he heard an anchorwoman announce, "Disturbing news out of Glen Cove, Long Island. A young woman has been found murdered inside her home in what appears to be a violent home invasion. Local authorities have no idea how long she's been dead, but she was found by a neighbor who had grown concerned after not seeing her for several days and decided to call the police. The victim, Takenya Admassou, a former child model and native of Ethiopia, was found in her bedroom early yesterday morning with a single gunshot wound to her head . . . ."

Hearing her name, Cane immediately stopped what he was doing and hurried into the bedroom to lay his eyes on the news. On the TV screen, they displayed Takenya's beautiful home swamped with police activity and yellow crime scene tape. He saw a glimpse of coroners removing the body from the home in a body bag and placing it into the coroner's van.

Cane was utterly shocked by what he was seeing.

"What the fuck?" His attention stayed fixated on the television and all kinds of feelings and concerns started to flood him. They mentioned her name again, so he definitely wasn't hearing things. Someone had murdered her? He was just with her. Cane didn't know what to do. He thought about the money—*shit, the money*. He became upset and emotional. Staring at the television and watching everything unfold, Cane couldn't help but to become a bit teary-eyed. Thing is, he really liked Takenya. She was a very beautiful woman, and she was different. She was smart. He was sure if the chance had ever come for him, he probably would have married her—yet, he didn't know much at all about her, not even where she lived. The crazy thing about that was he trusted her with his money. Takenya had this glow about her that he liked.

"Fuck me!" Cane cursed.

With a sudden and brisk motion of his hand, he angrily swiped everything off the dresser and sent all kinds of shit crashing to the floor. He had no one to call. Who was her family? Did she have family? Was he to make funeral arrangements for her?

Abruptly, Cane's knees became wobbly and he collapsed into a chair in the bedroom. He couldn't move. He was grieving. He was upset. Someone violently took something special from him—and that someone needed to pay. But for now, Cane was overcome with emotions that he never knew he had. He really did care for Takenya, and he trusted her too. He felt that he could trust her with his own life. Now she was gone.

Three hours later, he was still sitting in the same spot, naked and silent. He seethed, and he was sad. He then sighed, finally stood up, got himself right, and shook off the shock of her death.

"Fuck it," he said. *A dead person is still dead whether you grieve or not,* he thought.

Cane picked up the half-empty bottle of Hennessy from last night, poured a glass, and downed it. He needed to get his mind off Takenya. There was no use in moping all day. He decided to call Stacy back and apologize for his actions. Surprisingly, she answered and said she was willing to come back to his place and give him some pussy. He decided to make the best of a bad day.

Soon, though, he would find out who had killed his bitch and taken his money.

10

Apple stepped out of the bathroom wearing a brand new thirteen-thousand-dollar mink coat and YSL heels. She smiled at Nick, who was lounging on her bed in his boxer shorts with his eyes fixed on her. Apple decided to put on a show for him, and she opened the mink coat to reveal that she was completely naked underneath.

His face said, *Wow!*

"You like it, baby?" she asked.

"Damn, baby, I love it. Shit!" Nick replied merrily, his eyes matching the wide smile on his face.

"I knew you would."

They were celebrating tonight—a continued celebration. They had scored a half-million dollars. They had a reason to celebrate. They wanted to enjoy themselves, and that meant popping champagne, going on expensive shopping sprees, and having great sex. It was business and murder, but it was also fun and love.

"Damn, baby, you're making my dick hard. Do a dance for me."

Apple chuckled. "You want me to dance for you?"

"Yeah . . ."

Nick already had his hand in his boxer shorts grabbing for his growing erection. Apple completely turned him on. She was everything he dreamed of—sexy, beautiful, and a down-ass bitch. She was fierce and a go-getter. She could kill like him, and she could fuck like him—probably better.

Their age gap didn't matter; they were nearly equal in everything. Nick felt if he had met a woman like her in his earlier years, then they would've ruled the streets together—maybe the world. They would have been unstoppable—and, of course, she would have given him a few babies.

Apple started to seductively move around the bedroom for Nick. She dropped the mink coat down to her shoulders, her tits showing and her shaved pussy looking marvelous. She dropped eagle style toward the floor and started to bounce up and down. Nick was fixated on her. By now, he had his fist wrapped around his big dick and was jerking off in front of her. They both liked being nasty and freaky; it gave their relationship a spark. Nick's age wasn't a deterrent. In fact, Apple felt he came with the experience to handle her.

Apple started to twerk for him and she moved like the best of them. Nick's eyes continued to light up and his dick continued to grow. It started to look like a rocket ready to launch.

"Damn, baby, I can't take it anymore. You need to come over here and do something about this," he said.

"Oh, you want me to do something about that?" she teased.

"Hells yeah."

"Keep jerking off. I like that shit," she said.

Nick continued to masturbate as his arousal reached a magnitude that almost hurt. He grinned at her. "Baby, you know I need your help with this."

She laughed and strutted closer to him, dropping the coat lower down her curvy frame. It was sexy to see him masturbate. His erection was impressive, and he was definitely all man. He moaned while pleasing himself, and Apple felt he'd suffered enough. She finally allowed the mink coat to fall from her frame, dropping it to the floor. She left her shoes on and joined him on the bed.

"Stay on your back," she said.

She straddled him, pushed him on his back, and gradually placed his huge erection inside of her, feeling his profound width. Nick moaned from the glorious feeling of penetrating her nice and slow, and he gazed up at her in admiration with his hands reaching up and cupping her breasts as they started to fuck.

And the celebration continued.

The next day, they headed to Kola's place. Apple had been thinking about her sister lately, and she felt the urge to check to see how she was doing, especially since she was pregnant.

The drive from SoHo to Westchester was a somewhat drawn out one, and while Nick drove, they started to discuss Citi. Not a day went by that Apple didn't bring the bitch up, either in revenge, disgust, jealousy, or hatred.

"That bitch was at a Knicks game the other night," she told Nick.

"She was, huh?"

"Yeah, and she damn near had courtside seats," Apple added. "Let that bitch enjoy her life for now, cuz we're 'bout to fuck her entire world up."

Lately, Apple had been stalking Citi's Facebook page from a fake profile she created. Citi was easy to find and follow because she wasn't hiding. Any big event—playoffs, Knicks games, concerts at Madison Square Garden or the Barclays Center—she showed up highly protected and flossing in her trendy outfits. Apple would seethe seeing pictures of Citi looking glamorous and watching videos of her living the good life, cruising around in expensive cars like Maseratis, Porsches, Range Rovers, Benzes. She had them all.

And now Nick wanted in on the glory and success. Seeing the toys and the money that Citi had, he saw that Apple was right. She was sitting on a goldmine. Apple explained to him that Citi was nothing but a brainless tramp that she and Cartier had taken under their wing. Had it not been for Apple and Cartier, she wouldn't have anything. Nick wanted to take care of the bitch. He knew niggas like her who didn't put in work but wanted all the glory and the street credit. But behind the scenes, they were nothing but punk bitches.

"If we go after her, then we gotta start with her muscle," Apple said.

"So, you and me, going after a big organization like hers," Nick replied.

"Without her muscle around, it will make her vulnerable."

"I agree, Apple, but this isn't some light work. This isn't a home invasion with a few armed niggas here and there. This is an organization, where they got guns too—lots of guns—and I don't have the time to get my hands that dirty, especially to go after one bitch. This wasn't what I signed up for," Nick griped.

"So you just happy wit' that half a million we took from that bitch?"

"Absolutely. Look, I love you, bae, and I want you to be happy," he proclaimed. "I can't lie, this Citi bitch is a fuckin' goldmine, but I made promises too. I say we bow out while we ahead."

"You mean, *you're* ahead. Me? I'm still in the same position 'cause that bitch ain't dead yet. How you sound, nigga?"

"I learned that an eye for an eye will make everyone go blind. That revenge shit ain't for me. I jumped in for a taste of the pie. We ate. Let's bounce now and drive off into the sunset, ma."

"You're such a fuckin' hypocrite. Where was that eye-for-an-eye logic when your ass was locked up for murder? Did you preach that bullshit to Amir before he went and murdered that snitching bitch for you?"

Nick was quiet. No refuting the obvious.

"Thought so, nigga."

Apple sighed and rolled her eyes. She knew he didn't see the scowl on her face because he was driving. She was growing tired of his back-and-forth attitude about helping with her revenge project. One moment he would be hyped, excited, and down for her cause, and then the next moment, he was indecisive and preaching to her about the promises he made to get out the game.

"I thought you was an OG," she muttered.

Nick's head swiveled her way. "What? I am an OG in these fuckin' streets. Don't get shit twisted. I ain't scared of no one, especially some young-ass bitch."

"I know you ain't scared, baby, that's why I fuckin' love you to death." She placed her hand on his thigh.

Nick sighed. "Damn, you're lucky I love you, or am in love with you. A'ight, we take out a couple of niggas and try to roll up on her. I wanna make you happy, baby, but I don't want this shit to come back on us either."

Apple grinned. "You already make me happy. But for this, I'll suck your dick for two months straight and make you come in my mouth each time."

Nick laughed. She had already done that, but he was happy to hear the news.

They arrived at Kola's place late that afternoon. They rang her doorbell several times, but to no avail. It seemed like no one was home, but they were always home. Apple sighed. She really wanted to see the kids, especially her daughter. Plus, this was the first time she'd brought Nick by to introduce him to her sister.

She rang the bell a few more times and knocked on the door, but nobody answered. After that, she pulled out her cell phone and called Kola, but there was no answer.

"Something's wrong?" Nick asked.

"I hope not," Apple replied.

Apple tried calling Kola's cell phone again, but received the same results. She didn't want to worry, but where were her sister and the kids?

"Maybe they went out for a bite to eat," said Nick.

"She always answers her phone," Apple replied.

By now, Apple started to look through the windows and snoop around the house. Nick stood there watching her. He had a .45 concealed on him. He was always cautious, observant of his surroundings, and ready for anyone or anything. The fact they were in the suburbs didn't matter. He knew shit could pop off anywhere, even in the safest neighborhoods. Danger had no zip code.

Apple sighed. "This is fucked up."

"Just chill. I'm sure your sister is okay," Nick said.

Just then, Apple's cell phone sounded in her hand. She assumed that it was Kola calling her back. She quickly answered her phone with a sharp, "Where the fuck are you and the kids?"

"Apple, it's me, Kamel," she heard him say.

"Why do you have my sister's phone?"

"Listen, Kola is in the hospital," he said.

"What? What the fuck you talkin' about? What happened?"

"We left this morning. She's gonna be admitted overnight for observation of the baby and she'll be on bed rest because it's a high risk pregnancy," said Kamel.

Apple's stomach fluttered. "What hospital y'all at?" she asked.

"We're at Westchester Medical Center," he said.

"We're on our way there."

Apple and Nick rushed to the hospital as fast as they could. In a way, Apple felt relieved that it was only pregnancy issues. With the life they had lived, anything could come back on them. Apple feared that one of their many enemies had located Kola and done the unthinkable to her sister and the family. It was one of her biggest fears—retribution from an enemy.

When they arrived at Westchester Medical Center in Valhalla, New York, Apple walked through the hospital with a sense of urgency. She was concerned about her sister and the unborn baby. Her heels click-clacked loud and fast against the flooring, and she spewed questions at the staff.

"My sister, Kola Evans-Carmichael—where is she?"

She and Nick were directed to room 312. Apple hurried toward the elevator with Nick trying to keep up. The girl was moving like a thoroughbred race horse. They soon arrived at room 312 and Apple entered without knocking. She laid her eyes on Kola lying in bed and looking copasetic. Kamel was by her side looking worried, and the children had fallen asleep on the nearby chairs.

"Bitch, you about gave me a damn heart attack," Apple exclaimed. "You okay?"

"I'm fine, Apple," replied Kola.

"What happened?"

"It was just a pregnancy scare, that's all . . . just some spotting."

"So is the baby okay?"

"The baby's fine," said Kola.

"Well, whatever you need, I'm here for you," Apple said.

Kola smiled. "And by the way, I'm having a boy."

"Bitch, shut up!" Apple hollered excitedly.

Kola nodded. Coming from a family with all girls, it was exciting to finally have a swinging dick in their family. After everything they'd been through, finding out that Kola was having a son was wonderful news.

"I saw the ultrasound and he's beautiful."

"I bet you he is," Apple said.

Apple hugged Peaches and showed her affection. She and Kola continued to chat.

Nick was taken aback by Kola. She was definitely Apple's identical twin, besides the extra weight due to her pregnancy.

"You need to take it easy like the doctors told you. The only thing you need to be doing is getting rest, eating good, and having Kamel wait on you hand and foot—and eat that pussy too," Apple joked.

"Shut up, Apple." Kola laughed.

The two sisters were in high spirits. Apple couldn't stop thinking about her sister bringing a boy into this world. She smiled at Kola and said, "I got the perfect name for him."

Curious, Kola asked, "And what's that?"

"Koke."

"What? Koke?" Kola wasn't too thrilled by the name.

"Yes!"

"Are you serious, Apple?"

"Koke sounds cool and intriguing," Apple replied.

Kola laughed, but Apple was dead serious. "Koke and Kola."

"I'm not naming my son after a narcotic, Apple. That's insane . . . and ghetto."

Apple rolled her eyes. "And Kola is so highbrow and distinguished."

The sisters continued to talk, and Nick got to meet Kamel, and the two men seemed to hit it off. It was all love inside the hospital room. Being with Kola and her daughter took Apple's mind off of Citi and her desired revenge. She and Nick looked like different people, almost the perfect couple—joyous folks enjoying family and good news for once. Nick even laughed and played with Peaches. He missed the little princess being around, but business was business, and he had some murders to do.

Later in their visit, Kamel gently tapped Apple on her shoulder and asked if they could speak outside. From the look in Kamel's eyes, it seemed like it was really important. They excused themselves from the room and went into the hallway to talk privately.

Kamel fixed his eyes on Apple. "Could you do us a favor? We need help around the house. With Kola being pregnant and needing as much bed rest as possible, I was wondering if you could come and stay with us for a while to help us around the house and with the kids."

The nerve of him, was the look in Apple's eyes. "That's what you're there for, right? You signed up for sickness and in health, didn't you?"

"And I'm there for her as always. I love your sister, Apple, but this isn't easy," he replied.

"Nothing in life ever is," she smoothly countered. "You made your bed, so you lie in it."

Apple didn't sign up to become anyone's maid or nanny. She hadn't put the ring on her sister's finger, he had. She wasn't about to make shit easy for someone she felt was a bitch-ass nigga. Kola promised to take care of Peaches—those other rugrats weren't her problem. Besides, she was knee-deep in exacting revenge.

Apple's final words to Kamel were, "Go hire a nanny with Eduardo's money."

She pivoted and marched back into the room. It was time for her and Nick to leave.

Kamel hated his daily thoughts about Kola's twin. He wished someone would park a bullet in her fuckin' temple and put him out of his misery. In another lifetime, he would have been that someone.

11

Nick sat behind the wheel of his GMC truck for a moment and enjoyed a cigarette and a moment of solitude. It had been a tiresome five-hour drive to the Clinton Correctional Facility in Dannemora, New York. The day was brisk and gloomy with remnants of a previous snowfall still covering the small iron-working town.

Nick felt ambivalent about seeing his father. The old man had spent Nick's entire life inside a prison, and he never got to see Nick grow up. They had to build a father-son relationship under the eyes of the powers that be, and his pops did his best to guide and teach his son from behind bars. It didn't take long for the father to see that his son was a chip off the old block.

Nick lingered in the visitor's parking lot and set his eyes on the towering concrete walls that stretched for several blocks in different directions. Multiple guard towers had a sweeping view of people's comings and goings. It was an intimidating structure—maximum security at its finest. From the parking lot to inside, everything Nick would do was going to be scrutinized. He sighed and got out of the truck to get the process started.

He moved through the tight-knit security without any issues. He'd been coming to the prison for so long that he knew the routines like the back of his hand. He knew what was allowed and what wasn't. In an inexplicable way, Clinton had become like a second home to him—though he didn't want to make the place his permanent residence. He feared ending up like his father and best friend, serving life sentences and never seeing the outside world again.

Hence the reason he wanted to retire.

Nick entered the large visiting room and took his seat among the others there to see their loved ones. They were mostly women with children there to see a husband, a boyfriend, a father, or a brother. The chitchat wasn't too loud, and there were cameras everywhere. Unlike Rikers Island, the visitors at Clinton had access to vending machines, the kids were able to run around, families were able to take pictures with their loved ones, and the guards weren't too overzealous with their authority and instructions.

Nick sat coolly at the table and watched his surroundings, observing a few beautiful ladies there to give their men some needed comfort. He wondered if he ever got locked up would Apple visit him faithfully like some of the women he saw there on the regular. He really didn't want to find out, though. Nick planned on staying free. He valued his freedom, and it was one of the reasons he continually worked alone and was always extra careful when pulling off a robbery and murder—take shit fast and subtle and leave behind no witnesses. The dead can't testify against you.

Nick's father, Corey Davis, loomed into the visiting area. Like always, there was an air of power about him. Corey's hard frown transitioned into a slight smile when he spotted his son in the room. He moved toward Nick with a tiger's stride—confident and authoritative, like even the guards couldn't tell him shit. He was an original gangster who ran the streets with the best of the best, and he'd once had more money than he could count. Corey was sixty-six years old, but he didn't look a day over forty. He kept himself physically fit, had smooth skin with no wrinkles, and he hardly had any gray hairs. It was like Nick's father couldn't age—like he'd found the fountain of youth.

The two hugged ardently, showing a father-son bond that couldn't be broken. Corey was always proud to see his son, and Nick was always proud to see his father. Although their relationship had always been through prison visits, Corey had a knack for knowing how to guide his son through letters or visits from the time he was young, and he knew how to look out for his only son even from prison.

"How you holding up, Pop?" asked Nick.

"Same ol', same ol' . . . one day at a time, because you know the hardest prison to escape is your mind," said Corey.

"You still look good, Pops. They got you looking healthy in here. Shit, you're looking better than some free fools out there," he joked. "What they feeding you, steaks and ribs? I bet you eat better than me in here."

"It's life, but it's not home. I do what I need to do to keep myself free inside here," Corey said, taking his two fingers and tapping the side of his head. "You understand?"

Nick nodded.

"Do you?" Corey uttered sharply.

"Absolutely." Though Nick was a grown man with a violent past, to his father, he still needed guidance.

"So, in saying that, are you keeping that promise you made to yourself?" Corey asked. "Because I don't wanna see you in here with me, doing a life sentence. Don't make it a family reunion by coming here, son. Do you understand?"

"That ain't gonna happen. Trust me. I didn't travel this far to go nowhere. I've moved intelligently and stealthily and have gotten off scot-free," Nick boasted.

"Scot-free?" Corey smirked. "Nigga, is you stupid? I don't know if it's arrogance or ignorance speaking. But check this, young blood, there's always a toll on that get-money-quick road, either at the beginning, middle, or end of your life's journey. You'll pay on this side or the other for your transgressions. I'm paying with time. I don't want you paying with your life."

Nick nodded. "I hear you, Pops. I got this."

"So, what's your next move since you're supposed to be out of the game? Are you gonna open up that bar you always talked about?"

Nick stared at his father in silence, knowing he could never lie to him. "There have been some changes, Pop."

Corey's eyebrow lifted as he repeated Nick's word, "Changes?"

"Yeah, I got something brewing right now—something sweet that can net me a few million dollars so I can retire more comfortably."

Corey's face was expressionless. He wasn't impressed with his son's words. In fact, he coolly replied with, "Let me guess, that young bitch got you caught up in something."

Corey knew about Apple. Nick had told him about her, and when he called her a bitch, he could see his son looking disturbed by the word. The slight disrespect toward the woman he loved stirred up some distaste in their visit.

"She's good peoples," said Nick.

"I care about you, not her," Corey replied.

Nick continued to be candid with his father. Corey listened, but he didn't like his son's decision. Nick thought Corey would be impressed once he heard about the robbery and the half-million, but he wasn't.

"She's a ride-or-die, Pop," he said in her defense.

"You're too old to be fuckin' with some young girl and proclaiming her to be ride-or-die. And this shit she got you caught up in? Not good. It's gonna break you. You're pushing your luck, and you need to drop her, Nick. Drop that bitch now before you fuck up and end up in here with me, because that's what her pussy gonna do to you. That bitch spreads her legs, gives you a taste, and she got you lookin' at life behind bars or six feet deep," Corey said.

Corey was wise—been there and done that. Nick didn't like his father's approach, but Corey didn't care. He saw something that Nick couldn't see, even for a man his age. A bitch like Apple was nothing but trouble, and Nick was about to bite off more than he could chew if he continued to mess with her, despite his reputation on the streets. Good pussy had a way of making even the sharpest men vulnerable.

"You just need to meet her, Pops," he said.

"No, I don't. I know her kind already."

"Her kind?"

"No disrespect, but look at you—you're blinded by pussy," said Corey.

"I'm not."

Corey had never seen his son so flushed and infatuated over a woman. *Bitch's pussy must be made of gold,* he thought.

"If this woman really loved you, then she wouldn't drag you into a war that y'all can't win. You're smarter than this, Nick. At least I thought you were."

Nick continued to protest his father's words. He didn't want to hear it, but he remained respectful. They continued to speak like men, never arguing, but agreeing to disagree. He filled Corey in on his plan to take down Scar, Citi, and Cane and ultimately end up with his biggest score.

Corey was adamant about leaving Apple alone before he ended up in jail or dead and, most importantly, to leave Apple's beef with her. Nick, however, was adamant that it would never come to that. He wouldn't allow it. He wasn't going to slip up. He was a cautious man and would continue to be one—and he would retire from the game, but not right now. Also, he felt that Apple did love him like he loved her. She was something special. Nick was sure Corey would change his mind about her if he could meet her and see them together.

Nick knew his father was griping about Apple because he only wanted the best for his son. Growing up, Corey wasn't there to play catch with him in the backyard, or to teach him how to shave, or drive a car, or personally educate him on women. Nick grew up in the streets and followed in his father's footsteps. So, the only thing Corey felt he could do for his son was help keep him out of prison or the grave with some fatherly advice.

Nick left the prison that afternoon, but he didn't leave town just yet. He drove to the nearest motel and paid for a room. He would stay the night and make another visit to Clinton Correctional Facility to see Amir early the next morning. He couldn't drive all the way to Dannemora, New York and not visit his best friend too.

✳✳✳

Nick sat at the table and waited for Amir to enter the room. Same shit, different folks this time. While waiting, Nick thought about Corey's words from the day before. He didn't want to disappoint his father, but he had to make his own way, and he could never leave Apple. It was like she had a spell on him. He was reaching for a serious payday, and he knew retirement would come soon for him—just this last job and he would become a legit civilian owning his own business.

Amir entered the visiting room standing six feet tall and neatly clad in his prison attire. He was lean with sharp eyes, a gleaming bald head, and a grizzly looking beard. He and Nick exchanged looks of respect. Amir walked Nick's way looking chill and serious at the same time. Nick stood up when he came close to the table and the two men embraced in a brotherly hug.

"Peace, my brother," Amir greeted him.

"Peace," Nick replied.

They sat down opposite each other.

"Your pops mentioned you were upstate," Amir said.

"Yeah. You know I can't come see him without seeing you too," said Nick.

Amir nodded. "No doubt. But what's going on with you? I'm hearing shit about you, Nick. Fuckin' retire, my dude, and don't get caught up in no dumb shit."

Nick looked at his friend and thought, *Here we go again! Round two!*

"I'll be a'ight, Amir."

"Cuz you know what you're doing, right?" Amir quickly interrupted him. "You ready to be in here with me and your pops?"

"So you ready to lecture me?"

"I'm ready to help save your life, Nick. Look, being in here, this shit ain't life, yo. This shit is a fuckin' disaster . . . complete dystopia."

"We make our choices," Nick replied.

"We do, but this is a fucked-up choice. If I was to do it all over again, I would go to school and work for mine. Allah has shown me the way, and I'm thankful for that. Life in this bitch, it's hell . . . no place for a black man to be. You got an opportunity to get out and live your life right. So far, you beat the odds, my brother. The way I see it, you're either pussy whipped or stupid," Amir said to him.

Nick didn't take kindly to the harsh statement. He slightly frowned. Amir's conversion to Islam was nothing new to him. It was a gradual change, but now Amir wanted to dictate his life.

"I'm telling you this not to hurt your feelings, Nick, but because I love you and I don't want you in here with me," Amir added. "And the sad thing is, my brother, I'm in here, confined behind these walls and I'm freer than I ever been, while you are the one imprisoned by your actions and your mind. The money you have saved, the untaxed blood money, take it, get out, and just live your life. And if that means not coming here to see me and your pops anymore, so be it. Believe me, your father and me, we made our peace with our choices and we're living with it."

Nick couldn't admit it, but he wanted to live his life with Apple, and if he didn't help her, he thought another nigga would.

"I hear you, Amir, but we make our own choices. I love this woman, and I'm determined to help her and she's helping me," said Nick.

Amir sighed heavily. He realized that he wasn't getting anywhere with Nick. His friend was hell-bent on moving closer to self destruction.

"So you made your choice to stick with this woman. It's that serious with her?"

"It is," Nick replied wholeheartedly.

"Well, the only thing I can say to you now is be careful. I hear things in here, and I've heard about this Scar. He's a grimy dude, Nick—really dangerous."

"Damn, you work quick. I just told my Pops about dude, and in less than twenty-four you got his whole resume."

"His jacket is I-95 long, Nick. This nigga done put in his work. I heard he's a beast on them streets; dangerous, cunning, and takes great pleasure in dropping bodies. It ain't about the money for him, my brother. This fool a body snatcher."

Nick's jaw tightened and his eyes hooded over in anger. Finally, he replied, "So am I."

12

Cartier was dreaming of her beloved Brooklyn. Her old crew and right hand-bitch, Monya, was there, and it felt like the good old days. Cartier and Monya were two of the baddest bitches in the game—in Brooklyn period. The Cartier Cartel—her, Monya, Bam, Shanine, and Lil' Momma—had respect, influence, and power.

Then Head appeared in her dream, and it soon transitioned into a wet dream. She could feel his magnetic touch against her skin. She felt him move his hand between her legs and start to massage her while inserting two fingers inside her. She felt him caress the opening and he stroked her inner flesh with slow, dreamy rubbing motions. Cartier felt each convulsive clench of her pussy around his fingers. Her pussy was throbbing as he fingered her, his mouth licking and sucking on her nipple like he was dying for the taste of her. Her excitement started to build, and her body started to squirm. Her passionate dream of Head felt so real. She could feel herself about to orgasm as he continued to please her.

"Ooooh," she moaned.

Her body continued to squirm and she felt two fingers slamming in and out of her rapidly.

Suddenly, Cartier's eyes flew open to see a very intoxicated Edward against her—touching her freely. It wasn't a dream. He was groping her like a horny thirteen-year-old boy. It was *his* fingers inside of her. Her

T-shirt had been lifted up, her tits exposed, as Edward took advantage of her.

With a stiff foot she angrily kicked him off her and he fell off the edge of the bed to the floor.

"Ouch!" he hollered.

"What the fuck is your problem?!" she screamed.

"What is wrong with you?" he shouted.

Cartier jumped from her bed and hurriedly clicked on the lights, and she saw the most hideous sight. Edward was naked except for his knee-high nylon socks. His extremely thin dick was dangling between his puny, hairy balls. She was exposed too. Somehow her panties had been removed and she was feeling the remnants of his saliva on her nipples.

"Are you fuckin' crazy?" she shouted at him. "You fuckin' pervert!"

She couldn't believe that she had ever given this fool some pussy. The thought of his fingers inside of her and his mouth on her nipple while she slept made her fume. The mere sight of him made her want to throw up and then fuck him up for violating her body. But she restrained herself. She knew if she reacted violently, a bitch nigga like him would call the police. The last thing she needed was that kind of heat in her life.

With her face twisted in anger, she spewed, "Don't you ever fuckin' touch me again without my permission! You fuckin' hear me, nigga?"

"Permission?" he whined. "What is this, an authoritarianism?"

He thought he was so smart. He thought he could just touch her without permission and preach his big words to try and intimidate her. But Cartier was smarter than she looked.

"Nigga, my pussy will always be a dictatorship—fuckin' North Korea, you bitch-ass nigga!" she shouted.

Momentarily, he was confused. Being intoxicated, he didn't know how they started talking politics.

"Leave me alone!" he exclaimed—and then he stormed out of the bedroom to take a shower.

Cartier was left with bewilderment. She immediately locked her bedroom door. "What the fuck?"

She was literally counting down the days to something new.

She couldn't go back to sleep because her body felt violated. She heard Edward in the bathroom. She still wanted to punch that bitch nigga in the mouth. Now her body felt awake and aroused. What upset her most was that she was about to come from his abrasive touching. It made her miss Head even more. She sighed deeply and just sat there on her bed for a moment, thinking about her man.

A half-hour later, Edward emerged from the bathroom and walked back to Cartier's bedroom. He jiggled the doorknob to find it locked. He became incensed. His high was coming down, so he knew better than to pick a fight this late at night with Cartier for two reasons. First, they lived in a high-end building that didn't tolerate noise complaints. And two, the rent was due in two days, and he didn't want to give her a reason to withhold it.

The arrangement with Cartier wasn't working out for him. When she moved in, he thought he would have his cake and eat it too. He would have an unlimited supply of ghetto pussy and she would pay half of all the bills. Pleasure and help with his bills, that's all she meant to him. There were no special dates, no freebies. It was fifty-fifty between them, along with some perks for him.

But now she wanted to act funky. Did she not know who buttered her bread? Edward felt slighted by the bedroom door being locked. He wanted some pussy. This was *his* place—*his* shit! He owned every piece of furniture, every fork and spoon, the bed sheets and the towels. *Does she not understand that this is a barter system?* he thought. When his blonde white girl was being stubborn or prudish, Cartier was supposed to be his backup plan for receiving pleasure.

The following evening, Edward decided to invite some company over to let out some of his frustration. He and his frat buddies were in the living room drinking and hanging out. Without lowering his voice, he started to gripe about his issues with Cartier to his buddies. He called Cartier a hoochie mama and a whore while she was in her bedroom.

"That whore was an easy fuck," he boasted to his friends.

His buddies laughed.

"She was, huh?" replied a friend. "Will she fuck a friend too?"

"Maybe. You know how those whores from the ghetto are—so easy and will have sex with anyone, but they can be so damn complicated. I was the one doing that ho a favor. I gave that homeless whore a place to stay. I'm her welfare!" He laughed.

His buddies laughed too.

He continued to call Cartier all types of disrespectful names but stopped short of calling her a bitch. Ingrate, parasite, low-class—he went in on his female roommate to his friends while Cartier was listening to the noise and disrespect from her bedroom. She could have easily gone into the living room and shut him down and embarrassed him in front of his corny friends, but she decided against it. He was hurt. He had gotten a taste of some good pussy—something his white bitch couldn't give him—and he became addicted. She laughed at how he was hiding his feelings behind hateful words. The man needed a psychiatric evaluation for real.

The next morning, Edward left early for work. Cartier emerged from her bedroom and went into the kitchen to find a note that indicated that she could no longer eat any of his food. Cartier was somewhat taken aback by the note, but she laughed. The man took his sweet time to list all the food that he'd purchased.

So immature, she thought. She sighed at Edward's pettiness. Shit like this made her miss a real nigga.

Cartier left the note affixed to the fridge. If he wanted it down, then he would have to remove it himself. Just to be spiteful, she went inside the fridge and made herself a wonderful breakfast from Edward's food.

13

I t was late at night, and Apple couldn't sleep. She sat at her laptop and embedded herself into Citi's world. Apple clicked on one photo, and then the next, and the next. She was stalking Citi's Facebook page again and her Instagram too. She carefully observed Citi in each photo, trying to pinpoint locales. Each picture with Citi popping bottles in nightclubs, vacationing in exotic locations like Bermuda and Bali, and showing off Birkin and Gucci bags made Apple see blood red. Citi was living the good life on *her* stolen money.

Apple took her time to analyze everything about the bitch and try to pinpoint her next move, but she stumbled onto one problem. Citi wasn't as dumb as Apple thought her to be. None of the pictures on her social media pages were posted in real time. Some of the pictures were months, maybe a year old.

"Fuck!" Apple mumbled.

"Bae, come get some sleep," Nick called out from her bedroom.

"I'll be in there in a minute," she replied. She continued to click on a few more pictures and studied them like she was a photography expert. Still, there wasn't anything she could use.

Giving up for the night, she logged out of her computer and joined Nick in the bedroom. Tomorrow would be a new day for her.

In the bed, Nick said to her, "C'mere, let me help you get your mind off that bitch."

He disappeared beneath the covers, maneuvered his face between her spreading legs, and ate her out for nearly an hour. Apple had no complaints at all.

***

It was Apple and Nick's time-out from the chaos. Nick wanted to do something special for Apple, so he decided to take her out to eat at a nice restaurant. Apple had a thing for cheesecake, so they went to the legendary Junior's restaurant in Downtown Brooklyn. The two of them sat inside the rust-colored booth near the wooden bar and enjoyed a hearty meal, drinks, and the restaurant's well-known cheesecake. Times like this made them feel like a normal, loving couple.

The night was growing late, so they decided to complete their date night by driving back to Manhattan and strolling through Times Square—and then maybe later, get into some freaky shit.

Nick climbed behind the wheel of his SUV with Apple sitting shotgun and looking content with her man. Nick started the vehicle, but before he could pull out of the parking spot across the street from Junior's on Flatbush Avenue, he noticed a garishly colored Range Rover drive by them, followed by a dark green Yukon. Both vehicles then busted a quick U-turn on the wide avenue.

Apple and Nick watched the Range Rover and Yukon come to a stop near Junior's. It was like fate. Citi and Scar were in the Range Rover, and two of their shooters were in the Yukon. It was after midnight, and the night was cold, and Nick and Apple had the urge to suddenly heat things up in Downtown Brooklyn.

From across the street, Apple and Nick observed Citi and Scar climb out of the Range Rover. The two looked like they were out to enjoy a late night meal at the same restaurant Nick and Apple had just come from. Apple saw her opportunity to strike. They had the upper-hand, and

Apple wasn't about to let this chance at revenge pass her by. Nick was on the same page. Nick reached for the Glock 19 under his seat, and Apple already had a 9mm in her hand.

They exited Nick's SUV simultaneously, and with their guns in hands and their eyes fixed on Citi and Scar approaching the restaurant, they marched toward their two foes audaciously. Their arms became outstretched with the barrels of their guns aimed at the unknowing couple—and then chaos ensued.

Bak! Bak! Bak! Bak!

Bac! Bac! Bac! Bac! Bac!

A barrage of bullets went flying at Citi and Scar. Immediately Citi ducked and took cover behind a parked car as car windows exploded around her and shards of glass went flying everywhere. She tried to get the pistol she carried in her purse, but she was so scared, the weapon fumbled from her hands.

Scar took cover behind another parked car and he removed the .45 tucked in his waistband and heatedly returned fire at the threat. Pacho and Damon emerged from the Yukon and soon joined Scar in the intense gunfight.

Boom! Boom! Boom!

Bak! Bak! Bak!

The shooting sent a wave of panic throughout the area. Bystanders frantically ran screaming for cover, and the patrons inside Junior's freaked out at the gun battle echoing from the streets.

Nick and Apple were hell bent on killing everyone. They were in a murderous trance, aiming to blow Scar and Citi's head off. But their two goons provided cover fire for the couple and quickly made things complicated and dangerous.

Still cowering behind the car and not wanting to die, Citi managed to pick up the gun and made a beeline toward safety. Scar was entrenched in violence and the shootout, and with the .45 in his hand, he took going berserk to a whole new level. The pistol repeatedly exploded in his hand, and he didn't flinch as bullets dangerously whizzed by him. One bullet even struck a nearby bystander in his chest.

It being Downtown Brooklyn and a very active area, it didn't take long for police sirens to blare in the distance. The shooters were about to have NYPD company, and none of them wanted to be caught with a smoking gun in their hands.

Apple and Nick made their way back to the SUV, but as everyone was fleeing the scene, Scar and Nick locked eyes. Scar saluted to Nick with two fingers and a cynical grin, then climbed into the Range Rover and sped off. It was as if he took Nick to be a joke.

Nick knew that the nigga was operating on a different frequency than the average thug—psychotic and eccentric. Nick wasn't impressed, and it pissed him off that a fool like Scar had tried to clown him.

Scar had just made things personal.

14

Citi hurried into her lavish penthouse suite on the Upper West Side of Manhattan highly upset. There wasn't any way she was heading back to Astoria tonight in her frantic condition. She couldn't stop shaking or crying. Scar witnessed her having a full blown breakdown. She kept chanting, "What the fuck! They almost killed us! What the fuck! What the fuck!"

"Citi, just calm the fuck down," Scar said.

"I can't calm the fuck down, Scar! We were nearly killed out there! What the fuck! What the fuck!"

"But we wasn't, right?" he coolly replied.

She looked at him like he had two heads. "How can you just stand there and look so nonchalant?"

Scar shrugged, removed a blunt from his pocket, and sparked it up. The shootout was amateur town to him. It wasn't his first rodeo with death, and he'd been in worse situations and still survived.

"Gettin' yaself all worked up ain't gonna do shit—it ain't gonna fuckin' help, a'ight? I got this shit. We gon' fuck up some niggas' shit over this," he said with gusto.

She stared at him smoking his blunt. He didn't even break a sweat. He didn't blink or fold under the pressure. The nigga was extra, special crazy, and it was why she had him by her side and on her team.

"You think niggas gonna take shots at me and live?" he continued.

"But who?"

"I don't fuckin' know, bitch. But believe me, I'm gonna fuckin' find out."

Hearing the commotion in the living room, Cane emerged from one of the backrooms shirtless and looking laidback. He gazed at his sister and Scar. He noticed Citi's uneasiness and apprehension and asked, "What the fuck happened wit' ya'll two?"

"We were shot at," Citi said.

"What? What the fuck you talkin' about? By who?" Cane asked, suddenly amped.

"We don't know."

"What the fuck you mean, you don't know?" Cane shouted.

"I don't know!" Citi screamed. "I didn't see their faces. But one was definitely a bitch."

"A bitch?" Cane said.

Suddenly, an afterthought came to her. *A bitch.* Who else but those bitches would be bold enough to come at her and cause chaos in such a public place?

"What if it was Apple? Or Cartier? Or both?" she said with a look of wide-eyed panic.

Scar proclaimed that he didn't see any woman. "The only thing I saw was a bitch-ass, non-shooting nigga."

Citi paced back and forth inside the main room. She needed a drink. She poured herself a shot of liquor and quickly downed it. Cane was still trying to interrogate her, but Citi was in no mood to answer any of his questions. She continued to rant about revenge coming from Apple and Cartier, but Cane didn't believe her.

"Them fuckin' bitches are dead, Citi. They were killed by the Gonzales Cartel, so what the fuck you talkin' about, crazy?" Cane griped.

"No . . . it was them, Cane," she replied adamantly.

"You losing ya fuckin' mind, Citi," Scar chided.

"I think she is," Cane agreed.

"No, I'm not!" Citi shouted irately. "I didn't tell you the whole truth, Cane. We all faked our deaths so we could get out of Miami alive. I used that opportunity to steal Apple and Cartier's money and then helped perpetuate the lie that the Gonzales Cartel had murdered them. I felt in my heart that the cartel would see through the ruse and it would only be a matter of time before they were caught and murdered. But now, I am almost sure that it could be them."

"The whole truth," Cane shook his head. Shit just got complicated. "All you did was lie. All this time, Citi, and you kept your come-up a secret from me!"

"Calm down, Cane. She did what she had to do," Scar said. "And as I said, I ain't see no bitch. Citi buggin'."

Citi felt like she was having a panic attack. She didn't want to believe that she was losing her mind. She saw the woman aiming at her, and although she didn't get a good look at her face, she was adamant that it was Cartier or Apple gunning for her.

"I need a fuckin' drink too," said Cane.

He went over to the bar near the floor-to-ceiling windows and poured himself a shot of Hennessy and threw it back. Cane had a lot on his mind too—like his missing half-a-million dollars and the death of his bitch. But he kept those things secret from Citi and Scar for the time being. They already had a lot on their plate, and he didn't have any leads.

"Sis, you look like you need to relax. Go in your bedroom and chill for a minute . . . take a long bath wit' some candles or something," he said. "And a stiff drink."

"A bath?" Citi rolled her eyes. "I hate when men say shit like 'go take a bath, light candles, and have a glass of wine' like that will make every fuckin' thing better! And silly bitches play into that sick, stupid-ass man fantasy. Did you not hear I was almost killed tonight? How is water and some fuckin' bubbles gonna make shit better? Yeah, let me go wash my ass and now I feel great. Thanks for the advice, Cane."

"Yo, you wildin'. It was just a suggestion."

"Well, I *suggest* you find those bitches!"

"What bitches?!" Both Scar and Cane screamed. They were tired of hearing her voice.

Scar continued, "Citi, take your narrow ass to the back and chill. You fuckin' up my high wit' your paranoia. I told you there wasn't no bitch bussing her gun. Your scary ass was too busy hidin' to see shit anyways."

Scar began mocking how Citi was ducking for cover behind the car, and he and Cane erupted in laughter.

Maybe Scar was right. Maybe she was paranoid. He was there too and if he said he didn't see a bitch then maybe that's because there wasn't one. It had been a long night. Maybe she needed some rest.

"I'll be in my bedroom," she said to whoever gave a fuck.

Both men watched her trek down the long corridor and observed her disappear into the bedroom and close the door behind her.

"You think she gonna be a'ight?" asked Scar.

"She good. We come from strong genes, Scar," replied Cane.

"You wanna hit?" Scar said, holding his blunt up.

"Shit, nigga, you read my fuckin' mind."

Scar and Cane lingered in the living room and got high off of potent weed and sipped on some brown juice.

Meanwhile, Citi sat in silence on her king size bed in the dim bedroom for a moment. The curtains to her bedroom were drawn back, and she gazed at the illuminated view of Central Park in the distance.

Citi was filled with worries, and not just about her own safety. She thought about Pacho. He was there too, firing away and trying to protect her with his own life. She had no idea if he had been injured in the gun battle or arrested.

She picked up her cell phone and dialed his number. With the phone pressed to her ear, she heard it ring several times before it went to his voicemail. She hung up. She didn't like leaving messages.

Citi heaved a long sigh and gazed out the window. She decided to try Pacho again, hoping that he picked up this time. His cell phone rang several times again, and Citi expected to get his voicemail a second time.

Surprisingly, she heard him answer with, "Yo."

"Pacho! Ohmygod, are you okay?"

"Yeah, I'm fine," he answered coolly.

"Where are you?"

"I'm home."

Citi was relieved to hear that.

"I need to see you," she said.

"When?"

With Scar and Cane in the next room, it was going to be nearly impossible to sneak by them and see Pacho. What excuse would she have for leaving the penthouse so unexpectedly? But why would she need to give them an excuse? She was supposedly the one running the show and this was her empire and her money, and she was a grown woman.

Fuck taking a bath and moping in her bedroom. Citi needed to get out. She yearned to see Pacho. He would take her mind away from her troubles. She stood up abruptly and marched toward her walk-in closet, swung open the doors, and decided to change clothes.

An hour later, Citi walked into the living room to find her brother and Scar lounging on the large couch, and both men were high and tipsy. They were like two fools. She shook her head at them and continued to walk by them, leaving the penthouse unnoticed until she ran into two of Scar's goons that were on standby nearby. Seeing Citi exiting the penthouse alone, they grew concerned.

"You okay, Ms. Citi?" one of the men asked her.

"Yeah, I just need some time alone. I need some air. I'm going for a walk," she said.

"Then we need to escort you," said the other.

"I said I'm fine. I don't need an escort," she snapped at them.

"But Scar insisted—"

"You don't work for Scar. You work for *me*," she exclaimed. "And I said I don't need a fuckin' babysitter."

Both men were skeptical about her leaving the comfort and security of her place to go for a walk alone, especially after someone had tried to kill them earlier. But Citi was adamant. She gave them an order, and they had to follow it—or else. Both armed men watched Citi disappear into the elevator and hoped that letting her leave alone wouldn't come back to haunt them. The last thing they wanted was to be reprimanded by Scar. That could be a death sentence.

Citi strutted through the empty lobby and made her way outside into the brisk air. She looked stylish in a pair of fitted jeans that accentuated her figure and butt, a brown leather jacket, and knee-high boots. Pacho was parked outside the towering building in the idling SUV, waiting patiently for Citi's exit. Resting on his lap was a loaded SIG Sauer P226. It was poised for action with a bullet in the chamber—just in case. Pacho smiled when Citi came through the automatic doors. She was a wealthy drug kingpin, but to him, she was some of the best pussy he ever had, and she was his comfort and joy. He hated that they had to hide from Scar, but it was too dangerous to expose their relationship.

Citi happily strutted toward the SUV and slid into the passenger seat. They shared a quick, passionate kiss like they were two teenagers sneaking out their parents' house for a rendezvous.

"You good?" he asked her.

"I'm better now." She smiled.

Pacho drove off. To where, he had no idea yet. Citi wanted to escape with him, even if it was temporary. She felt comfort and security with Pacho. She was glad that he was home. Scar was a fearsome ally to her organization, but he couldn't provide the kind of comfort and sexual healing that Pacho offered, and tonight, she needed that kind of healing.

They checked into a room inside the Kimpton Ink48 Hotel, a stone's throw away from the West Side Highway. From their room was a dramatic view of the Hudson River and Midtown skyscrapers.

The two lovers kissed fervently, hugging and groping each other inside the contemporary room. Citi could lose herself with Pacho. His touch was riveting and his kisses on her lips and her skin were creating a ripple effect of emotions and urges. He slowly peeled away her clothes, yearning to see her nakedness like it would be the first time. That's what she loved about him. The way he looked at her was always the first time their eyes met and their bodies became entwined. She loved it.

Almost immediately, she cried out with ecstasy when she felt his soft, skillful tongue tunneling inside of her. She closed her eyes and squirmed in his grasp with her legs in the air and her fingers holding on to the bed sheets for dear life.

"Aaaah . . ."

Subsequently, Pacho thrust his hard dick deep inside her. It didn't take him long to find the special pleasure spots inside her, and they fucked like hardcore porn stars. They were young and energetic, and Pacho didn't disappoint her tonight. He always came with his A game—a big hard dick and perfect rhythm. After several strong orgasms, Citi collapsed with delight on the bed next to Pacho and exhaled.

The sex was great, but Pacho's love and intimacy was what she really cherished.

"Hey, let me ask you something. Did you see a bitch tonight? Or, bitches shooting at us?"

"Bitches?" Pacho thought for a beat. "Nah, no bitches. There were two triggermen, though. One was more aggressive. He's the one I tried to blow his fuckin' head off."

Citi nodded. She trusted Pacho implicitly, so his word was her holy grail. She could now move on and allow Scar and Cane to focus on getting at the niggas who tried to dead them. Feeling renewed, Citi wanted to feel Pacho's big dick stretching out her tight walls again.

And then her cell phone rang. Scar was calling her and ruining the mood. Citi stared at her phone with some contempt, but she didn't want Scar to become suspicious. She had told his two goons that she was going for a walk, and that was over two hours ago.

Pacho stared at her with some concern.

"It's Scar," she said.

"You gonna answer it?"

She sighed heavily and answered the phone. "What?"

"Where the fuck you at, Citi?" Scar griped.

"I went for a walk," she said.

"To where? Fuckin' Canada!"

"I'm a big girl, Scar. I don't need you fuckin' babysitting me," she retorted.

"Yo, look here—we got beef out there, and unless you Super-fuckin'-woman, I suggest you don't trek off all by yourself an' shit. I should fuck these niggas up for letting you go by them without them doin' shit."

"It's not their fault."

"I don't give a fuck who fault it is. You ain't fuckin' here cuz you out there."

"I'm on my way back," she said in defeat.

"Hurry the fuck up!"

Citi sighed so heavily that it felt like her chest was about to cave in. She looked at Pacho and said to him, "I need to go."

"He don't deserve you," he said.

"I know, but he's needed right now, especially after tonight's incident," she replied.

"I thought you was the one running things."

She didn't like that comment. Of course she was, but her position in the organization was tough. With a man like Scar by her side representing power and authority, they could appear and become untouchable.

Citi removed herself from the bed and started to get dressed. Pacho didn't want her to leave so soon. He felt that their night was only just beginning. Scar was getting in the way of their affair and he wasn't happy.

Dressed and ready to leave, Citi lovingly stared at Pacho and uttered the words, "I love you."

"I love you too," he said.

She dashed out the hotel room like she was a married woman running back to her husband. Pacho sat there and wondered how long could they keep up their affair before Scar found out. If he did, then that was surely a death sentence. Pacho wondered if Citi was worth dying over. Right now the answer was an emphatic yes. But he wondered if he would feel that same way with a .45 against his temple.

15

Nick sat in his living room contemplating his next move while puffing on a cigarette. Had they moved too fast on Scar and Citi? But the opportunity to strike had fallen right in their laps. He sat there with a bruised ego trying to convince himself that Apple wasn't bad luck. Did she fuck up his mojo? Never in his entire life had he pulled the trigger so many times and never hit his target. *How did I miss Scar?* Nick had a clear shot of Scar—clear enough to see the pimples on his face—and he'd missed.

While Apple was at Kola's place checking up on her sister and seeing her daughter, Nick sat there in the dark silence of his apartment going over every move they'd made that night. He and Apple took a huge risk by acting off emotions instead of strategy. Then he had to think about the witnesses that were outside during the shootout, and he worried about Apple and him being captured on surveillance footage.

The shootout at Junior's restaurant had made the evening news and it was a front page announcement in nearly every New York City newspaper. Nick had purchased the *Daily News* and read about the incident that he and Apple created. The bystander who had been shot in the chest was alive, but he was in critical condition. Witness accounts to journalists described the abrupt shootout like being in the wild, wild west.

"It was crazy," said one witness. "Bullets just started flying everywhere. It seemed like the shooting wasn't going to end."

Nick paid close attention to witnesses' accounts to see if there was anything that would connect the shooting back to him and Apple. So far the statements were vague and any surveillance footage in the area was unclear. The police had nothing to go on. They had no suspects.

Nick felt he and Apple had gotten lucky. Things could have gone terribly wrong for them, and he could have been sitting inside a jail cell right now with serious charges against him.

He dowsed his cigarette into the ashtray near him and stood up. He couldn't stop thinking about Scar. He couldn't take his mind off that salute Scar threw his way with a smirk on his face. Nick hated to be taken as a joke, and now he felt this young thug was laughing at him.

Two twin 9mm Berettas were on the living room table. They were ready for action, ready to aim directly at Scar's face and spill his blood. This time, Nick was going to make sure he wouldn't miss the fool.

Nick finished his night by smoking another cigarette, pouring himself a shot of Hennessy, and formulating a precise plan to strike. Nick felt he worked best by himself, and this time it would be calculated and spot-on. He loved Apple, but he needed to make moves alone.

***

The following week, Nick avoided Apple and her phone calls. He had been staying at his place until he wrapped up these last murders. He hit the streets with a strong motive on his mind. The first phase was information gathering and surveillance. He remembered the faces of the two shooters in the Yukon who tried to protect Citi and Scar. Their image was embedded into his memory and he knew that it was in his best interest to start from there. He needed to put names to the two faces, but he knew it wasn't going to be easy.

The first week he hit every bar, nightclub, strip club, lounge, and hole-in-the-wall searching for faces and information. What he needed was a name—any name—a location, any weak link that would connect him to someone affiliated with Citi or Scar. He passed a few bills around to get certain folks to talk. For that first week, Nick came up with nothing.

The subsequent week, he met a stripper named Candy, and she had something for him for the right price. He gave her a few hundred dollars and she gave him a private lap dance in one of the backrooms inside the club. Nick gave her Scar and Citi's names and she was familiar with their organization.

"Scar comes in here like a big shot. I rarely see him, though. He's mean and cheap and most of the girls stay far away from him and his kind. But his man Damon is a regular. He gets sloppy drunk and leers like a pervert, but he pays for a private dance when he's here."

"Tell me about him. What's his story?" Nick asked her.

"He's one of Scar's goons . . . a nasty and dangerous muthafucka."

"Where can I find this nigga?"

"He comes in here most Wednesdays and handles his business," she said.

"He fucks you?"

Candy smirked, "Never that. I got that good pussy that ain't for sale."

Nick raised his eyebrow skeptically. "Really?"

"I smile. I twerk. I shake my phat ass for these niggas and then go home to my kids."

"Anyone else? Anything you can think of?" Nick sounded desperate.

Candy shook her head. "I told you all I know."

Nick went back into his pocket and pulled out his huge wad of bills.

"I need you to do me a favor," he said.

"Go on," she replied.

"When you see him again, give me a call. I need to have a chat with him. It's important."

"How important?"

Nick peeled off several hundred dollars and placed it into her hands. "That important. And there's more where that came from when I get to see this Damon face-to-face."

Money talks and bullshit walks. Nick put five hundred more dollars in her hands and it was the easiest money she ever made. With the promise of more, Candy was willing to help him out. She didn't care what beef they had, as long as she got paid.

Nick was about to exit the room, but Candy called out to him with an addendum. She grinned at him and pulled back her thin shirt to expose her perky tits and said, "You know, if I did have sex with clientele I bet you'd be a memorable fuck."

Nick smiled. She was cute. He pivoted and exited the room. Apple gave him plenty of pleasure.

✳✳✳

The call from Candy came three days later.

"He's here," she said to Nick.

"Keep him busy," Nick replied.

Nick moved with a sense of urgency. He picked up a 9mm Berretta and a Glock 19 and marched out the door and to his vehicle dressed in all black, looking like some kind of Navy Seal Operator. He had one thing on his mind—killing. He and Damon needed to talk about some things.

✳✳✳

The black Ford Fusion traveled north on I-87. While driving, Nick listened to some old school like The Temptations, The Isley Brothers, and Marvin Gaye. The music put him in a calm mood. He sang along and nodded to the music. He felt one step closer to hunting down Scar.

He traveled thirty miles north of the city and reached a small town near Connecticut. He came to a dark wooded area, where there were no people and no homes, just a small lake, trees, grass, and animals. Nick navigated the Ford through a winding dirt road and came to a stop and killed the ignition. He observed the area and there was nothing around for miles.

"This should do," he said to himself.

He climbed out of the car and went to open the trunk. Damon was inside tied at his wrists and ankles. He had been badly beaten, and his face was bloody and bruised.

Seeing Nick towering over him, Damon immediately shouted, "We gonna fuck you up, nigga! You know who the fuck I am?"

Nick stared down at him coldly and put on a pair of black latex gloves.

Damon squirmed in his restraints, trying to free himself, but Nick had the zip ties extra tight around his wrists, and he'd tied thick rope securely around his ankles. Damon wasn't going anywhere. Damon glared back. He refused to be intimidated by the stranger that kidnapped him.

"You don't scare me, muthafucka!" Damon cursed.

Nick smirked. "In due time." He was about to show Damon just how scary he could be.

Nick had all kinds of tools in the car to assist with the interrogation. He walked away from the trunk and reached into the backseat to grab a few things, including a blowtorch. He then loomed back into Damon's view, displaying the goodies to his captive.

"I just want some information from you, that's all," Nick said.

"Fuck you!" Damon cursed.

"Fine, we'll do this the easy way. And in case you're wondering, I got a lot of time on my hands, and the only living things out here that will hear you scream are the birds."

Nick decided to start with the knife and the ice pick. He leaned closer to Damon and started with his bare feet—this piggy went snap, and so did the next.

"Aaaaaaaaaaah," Damon hollered. And then he hollered some more and some more.

Slowly but surely, Nick was deforming Damon's body from his feet, to his legs, to his knees. Then he reached his genitals, using the ice pick to puncture his balls and the blowtorch to sizzle the skin. It was agonizing pain, and Damon screamed like a banshee. There was the smell, but Nick was tolerant to it.

"You still a tough goon, nigga? Huh, Damon?" he mocked. "Ya'll still think a nigga weak? I'm a fuckin' joke? Huh, nigga!"

With his genitals burnt and grossly mangled, along with the lower half of him, Damon begged for death. He had no idea who this man was at all or why he was being targeted. "Please . . ." he panted. "Please . . . stop," as drool slid down his chin to his neck.

Damon's face was awash with tears and slobber as he screamed out in anguish and pain. How many times had he been the aggressor? Not so long ago, he'd participated in murdering one of his closest friends, Wise.

Nick indicated that he was going to start with his face next—kill him really slowly and make him suffer. Damon wanted to die. He gave up Pacho. He gave up Scar and Citi. Nick had his way of making the tough thug talk.

Nick spent an hour in the woods dismembering Damon's body and dumping pieces of him into the lake, and then driving a few miles away and burying what was left of him. He wanted to make the fucker disappear.

One down, three to go. Pacho, Scar, and then that bitch Citi.

16

Cartier released a deep sigh as she took a seat inside the break room after her shift. She had been on her feet all day, and it felt like she had been stepping barefoot on hot coals. What she yearned for was a massage. Working at the Starbucks in the city was starting to take its toll on her. The business was packed every day with non-stop foot traffic—sometimes the place seemed more packed than a nightclub. Those white folks loved their Starbucks.

It was almost dusk, and as no surprise, the sky was gray and overcast with looming rain. It was predictable Seattle weather, and Cartier wasn't looking forward to it, especially on a bicycle. But she had no other choices.

As Cartier was preparing to change clothes and leave, her coworker Cindy came into the break room carrying the tip jar. It was halfway filled. She smiled at Cartier and said, "It's about that time. Let's see how much these cheap bastards left us in tips."

Cartier managed a tired smile. Her friend spilled the money from the jar onto a nearby table, and from there, the two started to split up the cash. In total, there was $55. Cartier took her half, which was $27 in tips for her.

"Something is better than nothing, right?" Cindy said.

"I guess," she replied nonchalantly.

"So, what are you doing tonight?"

"I'm going home and relax . . . get some needed sleep," said Cartier.

"Why don't you come and hang out with us tonight? It'll be fun. And you might even meet some cute guys."

"I'll take a rain check on that, Cindy. The only cute thing that's going to have my attention tonight is my bed."

Cindy chuckled. "Okay, but you're missing out, girl."

Cartier simply smiled and continued to change her clothes. She kept things simple with her coworkers, most of whom were white. They walked around work young and carefree with their upbeat attitudes and their privileged lives. Working at Starbucks was the only thing Cartier had in common with them. She came from a different world than theirs. She had seen things they couldn't imagine—shit that would give the average person nightmares for life. To them, she was the quiet girl who minded her business and rarely went out. There were a handful of occasions when Cartier let her hair down, but in the back of her mind she kept her guard up, knowing her past could always catch up to her.

Cartier grabbed her mountain bike and trekked outside. Her bike was a far cry from the luxury vehicles she was used to. If her enemies could see her now, riding a bicycle to and from a mediocre job like Starbucks, they would gloat at her painful fall from grace. They might even let her live so she could continue to suffer in her new life. For many, death would be better than living a life like Cartier's.

She tossed her backpack over her shoulders and straddled the bike, and she started to pedal home. But then her cell phone rang. Seeing Edward's name on the caller ID made her sigh with distress. She reluctantly answered.

"What?"

"Hey, can you do me a favor and pick up some dinner tonight? I'm swamped at work, but I promise I'll pay you back," he said.

She rolled her eyes but said, "Okay, I can do that."

"Thanks. I owe you."

Of course, he did. But there went her tip money. Things were awkward between her and Edward—almost like a love-hate relationship, more hate than love. Edward gave her a place to stay, and she would always be thankful for that, but then again, he was mostly a grade-A asshole who wanted to control her life when she wasn't his to control.

She arrived home with Chinese food just in time before the downpour started outside. Cartier kicked off her boots near the door, dropped the food on the table, and left a trail of clothes from the door to her bedroom. All she wanted to do was take a shower, eat, lay around in her bedroom, and smoke weed and chill.

Edward arrived at the apartment an hour and a half after Cartier in a stank mood. He'd gotten caught in the rainstorm, not to mention that his girlfriend Jill was pressuring him to kick Cartier out. Jill didn't want Cartier gone because she wanted to move in, but because she believed there was something more between the two of them besides just being roomies.

Walking through the front door, he immediately saw Cartier's things spewed all over the place. First he tripped over her rain boots at the door, which caused him to start griping. Her messiness inside his apartment immediately added to his foul mood.

After the rain boots by the door, he saw the dishes in the sink and the mess she'd left from her breakfast. Then he saw her backpack on his sofa, and she left behind what black females called their hair in a doobie wrap with bobby pins. Edward pursed his lips tighter. The leftover Chinese food on the kitchen table sent him over the edge. He charged down the hallway and abruptly barged into Cartier's bedroom with her barely dressed.

"Didn't I tell you that I don't eat that shit! I hate Chinese food. Yet, you keep bringing home pork fried rice and chicken wings."

"Nigga, are you stupid? Don't be charging in my room beefing about no Chinese food," she hollered, cutting her eyes at Edward.

She donned a robe, marched right by him with an attitude, and went into the kitchen to get another helping. Edward was right behind her, yapping at her.

She spun toward him. "Eat spit, your fuckin' fingers, or my asshole, but don't kid yaself into thinkin' that I give a fuck!" Calmly, she added more chicken wings and rice to her plate. "I'm not in the mood for ya shit tonight."

"You fuckin' disgust me," he spat. "I've tried to class your ghetto ass up, but you're nothing but a damn hood rat!"

Hood rat?

Cartier continued to be sardonic toward him by smacking on her chicken wings, adding more hot sauce to her food, and licking her fingers repetitively out of spite. "Watch ya mouth, fool."

"Would it have killed you to bring home some sushi rolls and a bottle of red wine?" he complained.

Cartier continued to ignore him and continued to be spiteful by enjoying her Chinese food in front of his face and subsequently adding more hot sauce.

Edward continued to rant by saying, "Look at this place! You hardly keep it clean anymore. We barely fuck, you don't suck my dick, and now I can't get a decent meal in my own damn place."

She laughed at his rant. "If you want some pussy, then go fuck that white bitch Jill. Go put your little dick in that fuckin' snowflake."

There was a shocked pause from him. Edward had no clue that she knew about Jill. But he retorted with, "Maybe I will."

Cartier shrugged at his comment.

He suddenly lost it and got loud and belligerent with her. "You know what? Fuck you, you ghetto hood rat!"

Cartier was ready to knock him out if he even dared to put his hands on her. She continued to eat her wings and made herself another plate, taking the last of the wings and rice. It was a delight seeing Edward upset, because she didn't give a fuck. She was marching by him when her cell phone rang.

"What's up? Who this?" Cartier answered.

"Bitch, this is Apple."

"Apple! Hey, girl. What's good?"

"You monkey looking parasite," Cartier heard Edward shout in the background. He was irritated that he couldn't get under her skin. "Hang up the got-damn phone when I'm talking to you!"

"Hold on, Apple. Don't hang up. This won't take but a minute," she said.

Cartier coolly placed her cell phone on the kitchen counter, picked up a half empty Hennessy bottle, and swiftly pivoted, bashing Edward upside his head with it. It shattered to pieces and brown juice went spilling all over him.

"Ouch!" he hollered as he stumbled.

Little did he know, that bottle upside his head was only the beginning. Next came the skillet across his head, and then Cartier went berserk. Her fists went crashing into him harder than Mike Tyson's in the ring, followed by kicks to his side as he cowered in the corner, bleeding from his face and forehead.

"Please, stop! Ouch, ouch! Aaaah! Please!" he cried out.

"I told you, you clown-ass muthafucka, I'm not the one to fuck wit'. I'm tired of your shit!" she shouted.

"Aaaah! Please!"

When he tried to get up, she continued to pound on him. "Sit ya bitch ass down!"

He continued to cower in the corner with his loud cries. This was a side of Cartier that he'd never seen before. It scared him. She'd overpowered him and he thought that she was going to beat him to death.

Cartier stood over him while he was cringing in the corner, crying and bleeding. In her eyes, he was more bitch than man. It was a final relief for her—executing an ass-whooping that was long overdue.

She exhaled and went to retrieve her cell phone from the kitchen countertop to continue her phone conversation with Apple. Breathing a little hard, she heard Apple ask, "Bitch, you a'ight?"

"No doubt. I'm okay. So what's good?"

"You tell me. It sounded like World War Three in there."

"Nothing I couldn't handle. I just had to beat a bitch nigga's ass, that's all—put this bitch nigga in his fuckin' place," said Cartier pompously.

Apple laughed. "You had to lay those paws on a nigga, huh? I'm glad to see that you haven't lost your touch."

"You already know."

"It ain't Christmas, but I got something for when you come through. I'll be waiting," Apple said.

Cartier took a deep breath and replied, "Yo, I'll be back in New York in forty-eight hours. I'm done wit' this fuckin' wack-ass city. One."

17

From the non-descript Toyota Camry, Nick observed Pacho leaving his building and climbing into a dark blue SUV. Where Pacho went, Nick followed. Nick was determined to catch him alone and give him to the same treatment Damon had gotten the other day.

Nick took one final pull from his cigarette and flicked it out the window. He started the car, watched Pacho drive right by him, and then pulled out and moved forward. He stayed a car or two behind the SUV and carefully kept it in sight.

Nick spent the entire day following Pacho around in the city. He spent a few hours in the local bar, and then he met up with a jump-off in Bed-Stuy. He gambled with a few niggas outside a bodega and lost a few hundred dollars. After that, Nick followed Pacho around Brooklyn and watched him collect a few payments.

As dusk settled over Brooklyn, Nick still had his eyes on Pacho from a short distance. It had been a tedious and tiresome task, but Nick was determined to take out the next man and make him disappear. Pacho didn't have any reason to believe he was being followed, so he continued to move around town like he didn't have a care in the world.

With nighttime finally covering the metropolis, Nick was back where he started. Pacho arrived back to his Brooklyn home in East New York on one of the quiet blocks in the rowdy neighborhood. Pacho exited his vehicle and made his way back into the house.

The moment Pacho stepped foot into the foyer of his building, Nick lunged at him like a lion pouncing on his prey. Quickly, he placed a taser to Pacho's neck, sending nearly 50,000 volts into the man and promptly rendering him helpless to defend himself. Pacho collapsed right there, and Nick had his prize.

A few hours later, Pacho hollered from the shock of ice cold H_2O jolting him awake. He found himself naked and bound to a metal chair. His restraints barely gave him any wiggle room, but that didn't stop him from trying to free himself, but to no avail. Whoever kidnapped him had made sure he wasn't going anywhere anytime soon.

Nick walked into the cinder block room where he kept Pacho. The men locked eyes and Pacho tried to keep a gangster attitude, but he was in no position to challenge his captor.

"What the fuck you want wit' me, nigga?" Pacho growled.

"To talk . . . like I had a talk with your friend, Damon," Nick replied.

"I ain't telling you shit!"

"That's the same thing Damon screamed at me, and then we chatted like friends," Nick joked.

Pacho scowled and fidgeted in his restraints, but he wasn't going anywhere.

Nick came threateningly closer to his victim. In his hands, he displayed tools for torture, including an ice pick that had been heated up with a blowtorch. The metal was sizzling.

The sight of it made Pacho cringe. "C'mon, nigga. What the fuck I do to you?" he hollered.

Nick placed the heated ice pick closer to Pacho's eye. "I just want you to talk, then scream, talk some more, and scream some more."

Pacho tried to recoil from the threatening tool. His breathing became heavier and then his urine hit the floor like a waterfall. He had peed himself.

Nick laughed and then plunged the hot ice pick into Pacho's left eye. Pacho's screaming was piercing and loud, his swift agony bouncing off the concrete walls.

"We're just getting started," said Nick in an eerily sinister voice.

Six hours later, Nick pulled up to the remote lake upstate, in the darkened wilderness thick with trees. He opened the trunk to the Camry and removed several black garbage bags from the trunk, each bag containing bloody pieces of Pacho.

Duplicating how he disposed of Damon's body, he wrapped chicken wire around the garbage bag and tossed several of them into the lake. He subsequently drove ten miles north and buried what was left of Pacho.

Like Damon, he would never be seen again.

Nick added a body to his kill list. Next on his list was Cane. He had the information he needed—a trap house in East New York. And then it would finally be Scar's time to die.

***

Scar huffed and puffed and closed his eyes in delight as the cute, young thoroughbred slid her full lips up and down around his hard dick.

"Ooooh, keep doin' that shit, shorty . . . yeah, just like that . . . just like that."

Seated on the living room couch, his legs spread wide with his pants around his ankles and his dick inside the girl's gaping mouth, he took a quick swig from the liquor bottle and grabbed a handful of her long, black hair and pushed her face farther into his lap—making her open wider and almost gag. She felt him jerk inside her wet mouth, his flesh growing harder between her lips.

He was ready to come. He was ready to spray his semen like a geyser into her mouth and let her swallow every drop of him. The oral pleasure had his eyes rolling in the back of his head and made him squirm on the couch like he had an itch he couldn't scratch. His grip around the girl's long hair tightened. She was in her panties and bra, bent over in his lap, her ass up in the air—pussy protruding.

"Suck that big, fat dick, bitch," he commanded.

And then his cell phone rang, interrupting his moment. At first, he didn't want to answer it. He was busy. *Let it go to voicemail*, he said to himself. The girl continued stroking and blowing on his dick. His phone rang again.

"Fuck!" he cursed.

He looked at the phone and, surprisingly, it was Damon's baby mama, Stella, calling him.

"Damon didn't come home! Where is he, Scar? Where the fuck is he?"

"What? Bitch, you call me lookin' for that nigga like I know where he at. Fuck you callin' me for wit' this bullshit?"

"He's missing!"

"Go find the nigga then."

"I tried. I called all the precincts, the hospitals, the morgues, and he ain't in none of them. Where is he?" Stella screamed.

Her screaming put a damper on Scar's sexual mood. He made the young girl stop sucking his dick and propped himself on the couch. Stella got him upset, and his response was, "You need to fuckin' call Tina."

"Who the fuck is Tina?"

"That's his main bitch!" He ended the call abruptly.

So Damon was missing. Scar didn't know if the nigga was shacked up with his main bitch or a stripper, or just wanted to go MIA.

***

Not only was Damon missing, but when days went by and they didn't hear anything from Pacho, Citi and Scar started to grow suspicious. In

122

her gut, Citi knew Pacho was dead. She called his phone numerous times and he wasn't answering—and then his phone went completely dead. He would have never gone a week without contacting her. She became distraught and depressed. She locked herself in her bedroom most of the time, feeling her heart break. She knew she would never see Pacho alive again.

It was the drug game.

Scar believed Wise's brothers were seeking retribution for his sudden disappearance, but Cane and Citi weren't too sure. Wise's brothers were working men—civilians—and they had no ties to the streets.

Cane was adamant that their disappearance had something to do with the shooters from Junior's. And though he still hadn't told Scar and Citi about Takenya, he also wanted to connect their disappearance to her death and his missing money.

"Nah, we're being targeted," Cane deduced.

"Then by who?" Scar asked.

"Apple and Cartier," chimed Citi.

Cane stared at his sister with skepticism. "You need to forget about them," he said.

"I can't. Who else would have such hatred for us, or me, to come after us in such a brazen way? I know Apple, and she's the type of bitch that don't give a fuck."

"You need to chill."

"Don't tell me to fuckin' chill!" she shouted.

"What the fuck is wrong wit' you, Citi? Why you tripping?" Scar asked.

"Because we're being targeted by these bitches and y'all actin' like I'm fuckin' delusional and stupid," she rebuked.

"We ain't calling you stupid," said Cane.

"Then what the fuck? You think I'm delusional then?"

"I don't know what you are right now, but you need to calm down," Cane said.

"Fuck y'all both!"

She stormed out of the room. She was upset. She was emotional. So much was happening, and with Damon and Pacho missing—and most likely dead—Citi felt that no one was safe, especially not her. New York was becoming too hot. She could hide behind an army, but Apple and Cartier were deadly and determined bitches. If they were alive, they were out for revenge.

Scar didn't care who it was that was trying to kill them, he just wanted to murder people. It's what he did best.

18

"This Nick. Get at me," she heard his voicemail greeting say for the umpteenth time.

Apple frowned. For some reason, her man was ghosting her. It had been a couple weeks since she'd seen or heard from him. He had just up and disappeared and he wasn't answering his cell phone. Apple feared she had pushed him too far with her thirst for revenge. Now faced with the choice of losing Nick to another bitch or seeking retribution, a strong part of her wanted her nigga back.

Apple had gone by his apartment with her set of keys numerous times at various times of day and night, and he wasn't there and his SUV was nowhere in sight. The only evidence that he had been there were the dirty dishes, clothes strewn around, and current newspapers. Apple hated feeling like she was stalking a nigga, but she had a bad feeling. When someone in the game goes missing for more than twenty-four hours, they're dead. They are not locked up, in the hospital, or laying up with some random bitch.

Apple didn't know what to think. This was Nicholas Davis. He had survived these streets longer than most. He couldn't be dead. And if he wasn't, then where the fuck was he?

She paced around the bedroom with the phone clutched tightly in her hand and continued to reach out to him, but she continued to get the same results—his voicemail.

She was tempted to leave him another nasty voicemail but thought against it. Apple couldn't shake the butterflies in her stomach about someone murdering Nick but tried to convince herself otherwise. It was easier to be mad than sad. Instead, she sent him a text:

NIGGA, WHERE ARE YOU? CALL ME ASAP.

She tossed her phone on the bed and continued to pout.

It was night, it was cold, and she felt lonely. She wanted some dick tonight but had to pacify herself with her fingers. Apple finger-fucked herself and tried to imagine it was Nick, but her self-pleasuring couldn't come close to what she and her boo shared in the bedroom. Ultimately, she forced herself to go to sleep sexually frustrated. She had a busy day tomorrow. Cartier was flying back to New York, and Apple couldn't wait to catch up with her and reminisce on old times. From there, Apple wanted to continue her plot to destroy Citi.

✳✳✳

The following morning, Apple was up early, and still, Nick wasn't by her side. She had slept intermittently throughout the night; tossing and turning. Her heart was heavy and she had an ominous feeling as she looked at her cell phone. No message from Nick. She sighed and dialed his number again, but like so many times before, her call went straight to his voicemail.

"You fuckin' bitch!" she shouted.

She needed to get it together. Apple couldn't fret about Nick right now. He was a grown man and he could take care of himself, she believed. Whatever the reason for his impulsive disappearance, she figured the nigga had a damn good reason for it.

Her cell phone rang, but it wasn't Nick. She answered with, "Hey bitch, you back in town, right?"

"Fo' sure," Cartier replied. "My plane landed this morning. I'm on my way to a hotel."

"Cool. We can link up in Brooklyn at that diner you like after you check in."

"You mean Lindenwood? By the movie theater?"

"Yeah, that's the one," Apple said.

"Cool, what time?"

"This afternoon, say around three?" said Apple. "And I miss you, bitch."

"I miss you too," Cartier said.

They ended their conversation and Apple stood up and started to get ready for her busy day. With Cartier back in New York, it made things much easier for her. She and Cartier had always been on the same level, and Apple felt stronger about executing revenge on Citi with Cartier on board.

She opened her closet door and started removing ten-thousand-dollar stacks from the closet and tossing the cash onto the bed. In total, she placed $120,000 into a knapsack before heading out.

Apple maneuvered her car into the parking lot at Lindenwood Diner that afternoon and parked. The diner wasn't busy that weekday afternoon. Apple climbed out of her car looking dressed for a date with her man, rather than a meeting with a female friend. Clad in a cute Versace dress that highlighted her curvy figure and her stilettos striking the pavement like she was on the catwalk, she entered the restaurant looking classy carrying the knapsack that contained over a hundred thousand dollars.

Cartier was already there, seated at a window booth near the back of the restaurant. The two girls spotted each other and grinned. Apple strutted her way with a smile on her face, and Cartier slid from out the booth to stand and hug her friend.

"Damn, you lookin' all sexy and shit," Cartier complimented Apple.

"And you lookin' like a bitch that just came back from Seattle," Apple joked.

"Oh, fuck you, bitch."

"The blonde hair is cute, though."

The two shared a needed laugh. They sat opposite each other in the booth and started to catch up on lost and old times from when they were young and wild. Subtly, Apple handed Cartier the knapsack underneath the table. Cartier took a peek inside and smiled, knowing where the money came from.

"Good lookin' out," she uttered.

"Absolutely."

"So, the bitch is six feet under, I assume," Cartier said.

"No, not yet. I'm workin' on it."

"So, you're toying with this slippery bitch?"

"I was gettin' us our reparations."

"And I appreciate this more than I can express. Financially, I'm fucked up, so this right here will hold me down for a minute. But it doesn't matter if it's gonna cost you your life. No doubt you can hold ya own, Apple, but that bitch has something you don't," Cartier said.

"Like what?"

"A team of thorough killers. I would just feel better if you waited until you had a stable of loyal goons to protect you."

Apple understood where her friend was coming from, but she replied with, "I have the best killer in town—my man, Nick." She conveniently left out that he was missing.

"Nick? Where he from? I know of him?"

"He's low-key and from Harlem. You may know him 'cause he's on that Brooklyn shit, but he's much older than us."

"Brooklyn shit?"

"Yeah, he takes money from the best in the game and leaves no witnesses. He's not interested in flooding the streets wit' that potent shit or making himself known. Nick is the best body snatcher I know. His father ran wit' Nicky Barnes and them niggas. His pedigree is official."

"Head might know him. I'll ask when the nigga finally gets home."

"So y'all cool?"

"Dude tryin' to play hard-to-get-his-dick, but he knows what's really good, though." Cartier smirked. "But back to Nick and that psycho bitch, Citi. Nick is only one man, Apple. Think this shit through."

"Trust and believe we have. We depending on brains rather than brawn to take that bitch down," said Apple.

"It's gonna take something." Cartier shook her head because she could see that Apple had tunnel vision. "Just promise me that you will be careful."

"Don't you mean *we,* Cartier?" Apple said. She had just given Cartier a knapsack full of cash. Nothing in life was free. Apple was bartering that money for Cartier's participation. She didn't say those words, but she didn't think she had to.

Cartier remained silent and deep in thought as she sipped on her milkshake. She knew Apple would try to pull her back into the game if ever she got out. Apple had a hard time letting things go. After thinking it over, Cartier realized that Citi deserved the business end of her .380 and she would feel better bussing her gun by Apple's side than over her casket dropping red roses.

"Okay, I'm here for you, Apple. But this shit can't be fuckin' reckless."

"It won't be. I'm thinking ahead just like you."

"What you mean?"

"I want what you want wit' Head. I just want to see that bitch's blood spill, and then Nick and I are gonna retire from the game. He wants to open up his own bar—maybe a string of bars in different cities."

"That's wonderful, bitch."

"I guess we're gettin' too old for this shit, huh?" Apple joked.

"We're like two dinosaurs in the game," Cartier said with a chuckle.

"But I'm not tryin' to become extinct."

"You and me both," Cartier agreed.

They talked, they laughed, they ate, and they reconnected with one another. It was good to have a friend in town, Apple felt. But the next stop was Murderville. Killing Citi was next on the agenda.

19

The driver steered the luxury vehicle off the highway and navigated through quiet, tree-lined streets. Within minutes they would be at their destination. Scar sat back and inhaled the Purple Kush. He was feeling nice for the task awaiting his arrival. He had repeatedly been violated in the worst way, and tonight he would get a little payback. In due time he would get his hands dirty and show niggas that he was not to be fucked with, just in case they'd forgotten. No one takes a shot at Scar and lives. Period.

Quincy hopped out the driver's seat of Citi's baby blue Range and ran around to open Scar's door. The night was exceptionally warm, so both men were only dressed in hoodies, jeans, and Timbs. Scar was eager to get at these bitch niggas as he walked through the dilapidated double doors. Citi and Cane were already there, impatiently awaiting his arrival. They'd come in Cane's black Lexus.

The brothers were both snatched up from busy locations by Scar's goons. With a .45 pressed against their rib cages, the men had no other choice but to comply. They were driven for almost an hour to a deserted warehouse in Shirley, Long Island. The place was barren besides a few crates, steel barrels, and debris.

Scar looked at Wise's brothers, Marvin and James, and sensed their confusion. They had no idea why they were captured, restrained, and staring into the eyes of a psychopath. They were both roughed up and sweating profusely. As soon as Scar assessed the situation, he knew that they had nothing to do with the attempts on his life. But, fuck it. It was too late to turn back now. The show must go on.

Marvin and James always knew that their brother's profession would blow back onto the family. Tonight confirmed what the family had already known in their hearts was true. Wise was dead. The look on Scar's face sent an unwelcome chill percolating through their bodies. He didn't smile. He didn't explain. For several uncomfortable minutes, he just stared. Scar locked eyes with Marvin first, until Marvin looked away. James was next. He, too, couldn't hold eye contact. It was like a childish game of chicken. The eerie silence could frighten the hardest of niggas, and Scar was doing this to working dudes with wives and children waiting for the breadwinners to come back home.

The brothers noticed that all the men were armed with pistols of all shapes and sizes and Scar wasn't. He had a hammer and a profoundly intimidating smirk.

James spoke first. "Scar . . . what's up, man? Why are we here? We ain't done nothing."

"Shut the fuck up, nigga! You did whatever I fuckin' say your bitch ass did. You hear me, nigga?"

James was baffled. He stared blankly and trembled.

"I asked you a question, nigga!"

"Yes, I hear you, Scar."

"Put some respect on my name! Call me Mr. Scar, nigga!"

For a moment, James refused to play his game until Scar grabbed the 9mm from Cane's waistband and placed it to his temple. Marvin's panicky eyes pleaded with his younger brother to comply.

"Y-y-y-yes. I hear you, Mr. Scar."

Scar stood back and grinned. Citi was already over this scene and didn't know why Scar insisted that she be there for the dirty work. She knew just like every other goon in the room that these two squares didn't plot any assassination attempts.

"So what y'all niggas know about ya brother's murder?"

Marvin spoke. "We don't know shit. As far as we know, he's alive, Mr. Scar."

James chimed in with the ass kissing. "Wise was always loyal to you, Mr. Scar. He loves you like you're family. We all do. Even our kids love you. You know they call you Uncle Scar. We haven't seen you around lately, though. Could you please tell us what's going on?"

"What it look like, nigga? You 'bout to die." Scar was cold blooded. All that family talk fell on deaf ears, just as it had with Wise and his begging and pleading.

Both brothers began to whimper. It was all surreal.

"We ain't do shit!" Marvin screamed out. "We ain't in the game. Whatever my brother did that's his cross to bear. Let us be, Scar. You know this shit ain't right!"

Whack!

Scar smacked him across his face with the claw part of the hammer, nearly cracking his skull open. The white meat and blood oozed out, and his neck jerked like a bobblehead. Citi felt sick, but she knew she couldn't show weakness in front of her men. She stood there as if she had sanctioned these hits, as did Cane.

"I see the bitch nigga gene runs in the family. Y'all brothers just *see* a pistol and y'all lips start quivering. My bitch harder than y'all niggas! Ain't that right, bae?"

Citi nodded. It was time to play her part.

"Yo, who the fuck has been tryin' to kill us?" She knew it was a rhetorical question, but she was in too deep. She had six goons on payroll at that warehouse who needed to see her behave like a thoroughbred. "Y'all pussy-ass niggas had to hire out the hit. Who was it?"

Marvin and James were both afraid to speak. But, James felt he had to say something. Their lives were on the line.

"Ms. Citi, I swear we don't know what you're talking about. We would never try to hurt you or Mr. Scar or Mr. Cane. We are both clueless. Marvin and I aren't about that life. I work for transit, and my brother works at the post office. I promise it's a misunderstanding."

"I run one of the most efficient organizations in these five boroughs. I don't fuckin' misunderstand shit, nigga. You calling me a stupid ho?"

Scar cringed at her last statement, and under different circumstances, he would have beat the shit out of her for trying to play him. He knew she was trying to flex her authority and grandstand on him. His trigger hand was itching to fist up and smash into her smart mouth. He even considered whether he could get away with it. Odds were seven to one. Cane, plus the six goons that Citi had on payroll. Sure, they took orders from him, but they all knew that it was *her* money.

Marvin replied with, "Look, either kill us or let us go. No man should have to go through this! We innocent."

An evil grin crept across Scar's face. "You heard the man, Citi. Give them what they want. Show them how a boss bitch keeps her organization running efficiently."

"Excuse me?" Suddenly, Citi lost her bravado. She looked to her brother to step up. Cane felt her hesitation and went to snatch his pistol back from Scar, who blocked him.

"Nah, Cane. Citi got this."

Citi felt all eyes on her, even her victims'. She swallowed hard as she pondered her next move. She could hear her father's voice saying, *Bitch, you better represent.* She knew that she had walked herself right into Scar's trap.

"Come on, now. What we doin'?" one goon asked. "Is we killin' or is we talkin'?"

"I'm fuckin' bored," another one replied.

They were there for bloodshed. Someone was gunning for the organization, and these dudes' names came up on the kill list. Mistake or not, a message needed to be sent.

With measured steps, Citi inched closer. Marvin and James were lambs waiting to be slaughtered. She lifted her .45 to Marvin's bloody head and squeezed twice—*Bac! Bac!* Two bullets ripped through his forehead. His head slumped forward into his chest as he stopped breathing instantly.

James begged for his life. Her test had just gotten harder.

"Please, Ms. Citi! On my kids I didn't do nuthin'!" James hollered. He was screaming hysterically, and his screeching was coursing through her veins. "I don't wanna die! I'm beggin' you, don't take my life."

Despite his plea, Citi knew that his fate was written. James's cries tugged at her heart, but it wouldn't save him. Gripping the smoking gun tightly, she quickly inched closer and put the barrel to his head. James tried to wiggle free, but Citi fired—*Bac!* His head lolled forward. He was dead.

Citi stood near their bodies and felt contrition. But it had to be done. Scar had put her on the spot, and she had stepped up to the plate.

"Clean this shit up," were her last orders for the night.

20

Cane said to their men, "Yo, y'all niggas watch yourselves out there. We gettin' heat from both ends. Wise fucked us up wit' five-oh, and now niggas comin' at us tryin' to take our fuckin' heads off. I ain't playin' wit' you hardheaded niggas! Keep ya eyes peeled on any suspicious movements. We at war wit' a fuckin' ghost."

Cane was preaching to the choir. These men had survived wars against the most thorough goons the boroughs had raised up. Scar had handpicked them all; soldiers who would die over that drug money.

Cane was apprehensive because they were being targeted. There had been too many attempts on their lives, Pacho and Damon were missing, not to mention Takenya's murder and his stolen money. Cane wasn't fuckin' around. The shit had him carrying two pistols. He had a .45 tucked in his waistband and a snub-nosed .22 attached to his ankle.

The newest trap house was in a busy section of East New York, an area where various niggas going in and out wouldn't be so obvious. Tonight, everyone had a job to do. They had just received an enormous shipment of 150 kilos from Citi's Mexican connect, Caesar Mingo. His coke was that good shit—hardly stepped on and about 95% pure. There had been a recent drought, so the streets were extra thirsty, and their business ran on supply and demand.

"Y'all niggas make y'all drops and hit me up in the morning."

One goon nodded. "We on it, Cane."

Cane spoke directly to his top enforcers. "Pie, Ebo, Nut, y'all niggas keep my shit safe."

"Stop worryin', nigga. This what we do!" said Ebo.

"I wish a nigga would fuckin' try me. I will blow his fuckin' back out," said Pie as he brandished his Desert Eagle for everyone to see.

Cane took a drag from the blunt in his hand. "Y'all hold it down."

"A'ight, let's go feed the streets," said Nut, as the group began to disperse.

***

Nick sat patiently watching the trap house like a hawk. He knew most of Scar's men were inside, along with Cane—his primary target tonight. To Nick they were just grimy goons standing between him and retirement. It had started out as a favor for Apple, but now it was personal. Nick was a nigga with something to prove. His track record was zero losses out of thirty-seven licks. Whoever came on his radar died.

As the group dispersed, Nick noticed the dark figures coolly walking out of the trap house to their stash cars. He couldn't see who was who or if Cane was one of the eleven killers he counted because of the hoodies shielding each man's face.

Nick's left hand neared the MAC-10 on his lap while his 9mm was snugly tucked in his waistband. He knew he had the advantage, but he was one man and outnumbered. He had to move stealthily and catch his prey by surprise. Nick exited his vehicle and kept low, creeping up on the niggas.

Rat-ta-Tat! Tat! Tat! Tat! Tat! Tat! Tat! Tat!

Deafening bursts of gunfire came exploding from the automatic weapon. Nick's MAC-10 mowed down half of Cane's men and tore into Pie's flesh, pushing him forward violently. His Desert Eagle fell as his body dropped.

Nut opened fire, shattering the glass of parked cars on the street.

Bak! Bak! Bak!

A bullet whizzed past Nick's shoulder as he ducked for cover. He rebounded and caught Nut in the head and opened his chest cavity with six rounds. Nut's body slumped on a tricked-out Escalade as bullets continued to tear into the exterior of the vehicle.

Cane watched the horrific scene from the second story window of the stash house, his right-hand firmly gripping his .45. He knew he should go down and help his men, but he was frozen. His heart lurched as they were cut down one-by-one. From where he stood he could only see one man—a lean, dark figure stealthily attacking with accurate precision. Thunderous gunshots continued to crack through the air.

Boom! Boom! Boom! Boom!

Bak! Bak! Bak!

Ra-ta-tat! Tat! Tat! Tat! Tat! Tat!

Two more of Cane's men went down.

The remaining soldiers tried to retaliate, including Ebo. Windshield after windshield shattered and shards of glass flew through the air like confetti and blanketed the pavement.

Ebo found himself dead center in the middle of chaos. It was raining bullets, and one grazed his forehead. The blood slid down his brows, making it difficult for him to aim. "Fuck!" he screamed out, wiping the crimson liquid from his eyes.

Nick continued to storm forward, gun popping off, knocking goons down like bowling pins.

Ebo saw the shadowy figure coming through blurred eyes. Still, he fumbled for the Glock and shot wildly.

Bak! Bak! Bak!

Nick stood firm, outstretched his 9mm, and parked bullets in Ebo's face and neck. His body dropped quickly to the pavement. Nick walked up and slammed two additional rounds into the back of his head. Briefly, Nick admired at his handiwork. He was sure that one of the fallen soldiers was Cane.

*** ***

Cane gawked at the carnage below. He didn't see this hit coming—not like this. He knew it was likely because niggas were gunning for them, but he thought that he and his team would get a preemptive strike in.

"Bitch-ass nigga!" he shouted. And that bitch ass was him.

Within minutes the area was blanketed with red and blue lights. Within an hour the block was swarmed with men holding brass badges. This was a massacre. There were so many dead bodies it looked like a street morgue. White sheets covered the dead as chalk outlined what were once vibrant young men. Killers with families and friends who loved them. Killers who would no longer kill.

Frustration and angst overwhelmed Cane as the bullet riddled vehicles that held Citi's 150 kilos were towed away. The news coverage dubbed it the "Midnight Drug Massacre," and that pretty much summed it up.

21

Scar's gleaming black Escalade came to a stop on the Queens street and parked directly in front of the barbershop with loud rap music blaring. Just last night his men were murdered and Citi's coke was seized. They took a huge loss, but he still had a reputation to uphold. He still had to stay fresh. Scar climbed out of the opulent looking vehicle with the large chrome rims and dark tints, smoking a cigarette and conversing on his cell phone. He was the center of attention on the block, looking thuggish in a do-rag tied together in the back, beige Timberlands, a fashionable winter jacket, and his gleaming jewelry. With a 9mm tucked into his waistband and flanked by his goon Big Top, he walked into the popular barbershop called Nappy Cuts and gave dap to his favorite barber on the scene.

"Neak, what's good? How many you got?" Scar asked him, holding his phone away from his ear.

"Just this one in the chair," replied Neak. "But you know I got you, my dude. What you need?"

"Just a shapeup."

"A'ight, give me like ten minutes, and I got you," Neak repeated.

Scar nodded and eyed the customer Neak had in his chair. He was a young boy—just an average Joe that Scar could easily chew up and spit out. He posed no threat. With his menacing goon poised by the front entrance on lookout, Scar took a seat up front and curtailed his phone conversation.

The barbershop was semi-crowded with people waiting patiently for their favorite barbers to finish with their current customers. To keep their patrons entertained, the shop had a pool table in the back, a 55" flat screen mounted on the wall showing either movies or sports, and there was chitchat and gossip amongst the clientele and the three barbers cutting hair.

"Yo, you really think LeBron James is better than Jordan?" one of the customers exclaimed from the waiting area in the shop.

"Hells yeah, he better—ten times better than Jordan," another male shouted out.

"Here we go again with this LeBron and Jordan argument," chided one of the barbers.

"Man, that fool is just a LeBron hater. Look at the numbers, nigga!"

"But Jordan got six rings," boasted the second man.

"Nigga, that's always y'all defense with ya niggas dick riding Jordan's career. He got six rings and he never lost in the finals. But check this— Jordan couldn't fuck with today's game. It would be too fast for him."

"Nigga, is you crazy? You think LeBron could fuck with niggas back in the days—Ewing, Pippen, Robinson, Shaq, Barkley? They were no joke. Shit would have been too physical for LeBron's weak and crying ass."

"Nigga, you don't know shit!"

Other customers started to volunteer their opinions on the conversation, including Scar. At Nappy Cuts he was just a cool dude talking shit with the regulars at the busy shop on Jamaica Avenue. He even smiled and laughed during the shit-talking.

The conversation in the barbershop went from the NBA to bitches, and even politics. When someone brought up Donald Trump's name, one of the clients said, "You mean Donald Chump—because that's what he is, a fuckin' chump."

Everyone laughed, including Scar.

Neak finished with his young client's haircut and motioned for Scar to get into his chair for his shapeup. Scar sat in the chair, adjusting the gun in his waistband and removing his do-rag.

"So how you been, my nigga?" his barber asked him.

"You already know, my nigga. I'm out here gettin' this money and making these niggas respect what I do."

"I feel you."

"Yo, keep it light on the sides," said Scar.

Neak nodded.

While Scar was getting his shapeup, Nick sat parked across the street from the barbershop in an unassuming Chevy Cobalt. He'd had eyes on Scar all day via following him around town, and he believed that he'd found his opening. Nick felt the goon Scar had standing near the doorway was easy to take out. They wouldn't even see him coming.

He removed the clip to his Browning Hi-Power 9mm, and it was fully loaded. Then he had his backup gun, an 8-shot .45 ACP pistol. He keenly eyed the activity in the barbershop across the street through the large glass windows. He could see Scar in the barber's chair. Nick didn't plan on missing him this time—and there would be no smirk or salute from Scar once he pumped bullets into that arrogant fool.

As Nick sat back and waited, his cell phone rang, and it was Apple calling him again. He decided to ignore her call for the umpteenth time, knowing she would be upset with him. He didn't have a reasonable explanation for ignoring her call, but he wanted to focus.

Apple's call went to his voicemail. He sent her a quick text before tossing the phone in the passenger seat. He couldn't afford the distraction. Not now.

It took Neak fifteen minutes to finish Scar's shapeup. Looking at his image in the large mirror, Scar was satisfied with the results.

"Nice . . . you always had skills, Neak."

"I'm glad you like it."

Scar got up from the chair with the butt of his pistol peeking from his waist. It caught the attention of some of the patrons inside the barbershop, but everyone knew to keep quiet and mind their business. They didn't want any trouble with Scar.

Scar removed a large wad of bills from his pocket. He peeled off a few twenty-dollar bills and overpaid Neak for his shapeup. Scar always took good care of the people he liked.

Neak was grateful. "Good lookin', Scar."

"You know I always got you."

"No doubt."

Scar turned and gave a slight head nod to his goon standing by the entrance. Both men made their exit from the barbershop onto the busy Queens street. From their view, everything seemed copasetic, until it wasn't.

As they were walking to the Escalade, Nick made his move toward the duo moving about in public. With his 9mm tightly gripped in his hand, he urgently marched their way, outstretching his hand, the gun poised and aiming at his target. Big Top spotted the threat right away and became a barrier between Nick and Scar while reaching for his concealed weapon. But he was too late.

Nick exploded on them.

Boom! Boom! Boom! Boom!

Big Top took all four shots to his chest, collapsing to the pavement while Scar scrambled into action, ducking quickly and taking cover behind a parked car. He reached for his own weapon and returned fire.

Bac! Bac! Bac! . . . Bac! Bac!

Bullets went flying everywhere, as car windows were shot out and several bystanders were hit during the violent melee.

"Nigga, you back for seconds!" Scar shouted, taunting his attacker.

Nick continued to release a barrage of bullets his way. He was determined not to miss him a second time. Bullets whizzed closely by their heads, including several rounds striking and shattering the windows to the barbershop. Neak and the others inside had no choice but to hit the floor.

The reckless echo of gunfire pierced the public street, bringing the immediate attention of two nearby beat cops. They hurried toward the melee with their guns drawn and screamed into their police radios as they moved closer to the gunfire. They ran into two men shooting at each other.

Scar once again gave Nick his signature salute and then ran up the block. Nick fired wildly at him. The nigga couldn't get away from him this time. It was like the movies—loud shots, screaming, and people fleeing. Nick knew he should jump back into his vehicle and flee the scene, but Scar's arrogance drove him, and he angrily gave chase.

Scar darted through traffic, bullets still whizzing by him. Another bystander got hit in the crossfire. Scar stumbled for a second, but caught his footing and could feel Nick barreling toward him. Unfortunately for him, he was out of ammunition and the only thing he could do was run for his life. Today wasn't going to be his day to die. He was determined.

Scar ran like Usain Bolt on the public street, dodging and weaving through cars and people, even pushing a few out of his way and knocking some to the ground.

"Move! Get the fuck out my way!" he screamed.

Soon, he gained a greater lead on Nick.

Nick fired three more shots at Scar but missed, and then he squeezed again and heard his gun go, *Click! Click! Click! Click!*

He was out of rounds. But that wasn't the worst of it. From behind he heard, "NYPD! Freeze!"

"Freeze! Put the fuckin' gun down now!"

The two beat cops had their guns aimed at him, ready for a threatening movement by the armed black man. Nick had fucked up. He frowned. He was upset. He then pivoted suddenly toward the officers with the gun in his hand and before he could even blink, both cops lit him up with multiple shots. The gunfire resonated through the Queens street, and Nick went down from a hail of bullets slamming into his muscular frame. His lifeless body hit the concrete hard.

Both cops were awestruck. They had just killed a man. They'd felt threatened, fearing for their lives. There was a gun. There were shots fired, and several bystanders had been hit. They screamed into their police radios, as news of the police shooting started to crackle throughout the NYPD.

22

Apple was lying on her bed in a black corset and thong, looking extra sexy tonight. She had a bottle of Ace on ice, Nick's favorite champagne, and had ordered steak dinners from his favorite restaurant. Apple wanted to fuck and fuck some more. Nick had texted her this morning and said he would finally be over tonight and that he had something very important to tell her. She was both relieved and upset that he had disappeared without telling her anything. But she couldn't wait to see her man. She missed him. She wanted to curse him out, scream and yell, and then fuck his brains out. But she wondered what important news he had to tell her.

Midnight came and went, and Nick never walked through her door. Apple started to worry again. She called his cell phone and it went straight to his voicemail. And then she got angry. Why was the nigga toying with her? Was there a new bitch? Was that the news?

"What the fuck!" she shouted.

Nick was trying her last nerve.

***

Apple woke up shortly before 3 a.m. and her face was awash with tears. She'd had a bad dream that she couldn't really remember, just pieces of it. Someone had a knife and told her that she needed to drive them to Mexico and when she screamed, Nick appeared in the dream. He told

Apple that he wasn't fucking wit' her and disappeared on a horse. Apple had no idea what the bizarre dream meant, but she felt sick. It spooked her. She got up, grabbed her .45, and walked around her apartment to make sure she was alone. The darkness spooked her, so she began clicking on lights. Apple had never felt so vulnerable in her life. *What the fuck is going on? Why am I freaking out?*

She paced around the bedroom and continued to call Nick's phone, but still no answer. Something happened! Her gut told her so.

Apple didn't want to jinx her nigga, but she had to call local hospitals just to prove to herself that she was bugging. Thankfully they didn't have anyone there fitting his description or with his name. Reluctantly, she dialed the local precincts and gave his government. A sergeant put her on hold. Apple could feel the butterflies swimming around in her stomach—something was definitely wrong. What made her call the police? She knew she had to be desperate to do something like that. Someone got back to her and directed her call to a Queens precinct. *Queens—what the fuck!* she wondered. Once again, she was put on hold. A few minutes later, a different voice spoke to her. It was gruff and unfriendly. "You're the one calling about a Nicholas Davis?"

"Yes. He's my brother. Has he been arrested?"

"And your name is?"

Apple paused and then replied, "Lisa Davis."

"Well, Ms. Davis, I'm sorry, ma'am, but Nicholas was in a shootout today with an unknown assailant. He didn't respond to police demands to put down his weapon, and officers had to open fire—your brother is dead."

"What are you saying?" Apple was in disbelief. "He was killed by cops? He's dead?"

"I can't answer any further questions until we conduct a full investigation."

"Where is he? I wanna see him!" Apple screamed. "I want to see his body!"

"Look, it's late! I know it's hard to hear, but your brother is dead."

"No way is he fuckin' dead, you hear me?" Apple wailed. "No fuckin' way!"

The cop rudely hung up.

Apple was devastated by the news. She dropped the phone from her hands and stood there in disbelief. *Not Nick!* She collapsed on her bed. Her crying became so hysterical that she felt weak and nauseous. Apple ran to the toilet and began to vomit up the remnants of her romantic dinner. The pain from her stomach contracting couldn't match the heaviness in her heart. It felt like it would implode. Part of her wanted her heart to implode because she couldn't take the agony of continually losing those she loved. Did she ever tell him that? Did Nick know that she loved him before he died?

She needed this all to be a dream. She wanted to wake up tomorrow to her nigga in her bed.

"Why did you leave me?" she screamed out. But Apple knew the truth. Nick would still be alive if she hadn't pushed him to get involved with her plot for revenge. She was sure that this had something to do with Citi and Scar. If not, who else?

Now Nick was dead. What was she going to do?

✳✳✳

Scar rushed home from the shooting, and he was a bit shaken up. It was the second attempt on his life, by the same fool that tried to kill him at Junior's. What the fuck had he done to this nigga? Who was he? Scar intended to locate this elusive muthafucka before a third attempt. Sure, he felt like he had nine lives. But he didn't.

The Astoria, Queens apartment was quiet and safe, he supposed. But to make sure he was in good hands, he went into the bedroom and removed two Glock 19's and a MAC-10 from under his bed and kept them close. He made numerous phone calls to his soldiers on the streets to let them know what had happened. He roused his goons and wanted to execute his own sneak attack—his own revenge.

He stayed locked inside the apartment the entire day. To ease his apprehension, he poured himself a drink, preferring Hennessy. The brown liquor soothed him.

Scar contacted Citi to let her know what had happened and to warn her to be alert. Shit just went down and they had lost one man. He contemplated his next move. Someone had to be talking or snitching on him and his crew. He felt some disloyal fool had betrayed the organization. He continued to down the brown juice and think, and chill, and seethe, and laugh.

"Muthafuckas can't touch me!" he uttered. "I'm Superman, bitches!"

The following morning, Scar seemed a lot calmer. He turned on the TV to get his mind off his troubles, but they were only beginning. The shootout was on the news, nearly on every station. Footage of the incident in Queens had gone viral. The authorities were looking for the second shooter. Scar learned that three people had been killed outside the barbershop—one bystander, Nicholas Davis, and Scar's goon, Jason "Big Top" Williams.

Detectives heavily plagued the entire area, going to local businesses and asking questions. They subpoenaed any surveillance footage from the area, hopefully using it to apprehend the second shooter, and also asking anyone who may have captured anything on their phones to come forward.

Scar frowned. "Shit!"

He felt the pressure. It wasn't his fault that Nicholas had come at him. He was defending himself. But still, cops were looking to crucify the second shooter. He knew now would be a good time to make himself scarce from the streets. There were a lot of people around—lots of faces and cameras. But what troubled him the most were the niggas inside the barbershop. They knew who he was. They knew his face and his name. He didn't know if any of them would get cute and start talking to the police. Cops were putting up a reward for any information leading to an arrest, and that was trouble for him. That was snitch bait.

✳✳✳

Citi called a meeting with Scar and her brother. She was sick over losing so much product, her organization was down nearly six million, and there wasn't much more where that had come from. It would take years to rebuild. But she was somewhat relieved when both Cane and Scar said that their enemy was murdered.

Her organization had taken too many hits. And with the cops looking for the second assailant, New York was starting to feel small.

23

The shooting of Nicholas Davis made front page news and became a national headline—another black man shot dead by police officers. The video of Nick's death had been captured by several cell phone cameras, and it soon went viral via WorldStar and social media. The public felt that the police were racist and overzealous in killing another black man, although he was armed and dangerous.

Nick's father, Corey, sat among a few friends in the dayroom watching a *Lost* rerun. He was an old man, but he was still a dangerous figure with some clout and was well respected. He sat quietly in his chair, doing more listening to the other inmates and watching TV than talking. He always felt that silence showed strength. But today, he had a lot on his mind. He couldn't stop thinking about Nick and his son's future with this woman named Apple. Although Nick was tough, Corey felt that his girl was making him bite off more than he could chew.

Amir entered the dayroom, carrying the same respect as an OG like Corey. He and Corey shared a brief conversation about Nick. They were on the same page about his girlfriend Apple. They didn't like her, and they didn't trust her. She was trouble.

C.O. Mitchell walked into the room with what appeared to be a sense of purpose. His eyes scanned the dayroom for an inmate and he soon spotted him. He went up to Corey and said to him, "Come with me. The warden wants to see you."

Corey looked up at C.O. Mitchell with a look of confusion. "What's this about?"

"I don't know. He's just asked for you. Let's go. I don't have all day."

With a stoic look on his face, Corey slowly stood up and followed behind the guard, marching calmly toward the warden's domain. If he was worried, it didn't show on his face. In fact, he cracked a joke while walking the corridor with the guard. But the guard didn't laugh.

Corey was ushered into the warden's office. It was neat, it was nicely furnished, and the place seemed a world away from the prison. Warden Cacti was seated behind his desk in his leather chair, and he was dressed immaculately in a black suit and blue tie. He was a white male around Corey's age. Both men had seen their fair share of violence and bloodshed in the prison. Cacti had been around for nearly fifteen years, and sometimes he felt trapped inside like the inmates.

Corey wanted to get straight to the point. He stared directly at the warden and asked, "Why am I here, Warden? What's this about?"

Warden Cacti looked at him with a slightly despondent expression. "Have a seat, Corey."

Corey already knew that it was bad news. "Why?" Corey responded, showing resistance. "I would rather stand."

The warden took a deep breath. He knew there was no easy way to say it—no other way to tell Corey the grim news.

"I got word this morning that your son is dead," the warden said.

For a moment, Corey stood there frozen. Did he hear the warden right? Did he say that his son was dead?

"What the fuck are you talking about, Warden?" he finally spoke.

"Nick was killed in a shootout yesterday with the police."

Corey could only stare blankly and swallow his anger. His only child and only living relative was gone—murdered by the police.

"What happened?" he asked.

"The details are hazy, but from my understanding, he got into a shootout with some men and the police intervened."

"It ain't right for a parent to outlive their child."

"I know . . . it isn't. My condolences to you, Corey. I can only imagine what you're going through."

Corey cut his eyes at the warden. Fuck his condolences! No, the privileged fool would never know what it was like to be him. He went home to his family every day. He got to see and hug his children, while his was lying somewhere cold in a city morgue.

"Will I be able to go bury my son?" he asked.

"I'll see what I can do."

"That's it?" Corey asked roughly.

The warden nodded. "Yeah, that's it."

Corey pivoted and marched out of the office. Still, he kept his anger and his emotions contained. The last thing he wanted to do was show any emotion around other inmates. But he was angry. He wanted answers about his son's death. Who was Nick in a gunfight with, and why? Corey's intuition screamed at him that Apple had something to do with it.

C.O. Mitchell led Corey back to general population. He walked back into the dayroom looking normal and expressionless. He exchanged looks with Amir and then decided to leave the room. He needed to be alone, though it was difficult to find solitude in a maximum security prison.

Once Corey was alone in his cell, a few tears leaked from his eyes and trickled down his face. He quickly wiped them away.

It didn't take long for Amir to see what was bothering Corey. On the TV in the dayroom, the news showed the video of Nick's death. The entire room became up in arms because they knew Nick from his visits. They knew he was Corey's son.

One of the inmates even turned to Amir and said, "Yo, ain't that your man?"

Amir sat there calmly for a moment, but he was bubbling with rage that his best friend was dead. And then he stood up, and it happened—he erupted. He picked up a chair and threw it across the room, and then he unexpectedly attacked the nearest inmate next to him, punching the man in his face. Then Amir started attacking other inmates. His violent actions quickly incited the other inmates inside the dayroom, and chaos ensued.

The alarm sounded, and guards ran to defuse the violent melee that had erupted. Several guards clad in tactical gear charged into the dayroom and stormed toward Amir, beating him down with their batons until he was subdued.

Bloody and broken, Amir was dragged to solitary confinement, where he would spend the next thirty days—grieving and bitter.

24

Kola stood by her sister's side five months pregnant. She had to take it easy, but she wanted to be there for Apple—give her comfort and condolences. She held Apple's hand as they stood near the open grave in the Brooklyn cemetery. Nick's Onyx Ebony 18-gauge steel casket was readied to be lowered into the ground by the caretakers.

Nick didn't have many friends. He kept to himself mostly, living a clandestine lifestyle. But Apple wanted to bury her man in style, although there were only a handful of people present. She wanted Nick to be remembered.

The sky was clear, but there was a brisk chill in the air. Kola wasn't the only one there to give Apple support and comfort. Cartier was there too. There was no way was she going to allow Apple to put her man in the grave alone.

Apple sobbed and grieved. She felt it was all her fault. Nick had his million plus to start his own bar and lounge. He wanted to follow his dream and live a quiet civilian life and stay out of trouble. That is, until she came into the picture and convinced him that there was much more out there—money and her revenge.

One week after his death, the narrative turned on a dime. The media dug up dirt and began smearing Nick's name because of his past drug arrests and murder and conspiracy to commit murder charges from Malik Noland and Stephanie Hawkins years ago. Then there was Nick's notorious father and his violent reputation and best friend doing life for drug distribution. The media had a field day slandering his name. Public outcry was no more. No one felt sympathy for him. There were no boycotts, no outrage from the African-American community, no Black Lives Matter movement, no Al Sharpton preaching for justice.

Corey stood close by the grieving girlfriend and his son's casket. The warden did him a favor and pulled some strings. He was clad in a cheap gray suit and handcuffed with his hands in front of him. U.S. Marshals flanked him and showed some sympathy for the loss of his son.

Slyly, Corey cut his eyes at the woman he believed was responsible for his son's death. He had nothing but contempt for the young bitch.

After the preacher gave the eulogy and Corey watched his son being lowered into the grave, he went over to Apple to properly introduce himself.

"Can I have a minute of privacy with her, gentlemen?" he asked the U.S. Marshals.

They allowed him one minute to speak to the teary-eyed Apple in private. They took a few steps away but lingered close by.

Apple managed to smile at the old man and introduce herself and embraced him. But Corey stood there aloof and motionless. She thought he was being standoffish to her because he'd never met her and he was in mourning too. She had no idea that Nick had told his father everything.

"I loved your son," she said.

Corey didn't care for her words. He had some words of his own to share with her. He leaned in close to her ear and whispered, "Before I leave this earth, I will personally make sure you join my only son in death."

She looked at Corey in shock. *Did he just threaten my life?* she asked herself. It wasn't the reaction she expected.

Corey saw her quizzical look and added, "You think you can't be touched because I'm locked up? Think again, bitch. You don't know me."

With that, he pivoted and walked toward the two marshals, ready to be taken back to his cage in upstate New York.

Apple stood there silently, taking in his words. But she knew why he hated her—the same reason she beat herself up. He blamed her for Nick's death, and she blamed herself too.

Corey marched silently toward the federal vehicle parked nearby. He'd finally gotten a glimpse of Apple, and it was satisfying to put a face with the name. The U.S. Marshals placed him into the backseat and he stared at Apple with her sister and her friend. The three of them were in a circle near the grave talking about something.

Bitch, he mouthed to himself.

"Take me back to jail. I'm done here," he said, like he was giving the marshals orders.

The federal vehicle started to move away from the area, and Corey kept his eyes on Apple until she was out of his sight. The bitch was living on borrowed time. He knew a lot of old heads still on the streets with sons and grandsons that could put in some work for him.

＊＊＊

Apple knew she couldn't get distracted by grief. Citi was still alive, and she and Cartier had a purpose to carry out. She didn't have the time to worry about an old man with a grudge. *He ain't gonna do shit!* she told herself. Nick was gone and no amount of grieving was going to bring him back. That was facts! She had learned that firsthand when her sister was murdered. The only thing that could comfort Apple was finishing what she and Nick started. Citi still needed to die. She was sure Nick would want this now too.

Sitting alone in her bedroom, Nick was heavy on her mind, as was his father. Apple had planned on picking up where Nick had left off and depositing some money into his father's commissary each week. She wanted to take care of him. Nick would want that. But since he wanted to get cute at his son's burial and toss idle threats at her, she thought, *Fuck him! Let him rot in jail.*

Then a thought popped in her head. Apple bolted out of bed, got dressed, and drove to Nick's apartment. "Please, God . . . I hope the superintendent didn't clear out his apartment yet."

Apple couldn't turn the key in the lock quick enough. She was moving so fast she tripped over her own feet running inside. Nick was messy as hell, which was one reason he always stayed at her place. It took a few minutes for her to locate his stash. Behind the stackable washer and dryer combo were three duffel bags containing his million plus dollars. *Sweet Jesus!*

"Thank you, baby," Apple said to Nick.

She had fleeting thought. Maybe she should take a page from Nick's book and retire.

∗∗∗

Apple peeled her clothing off and decided to take a hot bubble bath. She sat soaking in the tub, drinking white wine and listening to some R&B. And then, all of a sudden, she was overwhelmed with emotions. She wished Nick was in the bathtub with her, holding her, bathing her, kissing her, and making love to her. He had gone after Scar on her behalf and gotten himself killed. Apple now had more of a reason to hunt Citi and Scar too.

It felt like her tears wouldn't stop. She had become an emotional wreck with Nick's abrupt absence. The only thing that was going to take her mind off him was seeing Citi and Scar six feet under.

For the next several weeks, Apple put all of her time and effort into hunting Citi, but the bitch had just disappeared. Her social media had gone silent for weeks, she wasn't at any of the hot spots in the city, and she hadn't attended any A-list parties. She was a ghost. But Apple refused to give up.

It was time to change up her game plan—maybe come at Citi a different way. Apple felt she had the help she needed with Cartier back in town. There was no way she was going to allow that young bitch to keep winning—not while she was still alive.

✳✳✳

It was over a month before Amir agreed to place Apple on his visiting list. She had written him after finding his contact info with Nick's personal items she had brought back to her place. Apple still found it hard living without him. Each night she would sleep in one of his shirts just to smell his scent. She would inhale her man and then mourn his loss all over again.

Lately, Apple looked like a hot mess. She was running around in the same jeans, sneakers, and dirty hair pulled back into a ponytail. But on this day, for the ride to Clinton Correctional Facility, she knew she had to pull herself together and represent her man.

Apple got her long hair washed and roller set, got a manicure and pedicure, and pulled a red Gucci dress Nick had bought her from her closet. It was sexy yet conservative enough to not get her kicked off the visit.

She hired a car service to drive the five-hour commute because she didn't trust herself behind the wheel. Her mind kept drifting off into dark places, reliving the good and bad, happy and sad times of her life's journey. Apple exhaled. No more fuck-ups.

As Apple walked through each security checkpoint she could feel all eyes on her. Male and female C.O.'s were gawking at the baddest bitch that had come through there in a while. Her beautiful face, high-end gear, and aloof attitude had folks wondering who she was and who she was affiliated with.

Apple sat perched at the visiting table waiting impatiently for Amir. Her long red fingernails tapped repetitively as several minutes ticked by. Nearly an hour had passed, and no one came looking for her. Apple asked a corrections officer if Amir knew he had a visitor waiting and he assured her that he did. Apple watched as the hands on the large, round clock circled until nearly two hours were gone. Her fuckin' pressure was up.

Finally, she stood up to leave when a lean, bald, powerful figure with a grizzly beard came thundering through. His eyes were filled with hate and rage as they met hers. Apple's eyes challenged his with the same level of contempt and anger. No-fuckin'-body kept her waiting, especially a nothing nigga with a lukewarm rep from decades ago. She was hardly impressed or intimidated.

Amir sat down without any pleasantries or apologies. He got straight to the point. "What the fuck you want, bitch?"

"Name's Apple," she replied. "But Bitch works."

"You think this shit a game?" Amir's face was so twisted he almost didn't look human.

"My man was murdered, so I promise you this is not a fuckin' game!" Apple told herself she wouldn't get heated. She needed to remain calm to avenge Nick's death.

"Your man?" Amir chuckled. "Bitch, he never mentioned you."

The lie stung.

Apple nodded. She knew Amir was hurting and felt helpless. He would have never agreed to meet with her had Nick not mentioned her to him. Also, his father calling out her name at his funeral was enough confirmation that his son had spoken of her.

Apple ignored his slick remark. "So the reason I'm here is that I need your help—"

"I can't help—"

"If you would just let me finish we could quickly end this visit. Unless you'd like to drag this shit out."

Amir had to admit that he had kept her waiting purposely. He was busy making a shank to slice her throat open. Apple wasn't supposed to leave Clinton alive. But when he saw the young, beautiful girl dressed in red with bright red lipstick, he immediately knew why Nick was open. She was stunning. And now Amir wanted back the two hours he had wasted on the shank.

Amir continued to smirk. He couldn't show his hand. "Keep talking."

Apple leaned in and whispered, "We both lost someone we loved. And I'm the first to admit it's my fault. But Nick was a grown man, and he made his choice to help me, and now he's gone. I can't sleep knowing the people who put him in his grave are still out there."

"What do you want me to do, shorty? You see I'm just a black man in a cage."

Apple nodded at the obvious. "You are. But you're also in the one place that information is traded freely. Everybody knows that gossip is disseminated first through iron bars before it even hits the streets, and right now I can't find that slippery bitch Citi or her nigga Scar."

Amir was ambivalent. Pretty bitches were manipulative. He knew she had purposely come up there looking like a beauty queen to get his dick hard and ask him to beg Corey to back off. She just fucked up his head when she mentioned Scar and Citi. This was a bold bitch. Did she not know that Corey's threat was authentic—that the old head still held weight on them streets?

"Yo, what about Nick's money?"

It was literally the million-dollar question. And how Apple answered would determine if Amir would give her a matching bow-tie to go with that red dress.

Apple was not surprised that he knew about Nick's cash. She also knew that money ruled everything.

She shrugged. "Nick left over a million. You want it? It's yours. Just help me find the whereabouts of Bonnie and Clyde. That's all I want—retribution for my man so he can sleep in peace."

Amir was impressed that she was straight up about how much cash Nick had accumulated. But he knew she wasn't going to give up that much money to a jail bird. No one would. But he played along.

"Nah, queen, you can't actually drop all that in my account, but you will hit me and his pops off until that shit runs out or you die. Nick would have wanted that."

"I know. And I've already blessed both y'all accounts. Check it when this visit is over."

"What do you need from me?"

"Any information you hear just call this number and tell me. It's a burner phone so you can speak freely. It won't trace back to me." Apple covertly slid a piece of paper his way, and he took it.

"You do know that our conversations are taped?"

"And?" Apple sucked her teeth. He was acting like an amateur. "So, they get you on a murder conspiracy? So, what? You already got life, nigga. What they gonna do? Bring you back from the dead and retry you?"

He chuckled. Apple wasn't a dumb bitch. "I'm lookin' out for you. I can handle mine."

"As can I."

Amir was beginning to warm up to her. "I'll see what I can do to help you on my end, but I promise you Corey won't be as forgiving."

"Fuck him. And I say that respectfully, of course."

Shorty was tugging at his heartstrings. If Nick hadn't been like a brother, Amir would have pushed up.

"All right, I'll help you. I'll see what I can dig up." Amir stared deeply into Apple's pretty eyes, and she didn't look away. "But one thing though, queen. Revenge is like a mistress. She will always try to take more than you're willing to give. You keep looking for an eye for an eye—"

Apple completed his sentence, "And everyone will go blind. Yes, so I've heard."

**

Amir quickly turned into a stalker. He repeatedly called Apple's burner phone, yet he never had any solid intel on Citi. Fifteen-minute calls morphed into hour long marathons with him chitchatting like they were best friends. At first, she welcomed his calls, excited about the prospect of getting closer to her prey. And when he had no information, she stayed on the phone with him because she liked the stories he would tell her about Nick and their childhood together in Harlem. But when those stories ran out and Amir began repeating the same shit, Apple knew she was being played for a fool.

The next dozen or more telephone calls from Amir went straight to her voicemail. She could hear the frustration in his voice. His tone and cadence had changed. The first messages his voice was soft and flirty like she was his bitch. "Queen, where you at? I miss hearing your voice." The next batch his tone was normal—he wasn't trying to seduce her. The message was brief. "Cut ya phone on so we can politick."

The last messages were laced with anger. Amir's voice was gruff and demanding. She was no longer his queen, and he was no longer on that religious shit. "Yo, shorty, I see you playin' games wit' a nigga. I got that for you, so you better open up this line before a nigga move on!"

Apple laughed. Niggas were all the same. She let him stew a couple more days before answering. As soon as she said hello she could feel his relief. Amir claimed he knew where to locate her problem but could only tell her in person because those peoples could be listening, talking about the feds or anyone in law enforcement. Apple was tired of his fuckin' games. Her nigga was dead and his best friend would fuck her if he had the chance.

"Fuck those peoples. Just give me the deets," she demanded.

"I said in person," he repeated.

"Amir, I'm not wasting ten hours of valuable time making a round trip for the information you can give me now in seconds, real-time, real talk. You made me a promise, and you owe this to your so-called brother that's rotting in the ground. Now once this situation is handled, I promise I'll come through at least once a month—show you some love like Nick used to do. Let people know you got peoples out here that care about you. But I can't focus until I get this shit off my mind."

Apple was lying through her straight teeth. This nigga would never see her black ass again unless she failed on her mission and her face was plastered across the television screen as a Jane Doe. But Amir fell for it and gave up all the information he had gathered. He wanted to hold out for a visit this week but settled for less and warned, "Next time a nigga call you better answer your phone."

Energized by the new development, Apple immediately called Cartier and told her that Citi had resurfaced and that she was doing it really big.

"Where that ho at?" Cartier asked.

"South Beach. You ready to take a road trip?"

"Absolutely."

25

The sign said, "Welcome to Miami." Apple and Cartier were back and everything looked the same. The weather was perfect and the blue water seemed endless. It was calm and picturesque with the white sandy beaches, the tall palm trees, the beautiful people, and the sun shining brightly over the city—it was awesome. But the girls weren't there to enjoy the view; they were there for retribution.

Cartier stared out the window aimlessly while Apple did the driving. She had a lot on her mind. Head had gotten into a serious brawl in prison and put two inmates in the hospital. He was charged with aggravated assault and got six months added to his sentence. It was news that broke Cartier's heart. *Dumb muthafucka must love the pen,* she thought. He could have come home to some warm and waiting pussy, but the nigga couldn't control his temper.

Cartier sighed.

Apple knew why her friend was quiet and gloomy. Like she missed Nick, Cartier missed Head—and she wanted some dick. But at least her man was still alive, Apple felt.

"You'll be okay, Cartier. Don't think about that nigga. He fucked up."

Cartier waved her hand in dismissal. "I'm good."

"I know you are. But you'll be even better once we hunt this bitch down and fuck her up. We 'bout to get paid, Cartier. You feel me? We didn't come this far for nothing."

Cartier slightly smiled. She then asked, "So, what's the four-one-one on this bitch?"

"Amir told me she's down here in South Beach doin' it up—living life out here like she fuckin' Beyoncé. Every day that bitch gets to breathe, it pisses me off," Apple proclaimed.

"Damn, I never thought I would be back down here," Cartier said, suddenly looking reflective.

For Cartier, there were too many memories, some good, but mostly bad. Miami was the place where her daughter, sisters Fendi and Prada, and her mother were murdered. It was where she went to war, and it was where she'd had last seen her best friend. Once upon a time, Cartier was living the high life in Miami, and then with the snap of some fingers, it all went to shit.

"Don't think about the past, Cartier."

"I'm tryin' not to," she replied.

"Look, we gonna check into a nice fuckin' hotel, on me of course, get dressed, and then we gonna have us a few drinks. And hey, we might find some cute niggas and do us," said Apple.

Cartier smiled. She was happy to see her friend was dealing with Nick's death.

The girls checked into the Retreat Collection in South Beach. They were content with their sophisticated suite overlooking the ocean, and the place featured a rooftop pool and a bar with skyline views.

Cartier toured the room and uttered, "God, I miss this."

She flopped down on one of the beds and stretched and smiled. The bright, opulent city and the luxurious suite were a far cry from mundane Seattle.

"What made you move to Seattle anyway?" Apple asked her.

"I just needed to get as far away from New York and Miami as possible. We were supposed to be dead, remember?"

"Yeah, but you know me. I couldn't go that far. I ended up in B-more. It was a'ight but it wasn't home. Something 'bout New York that other cities can't duplicate."

"I swear you ain't ever lie. I love my fuckin' borough. Brooklyn is in my bones. You can't take it outta me." Cartier thought for a second. "So if we love our home what the fuck are we doin' here?"

"I don't give a fuck, Cartier. That bitch played and used us, and I'd rather be dead than to allow Citi to live the good life while I'm still fuckin' breathing."

Cartier understood. She had killed for less. She was just grumpy about Head and his additional jail time.

The girls ordered room service, downed a few drinks, and talked and laughed. Apple wanted to go down to the bar and mingle. But Cartier kept in mind why they were in town—to hunt.

"We can't be seen like that," Cartier said. "I think we should at least try to keep a low profile."

After a couple martinis, Apple removed her laptop from her bag and logged on to social media. Again tonight, there was nothing. Citi's accounts were up, but they were quiet. Apple was out of ideas. Her intel had gotten them this far, and it was now Cartier's time to put in work.

"So what now?" Apple asked. "It's been a while now since this bitch posted. She's smarter than we gave her credit for. How we gonna find this ho?"

Cartier exhaled. Citi and her goons were playing for keeps. It was time for her to get her mind fully in the game. Their lives depended on being a step ahead because in this game if you get caught slippin', you're done. Nick was a prime example of how the game will turn on you.

Cartier got serious and leaned forward in her seat. "We know a few things. We know that she's in South Beach. We know this bitch got money and likes nice things. We know that they should feel safer here than New

York because I'm sure they know about Nick. We also know that people like us run in the same circles. So, bitch, I think we know a lot."

Apple was lost. She didn't get it. They didn't know shit. "I don't follow."

"Sooner or later this bitch gonna show up at all the hot spots. Think about it. Why does Harlem show up at the Ruckers game each year? Or the car show? Or a Funkmaster Flex party?"

Apple grinned. "'Cause we wanna be seen, bitch."

"Exactly. What good is being rich if you can't flaunt it? This Citi bitch will do her rounds, and when she does we'll pounce." Cartier was amped. "I wanna punch her fuckin' lights out before I shove my fuckin' gun in her mouth."

"No, bitch! I get to shove my fuckin' gun in her mouth!"

The two were tipsy as they bickered about who would get to kill Citi. Cartier decided to concede because Apple had taken more than a financial loss because of this bitch. She lost her nigga.

***

The following morning, Apple and Cartier were up bright and early and trolling social media. They found ten eateries that were popular, celebrity driven-hangouts. A few only served breakfast, while some were open through dinner. They also located at least five nightclubs and identified the top shopping center.

"You still got some of your Miami connects down here?" Apple asked Cartier.

"Maybe . . . I need to make a few phone calls."

"We need to be extra subtle on this. I don't want to alert this bitch that we're looking for her."

"I know. Believe me, I know," Cartier agreed.

Cartier thought for a moment. It'd been a while since she'd left town. Who could she trust? Hector's organization had turned on him and never fucked with her. She had made a few contacts, but none she could truly trust. Not with so much on the line.

Cartier made her final decision. "There was this bitch named Diane that used to do my hair. She was connected to all the dope boys. Her salon was always packed. Back then when I was wit' Hector, she was fuckin' wit' this baller named, Rah. He bought her that salon and laundered his drug money there. Now if anyone could point us in the right direction to Citi, I'd bet my life it would be her. Her place is a gossip spot, and bitches are always running their fuckin' mouths in there."

"Call that bitch, then. What you waitin' on?"

Cartier shook her head. "That's exactly what we won't do."

"Why the fuck not?" Apple's patience had long ago expired.

"Think, Apple." Cartier stood up and got animated. "How did Citi get the drop on us? That young stupid bitch outsmarted two bitches who'd been in the game for years. What did we do wrong?"

Apple nodded. "Trust. We trusted a bitch we barely knew."

"Exactly," said Cartier. She began clapping her hands as she spoke. "Down here we gotta recognize that we don't trust no-fuckin'-body but us!"

"We go to this Diane bitch and she'll set our asses up!"

"Get dressed," said Cartier.

"Where we goin'?"

"Wig shopping."

Apple smirked. "Lace front or custom?"

Cartier threw a pillow at her. "Bitch, get dressed."

26

Cartier and Apple drove around the hood of Miami-Dade until they found a local beauty supply store. Liberty Beauty wasn't far from Pork 'n' Beans projects and was owned and operated by Koreans. The establishment thrived in the heart of the ghetto and had steady business seven days a week.

Apple sucked her teeth. "This shit gets to me," she began as they walked through the aisles looking for cheap wigs. "Do you think we could go to Korea, set some shit up in their neighborhoods, and get rich?"

Cartier shrugged. "This is America."

"What the fuck does that mean?"

"It means I don't give a fuck. It means that I'm focused right now."

Apple cut her eyes. "I'm focused too, damn. That don't mean we can't chitchat."

The pair looked up at a buffet of cheap wigs in various lengths and textures modeled by Styrofoam heads. There wasn't any use in trying to find a cute one.

"Get something long, something that distracts from your face."

Apple picked up a long Jheri curl looking wig and smirked. She shrugged. "I guess I'll take this shit here, but is it necessary?"

"Most definitely," said Cartier. "I already ran through South Beach with a blond bob haircut, and your face done ran through these hoods twice between you and Kola. If we're gonna start frequenting the hot spots lookin' for this bitch, we can't be recognized. If we run into someone we know and it's unavoidable, then it is what it is. But let's not advertise that we're here."

"Facts."

Cartier grabbed something similar. Both were ready to bounce when Apple's burner phone rang.

Apple held up the phone. "This Amir."

"Cool. Get that, and I'll go pay for these. Meet me in the car."

Apple picked up the call and began walking to their vehicle. She listened to the recording before accepting his call.

"Whaddup, Amir?"

"Hey, queen."

"You got any more info?"

"On what?" he asked as if he had no idea what she was talking about.

"On those peoples."

"Nah, I was just calling to see what's up with you. Making sure you're all right." He was using his soft, "sexy" voice that irritated Apple.

"Amir, straight up. I don't have time for this!"

"What you mean?"

She knew she had to speak in riddles, and that was hard because she was a bitch who spoke bluntly. But for the sake of correctional facilities and their right to eavesdrop, she replied with, "Look, I'm down here for our boy—remember him? I'm tryin' to get this handled."

Apple hit the alarm on her cream Lexus and got in the driver's seat. She couldn't wait for the fifteen-minute call to end.

"You going somewhere?"

"What?"

"I just heard a car alarm. Where you going?"

What the fuck! Apple's rage had simmered and was now boiling over to erupt. No more Ms. Nice Bitch. She was about to curse his ass out

171

when Cartier got in.

Cartier saw the look on Apple's face and mouthed, "What happened?"

"Hold on. In fact, call me back later. I'm busy now."

Apple hung up on him, and the nigga called right back. She continued to let him go straight to voicemail as she calmed herself and steered her car onto the highway. She and Cartier remained silent until Apple was ready to speak. Cartier thought something terrible had happened up North—someone was dead or locked up.

"This nigga Amir is a problem. Dude is a thirsty nigga thinkin' he can bag a bad bitch like me."

"That's what got ya pressure up?" Cartier chuckled. "You know he ain't that crazy, though. I know plenty lonely bitches who done linked up wit' these lifers."

"That shit won't ever be me." Apple rolled her eyes. "And you should hear his fake ass wit' that 'queen' this and that and all his fuckin' preachin' like he's book smart. You dumb, nigga. That's why you got caught. You's a stupid muthafucka!"

Cartier laughed harder. She had missed Apple.

"And you think he give a fuck I just buried my nigga, who was also his best friend?"

"That's when they pounce. They come at you when they think a bitch all vulnerable."

"I can't do this shit any longer," Apple stated. "I was only keepin' the line open just in case he found new intel on Citi. But evidently, this nigga is too busy climbing up my asshole to focus on that bitch. I'ma get rid of this fuckin' burner. Fuck him. You hungry?"

Cartier nodded. "We got our wigs, now let's head to one of the hotspots on our list. Who knows? We just might see that bitch. That should cheer ya ass up!"

***

Apple and Cartier walked through a popular eatery on Ocean Avenue with their cheap, frizzy wigs. The place was packed, and they had to wait forty minutes for a table. They didn't care. They were scoping out the area. Once inside, they saw a couple Yankee players, a Miami Dolphins football player, and a few B-list actors. The hostess offered up that J-Lo was there earlier that day looking gorgeous.

Once they were seated and their food and drinks were ordered, Cartier got serious. She leaned in and said, "I've been thinkin' about Amir."

Apple cut her eyes. "Are you tryin' to ruin my meal?"

"He can still be useful."

"How you figure? Unless he can give us an exact address to find that cum-guzzling thief, then I'm deadin' him."

"Put your feelings aside. We're still down one man. Nick should be here too, Apple. So maybe Amir could connect us wit' some killers."

Apple thought for a minute. She liked what she was hearing. "We'd have to put them on payroll."

"Or give them some pussy," Cartier joked. "'Cuz don't nobody do shit for free."

***

The next time Amir called, which was shortly after their meal, Apple picked up. She, too, now had the soft, 'sexy' voice on.

"Yo, shorty, what the fuck happened earlier?"

"We got ambushed."

"Say word?" Amir was still using nineties vernacular.

"Word up," Apple played along. "We all right, though. But it was close."

"Was it that problem we discussed?"

"Of course. Who else?"

"True. True. Now you got a nigga worried, queen. I wish I was there for you."

"Me too," Apple replied in her sexiest voice. "But it's good to hear your voice."

"It is?"

"Yeah, you're the only one who knows what I'm goin' through. And like I said, if I make it outta this, I'm headin' your way."

"Listen, real talk. I don't know if I should even be saying some shit like this."

"What is it? Just say it."

"I've been thinking about you since you left. You and that red dress . . . those red lips . . ." Amir lowered his voice. "Got me having them dreams, if you know what I'm saying."

"I do . . ." Apple wanted to jump out a window. This was so pathetic in her eyes. "But like I said, as soon as I'm done I'm headin' home. I wanna see you too."

"Leave now and come see a brother."

"You know I can't. Besides, things are heating up, and we're outnumbered. I only have one person watchin' my back, and those peoples got a whole team on their side."

"You down there with one dude?"

"One female, a good friend."

Amir shook his head rapidly. "Nick said you were a hothead. I just figured that with that bread, you'd have a squad."

Apple exhaled. "I know, but I didn't have time. No niggas I could trust. New York can sometimes be a small place."

"Apple, give me until tomorrow to see what I come up with."

"What do you mean?" Apple feigned ignorance.

"Just sit tight. I'll call you this time tomorrow."

"Uhhh, ok. Tomorrow then."

"Tomorrow, queen."

✳✳✳

The next day Amir called with the news Apple and Cartier had hoped for. Amir had two dudes who had been released from Clinton within the last thirty days and were strapped for cash. They were starving out on the streets. They couldn't get gainful employment because of their records and they were too old to hug the block. They had pulled off a few robberies, but that didn't net them any real money.

"They good wit' that thang-thang?" Apple asked, talking in riddles.

"Thoroughbreds," replied, Amir. "And they know how to take orders."

"Good. Send them our way."

"Nah, not so fast," Amir added some bass to his voice and spoke with authority. "If your company's hiring, just note that they're highly sought after, and you may become involved in a bidding war."

Apple snorted. "A biddin' war, huh?"

"Yeah. You know construction jobs are pricey. Any remodel nowadays will have you breaking open that piggy bank."

"So how much we talkin'?"

"A quarter."

"Twenty-five hundred a week?"

Amir laughed. "For that three-story brownstone? No way, queen. Each floor is a problem. Especially with that killer fireplace that can't be extinguished. It was a tough sell, but two-hundred and fifty thousand will do it. A full demolish, and then you're free to rebuild."

Apple knew she was being hustled. For that kind of money, she could hire a dozen goons.

"That won't be an issue."

Amir was still in business mode. He spoke with authority and was loving it. "That number is per man. No negotiating."

Amir knew she had Nick's money and actually trusted his former cellmate Floco and Floco's cousin Whiz. See, Apple thought she was using him, and Amir felt he would use her too. The game is the game, and it was a matter of who reached the finish line first. Amir knew that Corey would never let the death of his only son not be avenged. Therefore, Apple's days were numbered. Amir couldn't let her die without getting his hands on at least some of that money. If he could get some phone sex and a few visits in the meantime, that was just extra gravy over his hot biscuits.

"Anything for Nick. They better be worth it."

"Cool. I'll give the green light. They'll arrive in forty-eight."

"I'll be waiting."

"Now that that's out the way, what's up with you, though, sexy?"

Click.

Apple turned to Cartier and said, "When this is over we got two more bodies to add to our list."

Without hesitation, Cartier replied, "Done."

27

Whiz and Floco arrived in South Beach one day earlier than expected. Apple had wired five thousand dollars for their travel expenses, which was to include car rental, hotel, food, gas, and tolls. Only the pair had stolen a car and slept a few hours in that stolen vehicle, all to cut costs.

Both had seen and done it all. They vividly remembered all the money they blew through when they were on the streets, hugging the blocks, murdering and robbing muthafuckas. When they got knocked they couldn't make bail and could barely afford legal counsel. Popping bottles, splurging on whips and women and jewels meant nothing when your attorney wanted a million-dollar retainer. If being locked up had taught them anything, it was that the fast life wasn't about shit. Whiz and Floco felt this last murder mission was just the kind of break they needed and the amount of money they were going to make would be just enough to help them live comfortably.

See, Amir thought that they were working for him and would ultimately give him a percentage of the half-million. But Corey, a man hell bent on revenge, had a better deal. Floco got in touch with the OG, thinking that he and Amir were working together and wanted to help avenge Nick's death. Corey pulled their coat to the million dollars Apple had and only had one request: kill the bitch and keep all the cash. Corey didn't want a dime. They liked what was behind door number two.

Floco steered the Nissan Altima to the address he was given. It was a modest, three bedroom furnished rental on the outskirts of town with an attached two-car garage. The key was left under the front doormat. Inside, they showered, prepared some food from the groceries that were provided, and chilled.

The house was sparsely decorated with just the essentials; a worn sofa, wobbly kitchen table and tattered chairs, second-hand televisions, and full beds in each room with rickety dressers. The cockroaches, spiders, and other insects didn't bother them at all. The place was almost paradise after the living quarters of the correctional facility.

Whiz dropped down and did three hundred push-ups. He was determined to keep his body and mind right. Feeling energized, he hopped up and asked, "You think this bitch got that cash down here in South Beach?"

Floco shook his head. "I wouldn't."

Whiz nodded. "It would make shit easier, though."

"We knew shit wasn't gonna be easy from jump. We do the hits and make it back up north to get paid. Stalk that bitch until we know where she lay her head at, get our bread, and snuff her out."

"I heard she a dime piece." Whiz stared straight ahead and then rubbed his dick thinking about how pretty this Apple might be.

"So is Rihanna. But I'll rock that bitch to sleep for a million crispy ones."

Whiz cut his eyes at Floco. "You mean a half-million, cuz."

***

Apple and Cartier arrived at the house shortly after nightfall. They were strapped just in case these fools tried anything. The women walked in and saw two good looking men. They hardly looked like experienced

178

killers who had been through street wars. Neither man had on a shirt, so Apple could clearly see no visible knife or bullet wounds, scratches, nicks, scrapes, or whatnot. Immediately she felt disappointed and copped an attitude. She and Cartier had been through several wars and had the scars to prove it.

Whiz spoke first. He was light-skinned with soft hair and full, pink lips, and his body was prison buff. Sleeve tattoos were painted on both arms and his throat tattoo of a black skull, cobra, and dagger was distracting. His face looked like Drake and his body looked like The Rock.

"So who's Apple?"

"That's me."

"And I'm Cartier."

Floco spoke. "I always wondered how to pronounce that shit. Whether it was 'ay' or 'air'." He smiled and couldn't take his eyes off the Brooklyn beauty. She was brown-skinned and pretty with an edge—just how he liked them.

Cartier drank in this thirsty looking fool and knew he thought he had a shot at some pussy. Floco stood six-one with a narrow face and dark eyes. His body was lean and athletic, like a runner's frame, and he had incredibly large hands and feet. The sweats he was wearing outlined his massive package. Cartier would have entertained a quick fuck, but she wanted her pussy to be tight when Head came home, and from the looks of Floco's shit, he could do some damage.

She said, "So I see y'all made it here safe. We came to take y'all to drop off the rental and get a new one with Florida plates."

"We didn't rent a car," Whiz offered up.

Apple smirked. She knew they specifically said that the five grand covered rental costs. "Then how the fuck y'all get here?"

"Look, ma, I don't like your tone. Now if we gonna work together there needs to be a mutual respect. I don't know what type of niggas you used to deal wit', but we ain't some fuckin' flunkies. Now we can either help you wit' this problem or bounce," said Floco.

Apple knew they weren't going no-fuckin'-where. Not with so much money at stake. She exhaled. "How did y'all get here? I still wanna know."

"We stole a non-descript toy. It's in the garage and we planned on dumpin' it and takin' off the plates."

Cartier and Apple looked at each other, befuddled. Did they want to go back to prison? Why would they take such an unnecessary risk, especially when it wasn't their money that was paying for shit?

"A'ight. So let's get rid of the car. We'll drop you to the rental place and then we figured we can do some recon." Apple pulled out several pictures she had printed from Citi's social media pages of her, Scar, and Cane. "These are our targets. And here's a list of nightclubs they might frequent. You and Whiz should stalk one or two nightclubs per night. Maybe buy one bottle of champagne to get near VIP, but don't ball outta control. If Scar is there, he'll take notice."

Cartier said, "The bottle service girls will have the most info on the high rollers. But information don't come cheap, so don't splurge on just any bitch. Some will lie just to get paid—"

Whiz interrupted. "Shorty, we got this. We were doin' this shit before y'all were born."

Cartier nodded. "Cool. Okay, so during the day, Apple and I will hit up all the eateries and shopping centers. That way we're all on the clock, twenty-four-seven. Sooner or later we gonna run into this bitch. South Beach ain't but so big."

"I agree," Apple continued. "And if you spot them use this burner to call me. I want to be there to take that bitch out."

Apple handed them a phone with her number stored.

"We good?" Cartier asked.

"Almost," replied Floco. "We need some money for our expenses."

Apple smirked. "What the fu—I mean, I already gave y'all five large for expenses."

"That was to get us here."

Cartier felt she needed to have her friend's back. "Not five fuckin' grand, nigga. Who you think you talkin' to? Y'all stole a fuckin' car, arrived here a day earlier so there's no way y'all booked a hotel room. I say y'all got plenty of fuckin' dough left for the clubs."

"No disrespect, shorty, but this ain't your bread so I don't even know why ya runnin' ya fuckin' mouth." Floco walked aggressively toward Cartier, and she did the same.

Apple jumped in between the two to quickly defuse the situation.

"How much will y'all need?" said Apple. "Cartier, go sit in the car. I got this."

"Whatever." Begrudgingly, Cartier exited the home and sat inside the Lexus with her hand trained on her .380.

Inside, Apple finished her negotiating with the cousins. She agreed to drop them three large in the morning.

"What about the rental? Y'all still want us to take you?"

"Nah, we a'ight. We can handle shit on our end."

"Ok then," Apple said as she exited to join Cartier outside.

When the ladies left, the guys couldn't help but to discuss them.

"You saw the look in that bitch's face?" Floco said. "She wanted to kill a nigga!"

Whiz laughed.

"I think I love her." Floco whistled. "Carti . . .yay . . . I bet she suck good dick and could fuck too. She look like one of them aggressive bitches in the bed, take charge on a nigga. Calling me daddy while I smack dat ass."

"Nah, that's Apple you describing."

"You must be crazy!" Floco exclaimed. "She look like she just lays there and want a nigga to do all the work."

"You sleepin' on her, cuz!"

"Maybe. She is pretty, though," Floco agreed. "Don't matter, 'cause soon she will be a dead pretty bitch."

***

The next day Apple dropped off the money as promised, and Whiz and Floco discussed strategy and finances. Whiz was running the numbers.

"So we got a little under forty-seven hundred left from the five grand, and with this three we just about up seventy-seven hundred. I say we cap our nightclub expenses at a hundred per week. Hopefully we find these fools by then. No bottle poppin'. We buy one drink each, a glass of Henny, and lay low. And we certainly ain't paying no bitches for information."

Floco added, "Do clubs still let muthafuckas in free before a certain time? We need to find out."

Whiz smiled at his cousin's brilliance. "And food—they got dollar menus now. And we can go to the supermarket and stock up on ramen noodles and frozen shit on sale."

"We doing all this, but what if that bitch is runnin' through all our fuckin' bread out here splurging in South Beach? You heard her say that they were in charge of stalkin' the malls and shit. Fuck around and when we get our hands on the million it won't be but half that!" Floco angered himself like he had ownership in Apple's blood money.

"There you go wit' that negative shit. Damn, nigga. All that does is motivate me to find this nigga Scar, his bitch, and her brother. The quicker we find them the faster we get paid. Let's keep our eyes peeled and show them how niggas in their forties get down."

***

182

For weeks they all worked around the clock trying to spot Citi, Scar, and Cane and kept coming up empty. Apple was highly frustrated, and Amir's calls and Floco and Whiz's begging wasn't helping. Working with these dudes was highly stressful, but she kept Nick at the forefront of her mind. Something had to give. And then she got what she considered a sign from her boo.

28

The Runaway Café was a popular spot with rich and tasty food. The décor was inviting, and the beach was just a stone's throw away. There was dining indoors and outdoors. The patrons were engrossed in enjoying their good meals and having good conversation under the setting sun.

Among the cafe's occupants were Citi and Scar. They were dining at an exterior table, enjoying smothered chicken, baked macaroni and cheese, and southern style biscuits. Three of their men sat nearby low-key, not wanting to draw attention or intimidate the other customers. For Citi, South Beach was the place to be. But it was Scar's first time there, and he felt like a fish out of water. He was a Brooklyn goon, and Miami, with the continuous sunshine, warm weather, and bikini clad beauties, was a stretch for him.

"So, you like it here?" Citi asked him.

"It ain't Brooklyn," he responded.

"I know . . . it's paradise," she joked.

Scar didn't laugh. Citi looked happy, but he had to remind her that being in Miami didn't mean that they were completely safe. This wasn't a vacation. It was business. After that shootout in Queens, he felt that it was in his best interest to let the heat die down in New York.

When they first arrived, Citi got straight down to business by reconnecting with Caesar Mingo and feeding the Miami streets. She was thirsty to make up for the losses she had taken. Soon she and Scar began to have differences of opinion on how to run her empire. Or, basically, who should be running her empire. Scar thought Citi quickly got lazy and preoccupied by tropical breezes and beaches, drop-top whips, nightclubs, and Spanish speaking dudes in flip flops and linen suits. He felt that the hot sun had fried her brain cells. She was snorting coke like she was guest starring on a 1980s *Miami Vice* episode. Scar had repeatedly laid hands on her, but she was a stubborn bitch. His beatdowns were no longer able to set her straight.

Citi's position was that Scar felt threatened by his second-in-command status after they were virtually run out of New York. He constantly felt like he had to prove he was a heartless killer who gave no fucks. Seventy-two hours after arriving, Scar had captured, tortured, and dismembered two men he said was following them. No one knew if that was true or false because nobody saw shit. The men feigned innocence, but that didn't stop Scar from putting on a show for all her men to see.

Scar needed to be the head nigga in charge. She knew that he was a ticking time bomb and if she gave him her connect, Caesar, she would be a dead bitch. Thankfully, Caesar would never do business with a thug like Scar. But she still had to think three steps ahead. See, Scar thought that she was slacking and moving less ki's per week. That wasn't true at all. She was still doing her numbers, but she kept some things in her organization a secret.

What Scar didn't know was that she was a sneaky bitch. She grew up knowing that you never let the right hand know what the left hand is doing. That's a mantra to live by. Citi needed to reduce Scar's bottom line because money was power. If she made that man too wealthy then she was expendable. Sure, Caesar wouldn't fuck with him. But there were the Colombians, Jamaicans, Panamanians, and rival Mexican cartels that just might give him some play.

Scar eyed Citi with a frown. She was an airhead to him, and he hated dumb fucks with a passion. "Remember, we ain't just down here on some personal shit," he said.

"I know."

"I'm still lookin' into who this Nicholas muthafucka was and why he was coming for me," said Scar.

"You and me got enemies . . ."

"And that's why we need—"

Before Scar could finish his sentence, the sound of a gunshot rang out.

Bak!

To Scar's right, one of his goons was instantly struck down by a bullet. And then a hail of gunfire followed that first shot.

Bak! Bak! Bak! Bak! Bak!

Pop! Pop! Pop!

Not again! Citi screamed to herself. She and Scar hit the ground hard and fast while their two remaining soldiers took up position and went into battle mode.

Scar's head was on a fast swivel as he pulled out the Glock 19 he had on him. Where was the gunfire coming from? It felt like it was coming from everywhere.

Apple and Cartier, along with Whiz and Floco, charged forward, desperately aiming for Citi as she tucked herself under the table with Scar trying to protect her. Citi's men shot back, and the scene abruptly transitioned from a peaceful outing to an all out gunfight. Many ran and took cover. There was screaming and absolute terror among the patrons and staff.

Boom! Boom! Boom!

Tables were overturned and chairs went flying everywhere. Cartier thought she had Scar in a losing position. There he was, crouched near a table. She was about to strike him center mass, but then he sprung up, pushed Citi toward safety, and took off running. He ducked and then angled his body and slid between a car for cover—on some stop, drop, and roll type of move. He was swift. He wouldn't be taken easily. He quickly recovered and shot back at Cartier. One bullet grazed her leg and she went down.

Apple tried gunning for Citi. She wanted to take the bitch's head off with a 9mm, but Citi was a slippery bitch. One of Citi's goons became a barrier between her and Apple, and he was fiercely firing her way. Apple had to take cover herself, but not before she and Citi locked eyes.

It was the first time Citi got confirmation that it was Apple and Cartier. She had stared the bitch right in her face. It was a what-the-fuck moment. She was praying that Scar or her goons murdered them both right there.

With Cartier injured, Apple had to retreat. They'd made the night ugly and violent, and they had the element of surprise, but it didn't pan out. Now Citi knew they were coming for her.

***

An area of South Beach had turned into Iraq. Surprisingly, the shootout only left one dead, Scar's hoodlum. But uniforms and detectives flooded the scene asking questions and collecting evidence. The culprits had managed to get away.

Although Citi survived another attempt on her life, it left an impression on her. Not only did they try to take her life, but she had lost her thirty-thousand-dollar Birkin bag during the violent melee. She was super pissed. She stormed into the luxury condo they were renting on South Beach screaming and kicking shit over, and she was ready to go to war.

Citi screamed, "I want them bitches kidnapped! I want them fuckin' tortured and ass fucked! I want them bitches raped and to finally fuckin' die!"

She screamed at everyone present like she was a mad woman. Scar and Cane glanced at each other and Cane mouthed, "Raped?"

Citi now had a face to her enemies. It was what she feared the most.

She continued, "Didn't I fuckin' tell y'all it was them bitches from the start? But, nooooooo, niggas wanted to label me a crazy bitch when I saw that bitch with my very own eyes! I can see, niggas!"

"Calm down!" Scar barked. He hated that she was right. "Cane, spark up that blunt. Citi, tell me 'bout these bitches."

"They're ghetto hoes," she began, trying to find the right description. She didn't know what Scar wanted her to say. "Cartier is from Brooklyn—a thug bitch. And Apple is from Harlem. That scar-face bitch thinks she so fuckin' cute!"

Cane took a hit from the blunt and passed it to Scar.

Scar looked at Citi like she was stupid. "How's that supposed to help us find them bitches? A thug bitch and a bitch who thinks she's fuckin' cute ain't much for the grim reaper to go on."

Cane and Scar chuckled.

"Look, y'all moron muthafuckas! These chicks went to war against the Gonzales cartel and are still breathing! They got fuckin' heart to even be here in South Beach again! They done murdered plenty niggas—I seen it wit' my own eyes! More niggas than you, Scar!"

That last statement got his attention.

"Fuck you mean, bitch!"

"I mean that you're a dead nigga if you don't stop actin' like you're six."

"A'ight bet. I'm all ears. How can we find Cardi B and Apple?"

"Cardi B," she hollered. "She ain't the rapper, you fuckin' retard!"

The weed had gotten to Scar and Cane. They both laughed hysterically at Citi's face. She was completely livid.

While Citi ranted and cursed, Scar and Cane poured themselves some Hennessy. Once again, Scar seemed too cool about the violent ordeal they had just gone through. He downed the liquor and poured himself another glass. It had been the third attempt on his life. He looked at Citi and said, "We got one, we'll get the others."

Citi fumed. "You can't underestimate these bitches, Scar. You already seen how lethal and sneaky they are."

"Bitch, I got nine lives, and they gonna get got," Scar countered.

Citi frowned. He wasn't interested in talking payback or it seemed like he didn't want to talk to Citi about it. Her life had been threatened like his, but Scar refrained from having any conversation about retribution. He was either stupid or insane. In fact, after pouring his second drink, he turned to Cane and asked about a new singer from Miami named Camila Cabello.

Cane smiled and remarked, "Yo, she can call me papi any day."

"I wanna see her Havana," Scar joked.

What the fuck! Citi's face became so tight that it looked like she was about to have a stroke. They both took notice that Citi was still in the room. She stormed out, but not before she grabbed the Henny bottle and smashed it against the wall.

"You know," Citi began. Her chest was heaving up and down as she was so irate. "Y'all are some ignorant negros. This shit ain't funny! It will never be fuckin' funny!"

Citi knew that if you wanted something done, then you had to do it yourself. Killing Apple and Cartier wasn't a priority for Cane or Scar. She didn't understand why.

But just as Citi masterminded stealing millions of dollars from Apple and Cartier, she would mastermind their deaths too, and they were going to stay dead. Starting today, her security would be extra tight. They weren't going to get a third chance to kill her, and she was going to put the word out that there was a bounty on these bitches' heads.

***

The moment Citi left the living room, Scar turned toward Cane. All signs of being goofy were gone.

"Yo, on my dead moms, I swear I'ma kill those bitches!" With blunt in hand, Scar paced back and forth. "I'ma cut their fuckin' toes off and shove them in their mouths! I'll take their eyes out with a muthafuckin' spoon! You feel me, Cane? I'ma inflict real pain, nigga!"

Cane nodded.

"We got a blowtorch?"

Cane smirked. "Nah, I don't think so."

"Get one, nigga. I'ma burn their fuckin' skin off down to the bone. I wanna see pain in those bitches' eyes, hear them beggin' me to stop. I need you on ya job, Cane. Find them bitches. They can't hide out here. We own fuckin' South Beach, nigga!"

Cane nodded.

Scar looked closely at Cane. "Yo, what the fuck is up wit' you nigga?"

Cane shrugged. "I'm high. You know I'm in chill mode right now, but I feel you."

"Nah, nigga, you ain't been feelin' me in a minute. You ain't been puttin' in work yet you collectin' a fuckin' check each week."

Cane sat up at attention. "I buss my gun like the next nigga. You buggin'."

The chronic had Scar paranoid. "How come you ain't never there when these bitches are gunnin' for us?"

"What the fuck you mean?"

"You heard me, nigga!"

Cane was confused. He was high and tipsy and he couldn't tell if these were Scar's words or the Henny talking. "I can't speak for them bitches, Scar. I ain't in their heads so I can't know when they gonna strike."

Scar was simmering with rage. "What happened at the trap house?"

190

Now Cane was aggravated. "Come on, man. Why you goin' there? You blowin' my high, nigga."

"How the fuck nearly a dozen of our most thorough goons get mowed down and let you tell it, it was one nigga?"

"It was!" Cane hollered, tired of the third degree.

"Why you ain't dead, nigga?"

Cane dropped his head into both hands. Scar's paranoia was evident. He was accusing him of something. If Cane was keeping it one-hundred, something was up with him. And it started that night at the trap house, or maybe with the news of Takenya's murder.

But if he had to put a name to it he felt he had PTSD. Watching Nick murder all those men right before his eyes—seeing those bodies drop—had affected him. Sure, he'd been seeing men murdered most his life. For some reason this was different.

Cane had been through a lot. He had lost his mom, dad, friends, and family. His brother Chris was doing life in prison and would never get to hit a blunt, fuck a bitch, drive a fast car, or have children. Cane was getting older and he wanted a future. He wanted a wife—a good woman—and some kids. His sister was a survivor, but he was the first to admit that she wasn't to be trusted. If she had to, Cane knew she would flip on him for the right price. She had sociopathic tendencies that he was well aware of. Citi was always one card short of a full deck, so he couldn't place his future in her hands.

Scar took his silence as an admission. When Cane looked up it was like slow-mo as he watched Scar dig deep in his waistband and pull out the .45. With his arm outstretched, Scar aimed and fired.

Cane's instincts were on point as he took flight.

Bak! Bak!

Cane took two to the back. He tried to crawl away, but Scar was on him.

Scar stood over a man that could have been his brother in-law and fired. *Click! Click! Click!* His gun jammed.

"Fuck!"

Citi heard the shots and came running out her bedroom with her 9mm ready for war. She thought Apple and Cartier had followed them home. When she saw her brother on the ground and Scar with a smoking gun, she quickly assessed what had happened.

"Scar, no! Are you crazy!" She ran to Cane's aid.

"That nigga snitchin'."

"What's wrong wit' you!" she screeched. Tears streamed down her face as she watched her brother try and remain awake. "Cane, don't go to sleep, you hear me? I'm gonna get you help."

Scar towered over them both as he thought two things. *When was the last time I cleaned my gun?* And, *Damn, that nigga looks fucked up right now.*

Citi ran and grabbed two head scarves and tied them tightly around her brother's open wounds to help slow the bleeding. "Help me!"

"You don't wanna hear this, bae, but I think he's workin' wit' them bitches."

"Are you insane! This is my brother!"

Scar smirked.

"I swear to God you better help me, Scar. He can't die in here!"

Scar took another look at Cane. His smooth brown skin was turning ashen. He looked terrible. "That nigga dead, Citi. Why you goin' through all that trouble?"

Citi ignored him and called two of her goons who were one floor below. "Cane's been shot. Get up here now!"

Ant and Bucky came running upstairs. Between the two they had four guns. They had no idea what they were charging into. Citi let them in and they saw a lifeless Cane bleeding out. Scar was back on the sofa chilling, sparking up another blunt.

"What the fuck happened?" Bucky asked.

"No questions!" Citi demanded. "We need to get him to a hospital. Ant, help me—help me stop his bleeding."

Ant didn't move.

Citi leapt up from the floor and slapped the shit out of him. "What the fuck are you waiting for!"

Quickly, both Ant and Bucky jumped into action. One ran and grabbed some sheets from out the closet and wrapped up Cane's body.

"On three, let's lift him up," Bucky said. "One, two, three."

"Be careful wit' his head." Citi was whimpering at this point. "If you die on me, Cane, then I'ma kill myself."

"Get this dramatic bitch outta here!" said Scar. "And that snitchin'-ass nigga too!"

Ant and Bucky had no idea what had gone down, but they did as they were told. They took the back staircase down to the underground garage and sped to the nearest hospital. They dropped Cane and Citi off at the curb, where she was able to get the attention of medical staff. She had to admit, shit looked fucked up.

29

Kola couldn't stop crying. There were no words anyone could say to her to ease her pain—not right now. She had lost her baby boy at nearly nine months, and it was one devastating event too many. She went into a deep depression and refused to be around any other children. Looking into their faces was just too painful, and Peaches and the others became a constant reminder of what she didn't have and couldn't have on her own—children.

Kamel was attentive and supportive. Every day he was by Kola's side, holding her hand, trying to comfort her, and trying to stay positive about the situation. It was his baby too.

"We should try again," he said to Kola.

"No!" replied Kola sternly.

Her doctors were clear to her. They were against her getting pregnant again. It was highly unlikely that she would ever carry a baby to term.

"Think about a surrogate then," he suggested.

Kola cut her eyes at him like he was crazy—*a surrogate?* She wasn't thrilled about some next bitch carrying her child. In fact, the thought of it angered her and she ripped into Kamel and cursed him out so bad it almost left marks on his skin. He had to leave the room.

Kola burst into tears again. She was sinking deeper into depression. She didn't want to interact with anyone. Day after day, she locked herself in the dark room and wanted to be alone. She didn't eat. Kamel feared that she was trying to starve herself—commit a slow suicide. He felt that his hands were tied. He loved his wife, and he hated feeling helpless.

He saw one last solution. Kamel called Apple to tell her about Kola. Apple was shocked to hear about the miscarriage. Why hadn't Kola reached out? Apple could only imagine how hard it would be to lose a child at thirty-three weeks.

Apple called Kola after speaking to Kamel, and the only thing her twin kept saying was, "Koke is dead, Apple. He's dead. Koke is dead."

"Sis, it's gonna be all right," said Apple.

"How? Koke is dead. My poor little man is gone."

"You know I'm always there for you."

"You're not here now," Kola griped.

"I know, I'm just tryin' to take care of some business."

"Where are you?"

Apple didn't want to mention her location, but Kola was in great pain. "I'm in Miami," she said.

"Miami? Why?"

"Like I said, sis, I'm handling some business out here."

"You mean you're going after Citi. I'm not stupid, Apple," Kola said.

"Okay . . . yes, I'm hunting that bitch down."

"I wanna help."

"What?"

"You fuckin' heard me. I wanna help you. I wanna fly down there to be by your side."

"I don't think that's a good idea, Kola. Now is not a good time to get involved wit' this shit. Besides, you got the kids to look after, especially Peaches," said Apple.

"And?"

"We can't afford to both get ourselves killed."

"Then we better be extra careful then, because I'm coming down there.

I don't give a fuck what you say. I can't stay here, Apple. I need to leave—I need to escape," Kola protested.

Apple knew there was no changing her sister's mind. They were both stubborn.

"Fuck it—just let me know when your flight lands."

Their call ended.

That same night, Kola and Kamel got into a heated argument. The kids could hear them arguing from their bedroom.

"You're not fuckin' leaving!" Kamel shouted.

"You don't fuckin' tell me what to do!" she shouted back.

"You're emotional, Kola. You ain't thinking rational."

"I'm thinking just fine."

"No—you and I—we're supposed to be out of that life," he shouted.

"She's my sister and I'm gonna always be there for her," Kola retorted.

"And what about us, huh? Do you give a fuck?" Kamel snapped back.

After hours of arguing, Kola finally relented and promised Kamel she wouldn't go to Miami. She would stay. She continued to cry over her miscarriage and told her husband that she was still upset and emotional about losing their son. Kamel promised he would support her and would always be by her side.

They reconciled, but Kola told him that she still needed some time alone. That night, he went to sleep in the guest bedroom.

Kamel woke up the following morning, and the first thing he did was walk into the main bedroom to check up on Kola. She was gone. He scurried around the bedroom to find some of her clothing missing from the closet, and he looked out the window to see that she had taken the Benz.

"Fuck!" he cursed.

***

Kola had left for Miami in the middle of the night. She decided to drive the twenty-plus hours from New York to Miami to clear her head. Her sleek Benz hugged the highway, speeding down I-95 South. It was a painful, emotional, and tiring trip. There were tears and apprehension. She had to stop halfway there, and she checked into a ritzy hotel on the outskirts of Savannah.

Inside the hotel room, Kola took a shower, ordered herself some room service, and downed some Henny on ice. She exploded into tears once again, thinking about her baby. She cried for hours. She felt weak. She believed that happiness wasn't meant for her. She thought she had done everything right. She'd changed her life around—for the better. She gotten married, she was raising her niece, along with Eduardo's kids, and yet, she couldn't have any kids of her own.

Eventually, she passed out on the bed. The next morning, she woke up feeling like she had an impetuous purpose, and she vowed to never cry over losing the baby again. She had done enough of that, and now it was time to move on. Reminiscent of her twin sister, she felt there was some unfinished business that she needed to tend to in Miami.

***

Kola arrived in Downtown Miami late that night. She climbed out of her Benz and looked around, feeling a bit of nostalgia. Being back in the city brought back a flood of memories for her. Long ago, she was queen bee bitch down here—money, power, respect, she earned that. But now, she was a shell of her old self. Everything done changed.

She took a deep breath and vowed to stay strong. *No more tears*, she told herself. She gazed up at the towering glass building. It was impressive. It reminded Kola of her old Miami residence long ago when she had paid 1.8 million for it—pure luxury from top to bottom. Not too far from the building, crowds were leaving the American Airlines Arena after attending the Miami Heat basketball game, where the Heat defeated the Lakers. The streets became flooded with foot and vehicular traffic.

Kola walked toward the building and entered the lobby, where there was security on standby. Kola, clad plainly in blue jeans, a T-shirt, jacket, and Nikes, caught the security's attention. One look at the twin, and the middle-aged man knew who she was. Apple had left her name and a spare key for her.

"You're definitely Apple's sister . . . very pretty," he said.

Kola wasn't in a friendly mood. She'd been through a lot and wasn't for the small talk. The man had to do a double take. They were identical, and he was in awe. Sensing her standoffish attitude, he kept his words short and handed the key to her.

Kola went up to the empty apartment. It was sparsely furnished, like a crash pad. There were several laptops and surveillance equipment on the table, some blunt wrappers, Henny bottles, and cartis spewed around the place, and there was barely any food in the fridge. There were guns in the bedroom—enough firepower to take out a small army. Kola wondered where her sister had gotten such high-end weaponry so quickly. She thought about calling Apple, but reveled in the alone time. She fixed herself a drink and turned on the television to watch some Netflix.

A few hours later, Apple and Cartier arrived. They'd been out to dinner. Kola and Apple locked eyes and then they embraced in a sisterly, tight hug.

"I'm sorry about the baby," Apple said sincerely.

It felt like they didn't want to let each other go. They'd been through a lot—lots of pain and loss. Kola kept her promise and she didn't cry. She huffed and kept strong.

After she hugged Apple, she looked at Cartier and they embraced. Cartier hadn't seen Kola in years, and she quickly remembered when Apple and Kola were at war with each other and she wanted to squash their beef.

Kola was equally happy to see the Brooklyn girl whose reputation preceded her. Cartier was the first bitch who the hood rumored wore sexy dresses and heels with a .380 strapped to her thigh. Cartier was known to be a beast on the streets—somebody not to be fucked with. She fought bitches and niggas hand-to-hand and busted her gun like a gangster. Kola remembered when she heard about Monya getting shot in the head while doing a drug run out of state. Like she and Apple, Cartier had been through some shit.

The three women, all shy of turning thirty years old, had been through some serious drama in their young years, but in Miami, all beefs would be settled. On that, they all vowed.

The next morning, Apple brought Kola up-to-date on their situation and their progress, or lack thereof. They told her about Whiz and Floco and how Apple planned on killing them once her enemies were dead. Most importantly, Citi, Cane, and Scar were still alive. Cartier had been grazed in the leg during the gunplay, and they had failed numerous times to kill, injure, or maim any of the three of them.

"Where did you go with that injury?" Kola asked Cartier, knowing hospitals were to report all gunshot victims.

"I ain't stupid, Kola. I've been in this game far too long. We paid a doctor to fix me up."

Kola nodded.

"Who is the strongest on their team?" asked Kola.

"That would be Scar," Apple said. "Without a doubt, that nigga is agile like a feline and his trigger finger is quick. It's like the muthafucka was born with Spidey senses."

Apple's run-ins with Scar were almost legendary.

"Then we take that bitch's legs out from under her," said Kola.

"But we need to get them alone," Cartier said. "We separate them, we better our chances."

Kola agreed.

"So who do we go after first?" Apple asked. "I'm thinkin' Cane."

"Cane?" Kola was taken aback by the comment.

"We catch that fool and lullaby his ass," said Cartier.

"Nah, we do that, and we put Scar on alert to hire more men and beef up their security, if they haven't done so already. No, Scar is the muscle. He falls first, and the others are gonna follow," Kola said.

Kola had her game face on. It felt good to be back. Kamel had been blowing up her cell phone, but she refused to answer it. She didn't want to talk to him and be reminded about her miscarriage. She wanted to jump back into her old self and start where she'd left off.

30

A black Chevy Impala pulled up to the small, yellow one-story home with a singular palm tree in the front yard on 9th Street in Liberty City. There were already several uniformed officers lingering around the property, and curious neighbors were gathering behind the yellow crime scene tape that had been put up to restrict the area. Something serious had happened on their narrow, inner-city block, and the looky-loos were flocking to crime scene.

Two detectives climbed out of the black Impala and approached the crime scene with soft eyes. Detectives Mitchell and Palmer were veterans with Miami-Dade Homicide, and they had over eighteen years of experience between them. Clothed in dark suits, they crossed the yellow tape and approached the yellow home. Already they deduced the house to be a trap house. The windows were darkened, there were security cameras perched near the entrance, and there was a pit bull chained up in the backyard.

"What we got?" Mitchell asked one of the uniformed officers.

"Seems like another home invasion. We got one down," the cop replied.

Mitchell took a deep breath and proceeded into the house. Immediately, he caught a strong whiff of death. A body was sprawled facedown across the wood floor, his blood pooling and staining the floor. The place had been ransacked. There were definitely drugs and cash involved.

Palmer crouched toward the body of the young black male, a face he'd never seen before.

"He's another one from New York," Palmer said.

"How you know that?" Mitchell asked.

"The tattoo on his right arm, the cross and skull—it's from a Brooklyn crew."

"What we got on our hands? A drug war with crews from New York?" Mitchell asked.

Palmer sighed. "I don't know, but whoever is hitting these trap houses, they're smart and they're fast—vicious too."

Palmer and Mitchell continued to inspect the crime scene. As usual, there were no witnesses—at least none who were willing to come forward. Fear and intimidation ruled the warm metropolis, and when it came to crime, everyone had amnesia.

This was the fifth trap house robbed in the past month, and the detectives speculated that it was a crew moving in violently on another rival drug crew. This reign of terror had left behind three dead so far, and the cops had no idea how much cash or drugs were taken. They were putting the squeeze on their C.I.'s and snitches. Something was happening in Miami, and they were determined to find out just what.

✳✳✳

"To my bitches," Apple hollered, raising her champagne glass in the air.

"To us!" Cartier said.

They all downed the bubbly champagne, but Floco and Whiz felt disrespected. They put in work too, but since this third bitch showed up, Apple had been letting her reckless mouth talk greasy to them. Whiz had to constantly remind Floco that the ends would justify the means and to keep his fuckin' mouth shut. Soon enough they would get their ultimate payday. In the meantime, they were earning a pretty penny doing these licks. Apparently, this Citi bitch had some paper.

The three girls and their hired guns were celebrating this evening. They had something to drink to and rejoice about. On the bed of a rented motel room was hundreds and hundreds of thousands of dollars—maybe in the millions, a few kilos of cocaine, and guns. They had successfully robbed another one of Citi and Scar's trap houses. The last one, they left one dead behind and took eighty grand and three kilos of heroin.

Whiz had a knack for surveillance, obtaining information, and plotting robberies. Together, they seemed unstoppable. They were adept, bold, and took risks and were tearing shit up in Miami. Drug crews didn't see them coming. Their crew was like a train barreling through a small town fast and strong, and then disappearing into the night. The cut was divided five ways, equally. And no one had any qualms about that because both sides felt that the other's share would be his or hers in due time.

Whiz and Floco watched the huge grins on the girls' faces and thought that all this celebrating was premature. They were older, wiser, and more disciplined. They knew they weren't getting any pussy here tonight, so they decided to take their cut and bounce.

"Yo," Floco began. "We out. We thinkin' we gonna go and do some more surveillance near the projects. See what's moving. I mean, these licks are good, but a nigga ready to head up north soon before our luck runs out."

"Luck?" Cartier snorted. "You think luck is what's gotten us this far?"

Everyone knew it was about to be another epic argument between Floco and Cartier, and no one was up for it tonight. They had been arguing every day for weeks now.

"C'mon, man. Let's just go," said Whiz.

"Why don't y'all just fuck already?" Kola assessed.

"Stop blowin' our fuckin' high!" added Apple.

Both Cartier and Floco smirked.

Whiz and Floco left to go and track down their intended targets while the ladies turnt up.

Kola downed the champagne and smiled widely. She was back to her old self. She and her girls danced to Post Malone's song with 21 Savage, "Rock Star," because that's what they felt they were—rock stars.

Kola's cell phone rang, and she saw that it was Kamel calling her once again. It had been weeks since she'd spoken to him. Apple sometimes would talk to him, but only to check on the kids. And though Kamel was frustrated and upset about Kola's sudden absence, he continued to take care of the kids without her. He had no idea when she would be back.

"You okay, Kola?" Apple asked.

"Yeah, I'm fine."

"Bitches, I need some fuckin' dick tonight," Cartier shouted out of the blue.

They all laughed.

"You ain't the only one," Apple replied. "If you run fast enough you might catch up wit' Floco and that big-ass dick he's waving around in them sweats."

"I would fuck the shit outta dude," Cartier admonished.

"Me too," said Apple.

"Me three," Kola replied, and they all laughed.

Apple opened another bottle of champagne and they stripped down to their skivvies and continued with their private party—girls only. Cartier went to the money on the bed and grabbed a fist full of hundreds and started to toss it everywhere, making it rain inside the room.

"Make it rain, bitches, make it rain," she laughed.

Apple and Kola joined in, tossing money up everywhere as it floated around the room. They danced around in it. Cartier leaped onto the bed and started to cover herself in money. It was a good time. The girls hadn't laughed so hard or had so much fun in months, maybe years. But tonight, they were like three teenagers enjoying the fruits of their hard labor.

Still, Apple knew that no matter how many trap houses they robbed in South Beach, how much money they took from Citi and Scar, or how many of Citi's men they killed, the only prize for her was seeing Citi dead. Then she could really let loose and celebrate.

While Kola and Cartier danced and drank, Apple began packing up the money and guns to go back to the duplex. As she scurried around the room she thought about Peaches. Apple missed her greatly. Though they were making moves in Miami, getting money and plotting her revenge, the life was taking a toll on her. She kept that undercover, though. She kept a rough and hardcore exterior, but being gone from Peaches this long was killing her inside. The streets kept her mind busy, so she would continue to rob, stalk, and kill to appease pain, but her heart was elsewhere.

Apple remained on the balcony for a moment, becoming lost in her own thoughts. The music blared behind her. Kola and Cartier were now drunk, and it damn near looked like they were going to have a lesbian exploit behind her. Cartier grabbed Kola from behind in her arms, dancing and swaying together, and then Cartier kissed the side of Kola's neck and cupped her tits. Kola laughed. The two continued to dance closely and then they fell against the sofa, entwined in each other arms.

While that was happening, her burner phone rang, and Apple answered.

Amir said, "How much you said you payin' fo' information on Scar again?"

"Ten," Apple reminded him.

"A'ight. I got sumthin'."

Apple was listening.

***

It took a miracle, but Cane had survived his gunshot wounds. One bullet passed through his side, and the other was lodged in his back, just barely missing his kidney. His surgeon went to great lengths to repeatedly tell him that had the bullet gone one-eighth of an inch to the right he would have been paralyzed. Cane knew he was trying to scare him into going straight. It worked too.

Each day his sister came to visit him surrounded by her security team, yet Cane still worried. Scar was a loose cannon, and being laid up in the hospital, Cane had no idea what was going on. He was still shell-shocked that Scar would accuse him of selling out his very own sister. That showed that he was unstable. Cane needed a way to get Scar out of Citi's life.

"I don't trust that nigga, Citi. We gotta get rid of him," he pleaded.

Citi looked around to make sure no one had heard her brother's treason. "We can't, Cane, and you know why. Those bitches are cuttin' me down day by day. I need him. It's not up for discussion."

"You take his side, even after what he did to me?"

"It's not about sides, Cane. Let's not act juvenile. You didn't die and that's all that matters."

"I just barely survived!" Cane thought he shouted, but his voice was low and raspy. His anger came out as a whisper.

"And Scar's sorry for what he did. He told me to tell you that."

Cane knew he couldn't get through to her. So, he had another approach. He'd set the nigga up to get knocked. It was a bitch-ass thing to do, but he was desperate.

"The losses y'all taken are crazy. Did you move the trap house?"

"Scar did."

"So where is it?"

"One of them hoods."

"But where, though?"

"Why, Cane? You're in no position to guard it."

"I'm your business partner. Or have you forgotten? Just 'cause I'm in here doesn't mean I'm out the game. I wanna know everything."

Citi exhaled. "Oh, Cane. You're lucky you're my brother so you get a pass. Just one, though."

"What the fuck you talkin' 'bout?"

"Why do you wanna know locations, huh? So you can set Scar up to get murdered? Call one of your amigos from Queens to come down here and murder my muscle? I told you that I needed him and when I no longer need him he'll be dealt with. But on my timeline. Not yours. *My* empire doesn't revolve around *your* revenge."

This dumb, smart, selfish bitch was on point. He would have to get at Scar another way.

✳✳✳

"How much did they take?" Citi asked.

"Close to a hundred thousand this time," one of her soldiers said.

Citi fumed. The heavy losses were crippling her organization. It was embarrassing. How were they finding out things about her? How were they coming after her?

"Fuck!" she shouted. She picked up her phone and flung it across the room, and it smashed against a wall.

She cut her eyes at Scar and glared at him. "Do something!" she screamed at him.

Scar retorted, "What the fuck you think I'm doin' out there, bitch! I got soldiers everywhere, I amped security at every location, and we got a fuckin' bounty on Apple and Cartie B."

"Cartier, you dumb fuck!"

✳✳✳

Apple felt the info she had received from Amir was a dud. Apparently, the old-adage is true, *there's no honor amongst thieves.* Scar had shot Cane up, and Cane was recuperating in a local hospital. Cane spoke with his brother Chris, who was doing time in Otisville and updated him on his situation. Chris wouldn't shut up about that nigga Scar violating his brother and wanting him dead. This looming beef quickly circulated throughout the state and federal prison systems.

Amir had a Puerto Rican mami who came to see him. She did her rounds through the correctional facilities and each year she was with a new inmate. Gabriella was a forty-seven-year-old mom of six kids by six inmates. She had low self-esteem and a penchant for bad boys that she felt she could control through commissary, collect calls, and letters.

Amir wanted Gabriella to be the go-between and deliver the message to Chris that they might be able to help him solve his Scar problem. All Chris had to do was help set him up. Amir and Gabriella had already put in the paperwork to get married so he would get conjugal visits. The money would help her get a house closer to the prison. Neither loved each other. It was just a transaction.

Apple was skeptical. "Now what's going on?" she asked Amir.

"Old boy is out of commission."

"Okay, and what?"

"And we think she can get Chris to fill in the missing pieces."

"You think?"

"Yeah, shorty, that's what I said."

"And why would he do that? Why would Chris snitch to the bitch that has an agenda against his peoples?" she replied, talking in riddles.

"Scar ain't his peoples," Amir snapped.

Apple felt Amir wanted to get his hands on it any way he could. He didn't give a fuck who ended up with it as long as it wasn't Apple.

Apple rolled her eyes. "So, what's my tab?"

"Twenty long."

"For what?"

"For the information!"

"What fuckin' information? You ain't tell me shit!"

"Yo, shorty—"

"My fuckin' name is Apple. I'm not your queen nor am I anybody's shorty!"

Amir bit down so forcefully that he nicked his cheek and shed blood. This bitch could really get under his skin. He felt like she had two sides.

"Apple, you owe a dime on that Cane information. If you don't want us to make a connection to Chris, okay, no problem. But send Gabby what you owe."

"Straight up, I'm not sending that bitch shit. Fuck I look like? Mrs. Claus? Nigga, don't call this line again unless you got some real shit to relay. Otherwise, eat a dick!"

Apple filled the girls in on the new information from Amir. She felt it was thin at best. Cane could already be dead or so fucked up that killing him wouldn't be a priority. And why was Citi still with the nigga that shot up her brother? They had no idea.

"I'll start calling around the local hospitals, see what I find on Cane," said Cartier.

As Cartier called hospitals, Kola had a thought. Maybe that information was useful after all.

"Apple, check this," Kola began. "If we find Cane alive we should go to him."

"And kill him at the hospital? I mean, damn, you trying to do life?"

"No, bitch. See if he'll help us find Scar."

Apple shook her head. "He'd be insane to help us."

"Maybe he doesn't need to be insane. Maybe he just needed to be shot."

***

Cane nearly peed his bed when Apple, a bitch who looked exactly like her, and Cartier walked into his hospital room. He wanted to bitch up and scream for help, but he had to remain defiant in the face of foes.

"Fuck y'all bitches want?"

Apple had a large bouquet of flowers and balloons like she was visiting a loved one. She placed the flowers on his empty table and could tell that he wasn't getting any love from his sister.

"We want to help," she simply said.

"Y'all bitches can't help me!"

"Stop yelling!" Cartier demanded. "Ain't nobody here to hurt you."

Apple continued, "Tell us where Scar is and the best way to get at him and our beef is over. We'll walk away from this. Too many have died already. We just want him."

"Y'all think I'm a dumb muthafucka? This whole shit is about my sister and I'll never give her up. Wit' me in here, Scar is the only one that will protect her."

"That nigga gonna kill her. You see what he did to you. She's next," Kola assessed.

"Yo, leave. Please. Don't make me ask y'all again!"

"You know," Apple inched closer to Cane, so she could see her rage up close. "Citi would speak about you, your brother, and your father like y'all were legends. As if your family was a family to be feared. All I see is that your pops got murdered by his friend, your brother is doing life, and you got shot in the back by your man. I don't see thoroughbreds. All I see is bitch."

"Get the fuck out! Nurse! Nurse! Nurse!" Cane hollered until damn near the whole nurses' station came rushing in. He thought the commotion would make the trio scatter. None of them moved an inch. They stood their ground and just glared. The nurses came in and looked at the pretty women and then to Cane.

"Get them outta here! Don't let no-fuckin'-body back in my room! Only my sister can visit me!" he began barking orders hysterically until they had to hit him with a sedative.

The women were politely asked to leave, and they complied.

The next day after the drugs wore off, Cane called his sister to warn her.

"Those bitches were here. Don't fuckin' come back or else you're dead."

31

Citi sauntered outside the opulent penthouse and onto the wide terrace that overlooked the blue ocean. Dressed in a sexy red double strapped string bikini and a pair of stilettos, she stretched out in a lounge chair with a cocktail in her hand and a deadpan expression. She exhaled. It was one of the rare times she got to relax and enjoy the sun and her wealth—and some solitude. The past few days had been quiet—no murders, no robberies, and no trouble. She felt it was the calm before the storm. Cane's message had spooked her, but she couldn't tell Scar about it. He would surely kill Cane, thinking that he was working with the enemy. So now that she wasn't running to the hospital, she had some me time.

Scar had become relentless on the streets, putting in work, searching for their foes, protecting their organization with an iron fist, and networking with the local drug kingpins to make peace in Miami. They were strong, but they were still outsiders in the Sunshine State—but they came bringing gifts—kilos of high quality cocaine and heroin at a discount price.

The beachfront property had a scenic and panoramic view of the Atlantic Ocean, Biscayne Bay, and downtown Miami. It had all the latest amenities, and high-tech security. Guards were subtly placed around the building for their protection. Citi felt safe there. The property became her haven and Miami became her playground.

She felt a strong connection to Miami, one that she never felt with New York. She loved the weather, the Latin men, the music, and the money. In Miami, she stood out as exotic. With her brown skin and long, soft hair, everyone was always mistaking her to be Dominican and thought she spoke Spanish. It was the kind of attention that she desired.

Citi needed an escape, and after losing Pacho, she needed something to help her escape—maybe a Latin lover. Her relationship with Scar had always been a façade. He couldn't hold a candle to Pacho—shit, he couldn't hold a candle at all. Scar was more of a thug than a lover—more killer than passionate romantic. He was good for the streets, but not in her bedroom.

Whenever he felt the need to fuck, Citi would spread her legs and give him some, but she never got off from him. Pacho had been her release. He was always there for her, sexually and mentally, when she needed to talk or a shoulder to cry on.

Miami brought about new potential men for Citi. Men who were gorgeous, Latin, and sexual.

She dawdled on the terrace in her bikini almost the entire afternoon, sipping on cocktails and getting a sun tan. She fiddled with her phone, posting on social media and once again boasting about her rich life. It was a habit of hers. She took a selfie of herself lying in the lounge chair in her bikini and posted it on several social sites.

Every day should have been like today, but for Citi, they weren't.

***

It was the third time Scar's phone rang in fifteen minutes—and then it continued to chime, indicating a text message was sent. Someone was really trying to get his attention. Citi glanced his way but kept quiet. Scar would glance down at a few text messages while driving, but he didn't respond. By the look on Scar's face, she knew it was a bitch—but who?

They had just left a popular spot on 2nd Avenue called Sneak Attack Miami. It was an upscale footwear shop that specialized in unique and collectable sneakers, in addition to street wear and accessories.

They rode north on 2nd Avenue in the baby blue Range Rover. Traveling behind them was a black Yukon full of their armed goons—Ant, Bucky, Lil Mike, and Coogie was driving. Scar wanted some privacy with Citi. There were some things to talk about. At first, Citi was talking to Scar about the new Fenty makeup collection, but he ignored her as usual. His phone became more important.

His phone continued to ring and chime, and Scar kept ignoring it.

"Who's blowing you up?" Citi asked.

"None of ya business," he sharply replied.

His response frustrated her. Her pussy was dry like the desert because she hadn't had any dick in weeks—yet, Scar was out there getting his dick wet by some bitch.

Scar continued to drive and Citi continued to fume. His phone rang again, and it was followed by a light chime.

"Who the fuck is that, Scar?" she asked again, offended and upset.

Citi had no idea why she was jealous of another bitch having Scar's attention. He was a lazy and lousy fuck. But if she wasn't having sex, then the bitch in her didn't want him to have any either. She wanted this nigga to be miserable like her.

Angrily, she snatched the phone from Scar's hand. Scar immediately lunged forward, while still driving, and mashed her head into the glass. "Stop fuckin' wit' me, bitch! What the fuck is your problem?"

Right away, the scene inside the Range turned into some Ike and Tina shit. Scar putting his hands on her and the constant disrespect from him made Citi go ape shit. She started to swing wildly at him, cursing and carrying on.

"Fuck you, nigga! Fuck you!" she screamed.

A few of her punches connected while Scar still had control of the steering wheel, but the Range started to swerve on the road. Citi didn't care that he was driving. Her emotions took over. He put his hands on her. She put hands on him, and it escalated.

"You fuckin' bitch!" Scar shouted.

The Range Rover continued to swerve on the road as the two fought inside. The men following behind them in the Yukon glanced at each other in bewilderment. They didn't have a clue what was happening. They were there for security but felt helpless to what Scar and Citi were doing to each other inside the vehicle.

Then it happened. The Range jumped the curb and struck a telephone pole at 30mph, and the front end became slightly smashed.

Scar heatedly jumped out from the driver's side, looking unscathed from the crash, and he ran around to the passenger side, angrily flinging the door open and pulling Citi from the front seat.

"You bastard!" she screamed out.

"You dumb fuckin' bitch!" he shouted.

Scar aggressively grabbed Citi by her neck and slammed her against the vehicle. The two cursed and fought each other in public. Lil Mike, Ant, and Bucky climbed out of the Yukon and stood there in awe. It was surreal, and it was dangerous. They all were exposed, and people were watching the fight between the couple like it was a pay-per-view match. The men wanted to intervene, but with Scar's temper, they didn't know what to expect from him. Should they let them fight it out and try to kill each other, or was it wise for them to try and get things under control?

Looking past Scar, Citi's eyes grew large with concern. She was the first to see them coming—five masked gunmen, and they weren't part of her crew. Desperately, she pushed Scar away from her and retreated into the Range to grab her pistol. Scar, now seeing the threat too, removed his gun and the two simultaneously opened fire.

Bak! Bak! Bak! Bak!

In a heartbeat, a full-scale shootout ensued on the public street. Bullets shattered the back glass of the Range Rover and pierced the side doors. Scar's men reacted with violence of their own. Bucky went down, shot in the chest.

The public street flew into a panic, and bystanders ran off or took cover. Bullets whizzed everywhere, and it felt like nowhere was safe to run to or hide. The streets of Miami started to emulate the days of when Griselda Blanco was in charge and put into practice massive bloodshed and public shootouts.

Among those trying to take out Citi and Scar were Apple, Cartier, and Kola. They were accompanied by the men they'd brought into their war against Citi. The trio tried to take out Citi, seeing her crouched behind the Range Rover, but shockingly, Citi had a surprise of her own. Citi was able to back them up off of her with her 9mm. The girls were amazed by how skilled she was with her pistol.

Whiz went down with a shot to his head, his body sprawled and displayed on the public street. Apple was determined to end this bitch's life once and for all, but Citi proved to be hard to kill. A round from a pistol nearly took her head off, so Apple had to fall back.

Boom! Boom!

The shots continued to echo on the streets. Citi knew she needed to escape or it was either death or lockup for her—and she didn't want to experience either one. She leaped from her hiding area, released several rapid rounds at her rivals, and dashed into the front seat of the Range. Lucky for her, the keys were still in the ignition. As bullets zipped everywhere, she desperately put the vehicle into reverse, removed the warped front end from the telephone pole, and then thrust the vehicle into drive and sped off. She did 60mph away from the threat.

With Citi gone, Scar took his opportunity to escape. Another one of his men, Ant, went down on the streets. He leaped from the area he took cover in, let loose a barrage of bullets at his foes, and hurried toward the

Yukon. He reached the passenger seat with his gun still emptying in the streets. He screamed at his man, Coogie, "Get the fuck in and drive!"

Coogie jumped into the driver's seat and pushed his foot on the accelerator. The Yukon sped off like a bat out of hell, leaving Lil Mike at the scene. Scar remained hunkered down in the passenger seat, the smoking gun in his hand and he laughed at his umpteenth attempt at escaping death.

"Muthafuckas can't touch me! I'm the real fuckin' untouchable!" he boasted to no one in particular.

Left behind was a bloody mess, three men dead, cars shot up with shards of glass everywhere, and the bystanders in complete awe at what had just happened. Police sirens were heard blaring in the distance. What was supposed to be a calm, beautiful day in Miami, once again turned into something out of Afghanistan.

✳✳✳

Citi left the bullet riddled and mangled truck parked in the underground garage. She didn't want to leave it on the street for it to be seen by the police or, worse, the people who were trying to kill her. She managed to make it home, but it was a miracle that she was still alive. Her adrenaline was still flowing. It had been fight or flight, and fortunately for her, she was able to do both.

Alone and still shaken up by another attempt on her life, she dashed for the underground elevator, the gun still in her hand, and pushed for her penthouse floor. Her breathing was heavy, and she tried to calm herself down, but it was difficult.

"Get it together, Citi . . . get it together," she repeated to herself.

So many worries flooded Citi's thoughts. How were Apple and her crew finding her? *Was it a GPS? Did they have a snitch in their crew? Was it Cane as Scar had suspected? Is he the snitch?*

Citi hurried into the penthouse, but even there, she didn't feel safe. With the 9mm in her hand, she worried about someone waiting inside the home to kill her. She went searching room to room for any threats, but it was still and quiet—nothing to worry about, for now anyway.

She stood in the center of the majestic living room and she screamed. She screamed loudly. She was about to have a nervous breakdown.

Although she and Scar had a violent fight, Citi became concerned about him. Did he make it out alive, or was he dead on the street? Trying to regain her composure, Citi tried to call his phone, but he wasn't answering. She tried not to think the worst, but that was impossible, because the worst kept gunning for them. If Scar was dead, then her chances of survival were slim.

✳✳✳

Hours had passed, and still no word from Scar. By this time, Citi assumed he was dead. She was in the kitchen making herself some chamomile tea when she heard a noise that startled her. Quickly, she grabbed her gun from the kitchen counter.

There was another noise, and Citi emerged from the kitchen with the pistol and warily marched through the penthouse toward the disturbance. Did they track her down? Did someone give up her location? Who was it—friend or foe? Whoever it was, they were about to be in for a very rude awakening.

Slowly and carefully, she entered the dark living room where she saw a figure in the distance. He moved about freely, and her adrenaline started to charge inside of her. She outstretched her arm and aimed the barrel of the gun at the darkened figure. *Does he see me?* she wondered.

"If you move, I'll fuckin' kill you right where you stand," she threatened.

"Bitch, now is not the time fo' fuckin' games," he shouted back.

She recognized his voice. Immediately, she flicked on the lights and confirmed it was Scar. For some reason, he was fixing himself a drink in the dark.

"Scar, what the fuck!" she yelled. "I tried calling you and you wasn't picking up."

"Shit got hectic out there and I lost my phone," he explained.

Damn, she was relieved that he was alive. She wanted to hug him but stopped herself from doing so.

"What happened? How did you get away?"

"Not with your fuckin' help," he grumbled. "You left me out there to die!"

"I didn't have a choice."

Scar glared at her then downed his brown juice and poured himself another. He said in a low growl, "I'm gonna burn this fuckin' city down to the fuckin' ground."

32

A hustler named Lynch parked in front of the Liberty Square housing projects, a sprawling complex in one of the roughest parts of Miami. The area was home to notorious gangs in the city, like the Zoe Pound and the Top 6. They were violent, but loosely organized and had no hierarchy.

Money and drugs moved quickly and at a high volume in the Liberty Square projects, and Lynch was the distributor helping Scar move product into the urban areas and everywhere else throughout the city. Lynch sold kilos wholesale to local crews and tried to rule the streets with an iron fist via murders and intimidation.

But since day one, the relationship between Lynch and Scar had been shaky. Scar believed Lynch talked too much and was too flashy. He was about money, more money, and nothing but money—pussy too. Lynch pissed Scar off with the way he would boldly talk about fucking Citi and doing other perverted things to her. He was a womanizer who ran through pussy like a fat kid went through a package of Oreos.

Lynch was a treacherous muthafucka who only showed loyalty to the almighty dollar. He was well-known in Miami, but some considered him a shady and untrustworthy dude. Many believed that he would sell his own mother and grandmother out to make a fast dollar.

Lynch was known for sporting a platinum and diamond Rolex around his wrist, a diamond pinky ring, and a diamond front grill that cost more than most houses in Miami.

He sat in his idling dark blue S-Class Coupe smoking on a Black & Mild. Seated next to Lynch was his trophy bitch, Miranda—a striking woman with long legs, exotic eyes, rich brown skin, a big butt like J-Lo, and a flowing weave. Lynch's cell phone rang nonstop.

He puffed on his Black and griped into his phone, "Yo, fuck that nigga Scar. He a guest in Miami and he needs to be reminded of that. I *let* that nigga rock in Miami, and besides, that muthafucka is bringing too much heat on everyone. I heard that nigga almost got his head blown off the other day by some gangsta bitch . . . Word up, a bitch named Apple. Yeah . . . I know, right? That nigga pussy . . . Nah, I ain't met that bitch yet, but I heard she hardcore. We get money, my nigga—*been* fuckin' gettin' money down here, but these New York muthafuckas need to understand how we really do. If they wanna walk around town with their chests puffed out, a fuckin' bullet gonna push that shit right back in."

While Lynch griped and talked shit about his drug connect on his cell phone, Miranda busied herself by applying more makeup to her pretty face and looking at her image in the visor mirror.

"Baby, how long we gonna sit and wait here? You know I got things to do," Miranda moaned.

Lynch cut his eyes at her and barked, "Bitch you in a fuckin' rush? You got shit to do, besides spend my fuckin' money?"

"I'm just saying, baby, I'm too cute to sit around in the ghetto looking crazy," she protested.

"Walk somewhere then. I got fuckin' business to take care of. Don't fuckin' rush me, bitch. I don't fuckin' know what you think this shit is."

She sucked her teeth and rolled her eyes and then sighed. She wasn't walking anywhere, especially in a pair of $600 heels.

Lynch went back to his phone conversation. "Nah, not yet. I got Steel meeting up wit' me right now. That nigga must be crazy! He been talkin' greasy 'bout me for some time now, but when I see that ugly, dead-eye nigga he don't never do shit! . . . Who? In my city? Scar is more bitch than his bitch. If he wanna see me, he know where the fuck I be. I'm right here all day ev'ry day in my fuckin' hood. These niggas love me out here. They fuckin' worship me! I wish a nigga would try me . . . Yeah, but I'ma see him and his bitch. Nah, man . . . Citi, I'm gonna fuck that cute fuckin' bitch," he said in front of his trophy jawn.

Now Miranda was the one cutting her eyes. "Nigga, you seriously gonna talk that cheating shit right in front me? That's so fuckin' disrespectful, Lynch!"

"Like I give a fuck, bitch!" he retorted.

They argued briefly while a black-on black Beamer with chrome rims rolled up on the block and parked right in front of Lynch's Benz Coupe. It was his right-hand man Steel arriving on the block to meet with him on an imminent issue with Scar.

Lynch opened his door and placed one foot on the ground. He was about to exit the vehicle to meet with Steel on the street, but Miranda continued to curse at him, and she was making him upset.

"Look, bitch—" he started.

His girlfriend's fury swiftly shifted into full-blown panic—something out of the blue had gripped her immediate attention. A masked gunman came from out of nowhere, his right arm extended and a SW99 pistol gripped in his hand. Lynch had his back turned to the threat, as he was fussing with his girl. Her eyes widened in terror, and before she could warn him or scream, it happened—gunshots and turmoil.

Bak! Bak! Bak! Bak!

The back of Lynch's head exploded. His blood splattered everywhere, and the force of the bullets thrust him into Miranda and left his cranium dropping against her lap. She released a deafening scream. She was terrified that she was going to be next, as she locked eyes with the masked gunman.

Pandemonium soon followed the explosion of gunfire. Covered in her man's blood, Miranda hurriedly ejected herself from the car and flung herself to the concrete, scraping her knees and elbows.

Steel immediately flew out of his Beamer with a pistol in his hand. Lynch was down, and the killer was dead in his sights. "You muthafucka!" he screamed as he released a barrage of bullets at the masked man.

Boom! Boom! Boom! Boom! Boom! Boom!

Steel scowled and rushed forward, gunning for the killer.

Miranda continued to hug the concrete and scream, trapped in a hail of bullets from different directions. Locals took cover, but the sound of gunshots and murder wasn't new to them.

Steel continued to rush wildly toward his target, hell bent on retaliation for his friend's death. But unbeknownst to him, there were two shooters instead of one. The second gunman craftily came from behind and opened fire on Steel, striking him multiple times in the back and in the back of the head. He collapsed forward, lying facedown against the black pavement.

The second shooter stood over Steel's body and pumped several more rounds into him. He then glanced at his partner in crime and they both ran off and jumped into a black Crown Vic that came to a screeching stop. The car took off, and Lynch's girl was left there on the sidewalk completely traumatized.

Seated in a SUV a block away was Scar. He had witnessed the entire thing unfold. It was his order to take Lynch out because he believed the man was a snake and partially responsible for the violent attacks against him. If Scar even thought you were about to cross him, or if you dogged his name out on the street, he was coming for you.

Appeased by what he saw, he grinned and said to Coogie, "Let's get the fuck outta here."

33

Scar and his goons fucked up leaving behind an eyewitness. Miranda knew everything. Scar had murdered her nigga and she wanted revenge. Overnight she went from being a hustler's wife to just another project broad. In less than forty-eight hours she found Apple. She began running her mouth like it was a marathon. Cartier, Apple, and Kola had listened to a long, drawn out epic saga detailing how she and Lynch met, how he was gonna marry her, how she was trying to get pregnant—all delusional, heartbroken shit.

"Kill that nigga," Miranda said, her face awash in tears. "Kill him fuckin' dead!"

"We need to know where that nigga sleep at," Apple calmly began. "Catchin' that slippery nigga on the streets is proving to be difficult."

"I don't know where he live at."

Cartier snapped. "Then what do you know!"

"I know shit," Miranda said, and cut her eyes at Cartier. "I know about a bitch he checks up on at club Floss. It's not his home, but it's something!"

Floss was located off Alton Road in Miami Beach. Night after night, they worked in shifts, either Floco and Cartier or Apple and Kola. It didn't take long for Scar to show up, only he wasn't ever alone. He came two dozen deep. Goons were guarding him like he was President Trump doing a speech at a Black Panther rally.

Floco and Cartier were able to follow him to a residence and Floco, still hot over the death of his cousin, wanted to get out and just start blazing.

"Are you crazy?" Cartier barked. "That's fuckin' suicide."

"That nigga killed my cousin! I'ma blow his fuckin' brains out!"

"I know. Just not tonight!"

Cartier felt Floco was a loose cannon. He was showing unstable tendencies, and his patience had dissipated weeks ago.

Floco missed New York, wasn't getting steady pussy, and now he was down his fam. Floco wanted to hurry this shit along because he still had an agenda. Apple needed to die and now the pot of gold at the end of the rainbow would be all his.

The next day, Cartier, Apple, and Kola sat inside the Lexus and from across the street, they keenly surveyed the quaint home on Virginia Street in the Coconut Grove section of Miami. The area was somewhat middle class with its smooth paved roads, medium homes, and tree lined streets. It was mid-morning, and the area was quiet. They observed Scar pull up to the charming residence and climb out of the Escalade. He didn't come alone. Four dark colored SUVs with tinted windows pulled along the curb and waited for their boss.

The girls were on the same street as Scar, only a few homes away from him. They were tucked away in the shade of palm trees and shrubbery. Scar moved from his SUV to the modest looking home, unaware that he was being watched. But he moved carefully, his head swiveling as he keenly scanned the area. The crazy killer had two guns on his person, a Glock 34 and a Sig 226.

Scar knocked and the front door swung open. A Latina girl loomed into view. She was pretty and voluptuous with big tits, a flat stomach, and a curvy ass. It appeared that she'd had some plastic surgery done. Scar hugged her, and even though her arms were wrapped around him intimately, Scar kept his reach close to his guns—always alert, eyes open.

She ushered him into the home. The girls watched the door close. Now they had a beat on Scar.

"This dumb fuck is gonna die over some pussy," Cartier said.

"You see how niggas be cheatin' and shit," Kola said. "Citi waiting at home on this ugly ass, dead-eye nigga and he up in here eating the next bitch's pussy."

"Oh please, Kola," remarked Apple. "How many next bitches have you been in your lifetime? You sittin' here actin' all innocent and shit."

Kola cut her eyes at her sister. "You still salty that I took your man all them years back, bitch?"

"And you see how that shit turned out, right?" Apple came back with.

The two started bickering inside the car, until Cartier had to shut them up. They were like the two young siblings that she never had, but enough was enough already.

"We're supposed to be focused, not arguing," Cartier spat.

The sisters knew she was right. They tossed a halfhearted apology at each other.

"How long you think he gonna be in there?" Kola asked.

"Don't know. Maybe all night. But now we got a location on this fool," Cartier said.

"Yeah, but it won't be the first time," Apple said.

"He got lucky before, but his luck is about to run out," said Cartier.

34

Precision Auto was a popular body shop on 7th Street in Little Havana, and Citi had her mangled Range Rover towed there for repair. The baby blue SUV was one of her favorite vehicles. Miami was becoming more of a nightmare than the paradise she expected. Trouble had followed her from New York, and if Scar didn't do his job, then she would have no choice but to replace him—if that was possible.

It was a clear, hot, and sunny day, and Citi climbed out of the E-Class Benz looking stunning in a black spaghetti-strap mini-dress, boasting her long legs and showing off her red bottoms. To everyone inside the mechanic shop, her appearance screamed money and power. She was a stunning woman—the type of woman who seemed out of place in the auto body shop. But not too far behind her were two men, not the type of men to take lightly. They read trouble and killers.

Right away, the owner of the shop approached Citi. His name was Manuel. He was a carbon copy of Ricky Martin—tall, handsome, bearded, and he looked more hands-off with the cars than hands-on.

"How can I help you, miss?" he asked Citi.

For a moment, Citi's eyes were stuck on how handsome he was. The mere sight of him lit a fire inside of her that was going to be hard to put out. She had to take a deep breath and try not to stare so hard at him.

"I need help," she at last said.

"I can see that. What happened?" he asked, staring at the wrecked blue Range Rover that had been towed to his shop.

"I want her up and running."

"We can make that happen. We know how to work miracles here," he said.

I bet you do, she thought. She smiled at him.

Manuel smiled back, being nice. Citi was a very pretty woman, but he instantly knew what she was about. He knew drug money when he saw it, as he was former player in the drug game. Manuel had gone legit a few years ago, after serving some time in prison and almost losing his life in a bad drug deal. He took his earnings and opened his shop.

For a moment, Citi created a distraction inside the shop, as all eyes were on her—her sexy black dress, her long legs, her luxury Benz in the background. She was the best thing they'd seen all week. But while Manuel's employees were ogling her, Manuel remained cool and kept things professional. He wasn't swayed by her beauty and her flirting.

"So handsome . . . . How long until she's fixed?" Citi asked. She stepped closer to him and placed her hand on his chest. She could feel his muscles through the fabric.

Manuel coolly maneuvered himself from her flirtatious touch, taking a few steps back from her. "I need to do an estimate first," he said.

"That's fine, handsome. I got time," she said, still smiling his way.

He didn't know much about cars, but he did know how to operate a business. He had his mechanics to help him, and they were some of the best in Miami. Citi continued to flirt with him, and he treated the young beauty with the utmost respect. He decided to put his best man on the job.

"Irving, come over here," Manuel called out to one of his mechanics.

A young black man with light brown skin, glasses, and a trimmed beard with soft hair braided back into cornrows approached them. Citi looked his way. He was cute, looking like a young Malcolm X, but it was Manuel who had her undivided attention.

"This is Irving, and he's my best mechanic here. He'll be the one to fix you up," said Manuel.

Citi gave Irving the once-over, and he looked like he'd never done a dishonest thing in his life—complete square. His father was a pastor who also owned a body shop back home in Connecticut.

"Hello," Irving said politely.

"Hey," Citi replied dryly.

"He'll take down your information, and whatever you need, he'll take care of you from now on," Manuel told her.

"And he's the best?" asked Citi.

Manuel nodded. "He'll have your Range Rover looking brand new in no time."

"Money is no issue for me," she said.

"I understand," Manuel replied.

"I'll keep you updated when the parts come in for your Range, ma'am," Irving chimed.

Citi chuckled. "Ma'am—that's cute."

Irving was respectful. On her way out, he opened and held the door for her. He continued to greet her with "ma'am," and it was unreal for Citi. He was sweet boy, but not her cup of tea at all. It was Manuel who she had her eye on. Citi was sexually frustrated, and she saw Manuel as her opening to pure pleasure and a good dick down. He was something to take her mind off her troubles. She needed the sexual escape.

When she walked away, approaching the E-Class Benz parked on the street with her two thugs standing nearby, Irving and Manuel watched her.

"She sure is pretty," Irving mentioned.

Manuel looked at him and snapped, "Get back to work."

*** *** ***

Two days later, the E-Class Benz came to a stop in front Precision Auto. Citi exited the car looking too cute in a red designer dress and a pair of Fendi heels. Manuel had been on her mind since the day she saw him. And like most, she loved a challenge. She knew Manuel wasn't feeling her and that he was married, and it made her want him even more.

Unfortunately for her, he wasn't there that day. But Irving was. He greeted her with politeness and chivalry.

Every couple of days, Citi made it her business to show up at the body shop out of the blue, and she made sure the outfits she wore there were sexy and eye-catching. But the moment Manuel would spot her, he would make a quick exit from the shop. He didn't want anything to do with her, but he valued her business. He wanted Citi and her associates to use his repair shop for their business—stash boxes, insurance scams, the works.

Unlike most men, who would have fucked Citi for bragging rights, Manuel loved his wife. She held him down when he did a long bid and he never cheated on her once he came home. He didn't want to break up his happy home for a cheap affair. Citi was beautiful, but she wasn't worth the heartache she would bring. Besides, he wasn't attracted to her type.

It was Irving whose eyes lit up each time Citi walked into the shop. He would smile, and his heart would swell with emotions. Seeing his eagerness for her, Citi would try to use Irving to make Manuel jealous. She and Irving would laugh and talk. She even gave him a few hugs inside the shop, but it wasn't Manuel that was stirred with jealousy, it was Irving's coworkers. To them, it seemed like Irving had formed some kind of odd friendship with the young beauty.

But the more Citi thought she was using Irving, the more she started to respect him. She realized that he was running the place. All the workers came to him for advice on how to fix certain things. If they second-guessed a repair, Irving would advise them on what to do and what not to do. He was a savant when it came to repairing cars. Yet, she noticed that he wasn't in a managerial position.

Unexpectedly, while he was on his lunch break, she asked Irving, "How much do you make an hour?"

"You mean me?" he said incredulously, looking embarrassed that she asked him. His eyes darted down to the ground, the introvert in him coming out. He knew that he could never afford someone as fancy and stylish as Citi.

"Who else?" she snapped.

He huffed and replied, "I make close to five hundred a week. But I'm supposed to get a raise soon."

"And what about him?" She pointed to the head mechanic, another Hispanic male.

The man was old, lazy, and smelly. He was always stuffing Spanish food down his throat with his greasy fingers and dirty fingernails. Citi immediately took a dislike to him. He never spoke English, like he hated the language, and he was rude. She heard that he was related to Manuel somehow.

Irving whistled and replied, "He makes a lot more than me."

"You're letting these Mexican muthafuckas play you," she stated. "Don't ever let anyone tell you your worth."

"They're Cuban," he corrected.

"Who gives a fuck what they are? You're too smart for them to play you, Irving," she exclaimed.

He wished she would lower her tone. He didn't want to start any trouble with his coworkers. He liked his job and he didn't want to get fired.

Citi peeped his nervousness and she felt sorry for him—the good-hearted underdog. She saw something special in him and felt the urge to protect him.

***

The following day, Citi showed up at the auto body shop again, but this time she no longer looked for the owner. She was there to see Irving. Mistreating the only black guy in there who was singly-handedly running the shop—shit like that irked her. She remembered being treated as such, as if she was nothing.

Irving appeared in front of her wearing a white tank top under his dark blue overalls, which he removed due to the Miami heat. Citi stood there in awe, seeing his muscles bulging from his shirt. He wasn't brawny like Michael Jai White, but he was slim and physically fit. She thought he needed protection, but physically he was appealing. Mentally, he was shy.

Suddenly, Irving was worth a second look. Citi was horny, and she craved someone that could make her feel good in the bed. Scar had his whores and he wasn't a real factor in her sex life. She had spent several months in Miami, and not once did she have an orgasm.

"How are things coming along, Irving?"

"They're coming along fine, ma'am. The parts should be here in a few days."

"Irving, do me a favor. Stop calling me 'ma'am.' I'm not my mother. Shit, do I look like a ma'am to you?"

"No, ma'am—I mean—"

"Just call me Citi."

He smiled.

Citi noticed that all eyes were on them. His coworkers were turning green with envy because he had her undivided attention. To them, it didn't make any sense—a beautiful and rich woman like Citi giving Irving some attention. For once, they wished they were in his shoes.

She continued to openly flirt with Irving and felt the need to take things further with him. All kinds of naughty things roamed through Citi's mind, and she wondered what other kind of surprises he was concealing from her. She stared down at his crotch and noticed the dick imprint through the fabric. It was hypnotizing—and from her view, he seemed to be impressive. Manuel easily became irrelevant.

Citi smiled and said, "I'll be back. I'll let you work."

She strutted out of the body shop with all eyes glued to her curves and plump backside. Even Irving was stuck on stupid for a moment.

Hours later, when Irving's shift ended at the shop, he walked outside to find Citi's Benz idling out front. She sat in the backseat. The rear window rolled down and Citi amicably gazed at Irving leaving the building. She smiled. He smiled.

"Get in," she said to him.

His co-workers couldn't believe what they were seeing. *Lucky muthafucka,* they said among themselves. Irving clutched his knapsack and tensely approached the sleek Benz, and Citi opened the rear door for him. It was an invitation to come see her world and have some fun.

"Are-are you sure you w-want me to?" he stammered.

"Irving, I'm not gonna ask you twice. It's your choice."

He glanced back at his co-workers and there were looks of jealousy and contempt. He decided to take Citi up on her invitation. He slid into the backseat of the luxury Benz and joined a beautiful woman.

***

"Damn . . . this is really nice," Irving said of the penthouse suite.

His eyes glittered from the luxury he was seeing. He had never been in such an opulent home. He was a poor kid from a poor neighborhood who could barely afford his own car. It was seventh heaven in his eyes.

"You own all this?" he asked.

"Yes."

"Wow—I mean, I wish I could afford something like this."

"Maybe one day you will," she said.

He laughed. It was unbelievable to him. "I'm just a mechanic working and repairing cars."

"So, open up your own shop."

"I'm not that smart at business . . ."

"You can be," she said.

"And besides, I don't have the money."

"You need to stop making excuses for yourself. You got skills, Irving. But enough of the small talk," she said.

She wanted some dick. She didn't bring him there for chitchat. Her hormones were raging, and her pussy was throbbing. She wanted to see what Irving was working with and if she'd wasted her time bringing him home or not.

She approached him and placed one hand against his chest and the other dipped low, grabbing his crotch and squeezing. Irving was completely taken aback by her assertive approach.

"Oh shit," he murmured.

"Damn, Irving. I feel something nice there."

For a moment, he stood there stuck on stupid as Citi fondled him. She unzipped his pants and pulled out his dick, and it was long and thick. She was impressed. She toyed with his chest and started to stroke him nice and slow, evoking a moan from him.

"You like that?" she asked him.

He seemed speechless.

"You wanna fuck me, Irving?" she teased.

Of course, he did. What man wouldn't?

Citi's manicured hand continued to work his dick, constructing a huge erection in her fist. She stepped back from her young stud and started to peel away her clothing. She wanted to entice him and show him what she had in store for him. Her tits and ass were perfection. He stood there in awe at her nakedness and it seemed like seeing her naked body added an extra inch or two to his size.

"Damn!" she said. His manhood was impressive. "Undress," she said.

He continued to stand there bashful, but with his hard dick showing. And he was too polite. She didn't want polite. She wanted raw and nasty, crazy and hard inside of her. She went up to him and they kissed passionately.

"I want you to fuck me," she whispered into his ear.

Right there, they dropped to the floor. She nearly ripped his clothes off and like his dick, the rest of him was impressive. He worked out—his physique was pure eye-candy, so why was he shy?

She slid a Magnum condom onto his erection, and slowly lowered herself onto his hard dick. She felt every inch of him penetrating her and she slowly started to ride him like a piston in a cylinder.

"Mmmm . . . Ooooh . . . Ooooh . . . shit, nigga, fuck me," she cooed and then flicked her tongue into his mouth and continued to moan. "Fuck me!"

He cupped her ass as she continued to ride him. She felt the fullness of his big, hard dick inside of her. Her fingernails dug into him as she thrust herself up and down, her walls clenching against his moving flesh inside of her.

Irving grunted and moaned. For him, it was a dream coming true. Their bodies rubbed and smacked together, creating a fleshy sound. They twisted and turned, sexually contorted on the floor and transitioning into doggy style where Citi wanted him to smack her ass from the back and pull her hair. Irving seemed shy from doing something like that, but Citi assured him it was okay. She wanted it rough. She had to tell him what to do, what she liked. Although he wasn't the Latin lover she wanted in Miami, his hard dick made up for her disappointment.

Irving caught on quickly to what she liked, and he slid his dick in and out of her pussy at a steady pace. He had stamina, which was another bonus for him.

"I'm gonna come!" he announced.

She could feel him engorge as his orgasm was building inside of his shaft. She was ready to explode. Her mouth was agape and her face in ecstasy as she rode the dick again, toppling forward and smothering him in her tits.

They both exploded. She came hard, and he was quivering with delight. It felt like he would never stop. It was some of the best sex she'd ever had, and Irving was beyond blown away.

Shockingly, Irving was ready for a round two and three. He was like the Energizer Bunny. Citi knew she'd made a smart move by choosing him.

They continued fuck long after her Range Rover had been fixed. Irving gave her what she needed, and she was gradually turning this boy into a man. They made it their business to meet each Monday before her hair appointment. He started to call their tryst Black Love Mondays. It was something he looked forward to. It got him through the week.

After some time, using condoms between them became a thing of the past. Irving and Citi connected in ways they never imagined. She didn't want to admit it, but she was falling for the young, broke mechanic.

35

Luxe & Beauty Salon in Coconut Grove was impressive. The front reception area had a juice bar, coffee, pastries, and a large lounge area with a 60-inch TV mounted on the wall. The middle section was massive with twenty leather stylist stations, and in the back were eyebrow and eyelash stations, manicures, and pedicures. The high-end beauty salon took in $400,000 monthly, had won numerous hair shows, was once featured in *Essence* and *Hype Hair* magazines, and some of their clients were A-list celebrities.

As usual, the place was swarming with female customers. The gossip was flowing, and the money was too.

The day was winding down to closing hours. It was nearing midnight when Apple casually strolled on the pavestone in five-inch Louboutins just as the last patron was leaving the shop, her hair and makeup on point.

The owner was flipping the *"Closed"* sign over and was about to turn the locks, but Apple pushed her way inside. Nikki stood there in shock.

"Kola is that you?" she asked in disbelief.

"Do I look like fuckin' Kola?" Apple scoffed.

"Apple," Nikki squealed. "Oh shit! They said you were dead. What are you doing here?"

"You sound happy to see me."

"I am." Nikki reached out to hug her cousin, but the love wasn't returned.

Once again, Nikki went to lock the door, but once again, she was interrupted from doing so. Kola and Cartier pushed their way inside the shop, startling Nikki. There was no mistaking it. It was Kola. She took a couple of steps back and suddenly found herself surrounded by the three women. Her false joy soon turned into horror.

"Hey Kola," she greeted nervously. "I haven't seen you in a minute."

"I know . . . since I got knocked."

"Wow, it's been that long," Nikki replied. She moved deeper into her shop and they all followed. "Come in, y'all, so we can catch up."

The tension could have been cut with a knife. However, Nikki tried to play it cool and pretended not to notice. She removed a bottle of red wine from a nearby shelf and offered the girls some with a nervous smile.

"Nobody drinks this shit," Kola barked. "Look at this bitch, acting like she got some class now."

"Oh, y'all want something stronger?" Nikki tried to joke. She didn't wait for their reply, adding, "Don't worry, I gotchu."

She went into the backroom and came back out clutching a bottle of Hennessy and some shot glasses. Kola carried a deadpan expression. Their cousin was trying to make peace somehow—break out the southern hospitality. She poured some of the brown juice into the shot glasses and handed them out.

"Let's drink and talk and catch up on old times," said Nikki.

"Yeah . . . let's do that," Kola replied.

And they did that. The girls took a seat in the chairs and downed the liquor, and as the brown juice flowed through their veins, they caught up on old times with their cousin. They all sat in the stylists' chairs and talked about men, fucking, money, hustlers, cartels, and more. Nikki bragged about her come-up and expressed how well her business was doing and named some of the celebrities who frequented her shop.

"I once did Beyoncé's hair," Nikki boasted.

"Bitch, stop lying," Apple said.

"No, I'm for real. She was in town for her concert and she needed an emergency stylist and my name came up. Girl, that bitch is gorgeous fo' real. She came up in here with her entourage and you would have sworn it was the President in town," Nikki proclaimed.

More Hennessy was poured into glasses, and the gossip continued. For a moment, it seemed like all was well between Nikki and her cousins—like they were trying to scare her in the beginning—put on a show by showing up at her shop unannounced. But Nikki felt relaxed. They were family.

When they could laugh no more, and reality was no longer a joke, it was Cartier who decided to shift the mood inside the salon. Her eyes cut over at Nikki and she said, "You know you gotta answer to Kola, right?"

Nikki swallowed hard. She stared at her cousins. "What is she talking about?"

Kola erupted with, "Let's start with how you set me up to get busted! You fuckin' lied about the feds raiding our fuckin' place. You stole my fuckin' money, and then you left me to rot in jail. Does any of that bullshit sound familiar?"

"That's fuckin' bullshit! That's wasn't me!" Nikki vehemently denied everything.

"Bitch, you gonna sit there and lie to my fuckin' face like I'm some stupid bitch?"

"You got sloppy, Kola!" Nikki exclaimed.

"Sloppy?" Kola abruptly lifted herself from the chair and looked like she was ready to charge at Nikki. "You fuckin' played me, bitch!"

They argued. Nikki continued to deny everything, but Kola looked around her cousin's immaculate salon and she saw where her money went.

"Bitch, I should fuck you up!" Kola screamed.

"Don't come in my shop with that bullshit, Kola. I ain't the fuckin' same," Nikki warned her.

"What, bitch?"

"You fuckin' heard me," Nikki retorted.

Kola had heard enough. She couldn't stand the sight of her cousin anymore. She swiftly charged at Nikki, ready to tear the weave out of her head and bash her face in. But Nikki had something for her cousin and the others. She quickly pulled out a pistol that she'd gotten from the back when she got the Hennessy and she opened fire wildly at her cousin.

Pop! Pop! Pop!

Luckily for everyone, Nikki was a lousy shot and was too afraid to aim straight. Kola, Apple, and Cartier quickly took cover. Nikki continued to fire wildly. She screamed and cursed at them. This was her shop and she wasn't about to be bullied, threatened, or harmed.

"I ain't scared of y'all bitches!" Nikki shouted.

"You fuckin' cunt!" Kola screamed behind one of the chairs.

Nikki fired her way and the bullets slammed into the chair, barely missing Kola.

"Get the fuck out my shop!" Nikki screamed. "Fuck you!"

Pop! Pop!

As Nikki was distracted by aiming at Kola, Apple snuck up behind her and thrust a .380 to the side of her head and parked a bullet in her temple. Nikki collapsed right there, dead.

"Bitch," Apple uttered with disdain.

"What the fuck, Apple!" Kola hollered.

"What?"

"I wanted to kill that bitch myself."

"You seemed busy ducking," Apple mocked.

"I had it under control," Kola griped.

"Really? It didn't seem that way to me. And besides, you weren't even thinking about the bitch all these years, cuz you were too busy playing house wit' your husband. It was me that said this bitch ain't gonna live her life while I'm in South Beach again," Apple proclaimed.

As the twins fussed, Cartier had the idea of going through the cash register and taking all the day's earnings. "I bet this bitch got a safe in here somewhere too," she said.

The sisters ceased their argument. Now wasn't the time for bickering, they felt. They had a dead body on the floor in a well-known beauty salon in Coconut Grove.

"C'mon, we gotta do this shit fast," said Cartier in a hurry.

After ransacking the place, the girls found the safe in the back. They locked the doors and dimmed the lights. Kola went and pulled the car around to the back door and they used a dolly to haul the safe out of the salon under the cover of darkness. It took all three of them to lift it and place it into the trunk. After that, they went back into the salon and wiped away their prints and whatever they touched, it left with them in a plastic bag. They took the surveillance footage and left Nikki's body sprawled across the floor in the middle of her shop.

36

pple took the first shift in following around Scar's mistress around town. She rode in an unassuming Ford and wore old jeans, a bad wig, and a baseball cap as she followed Scar's mistress to work, to the mall, and various other places.

The girls took turns, and Cartier had the late shift.

That night, Scar's mistress exited her home looking glamorous in a tight red dress and a pair of high heels. She climbed into her Audi and sped off. Cartier was close behind. Twenty minutes later, she followed the girl to a nightclub in South Beach called Twist.

From the car, Cartier observed the woman strut into the nightclub, and then she made the call to Apple and Kola.

The girls entered Twist separately. Twist was a large club on Collins Avenue with a long black bar and many VIP areas, and there was a large gold couch in the middle of the club. The music was techno and disco, and the trio noticed that the girls were dressed extravagantly in dresses and gowns, and their faces were beat. Men and women were mingling, but there was something off about the place. The disco lights flashed and there were a few men vogueing in the middle of the dance floor.

"What the fuck is this place?" Apple questioned.

When a couple took to the stage to sing a Gloria Estefan song, it was then that they all realized that they were in a drag queen club. Seeing Scar's mistress up close, they realized that *she* was a *he*—and he was transitioning.

It was a what-the-fuck moment. All three of them were completely in shock. Was Scar gay?

As the night progressed, Kola and Cartier started a conversation with one of the male bartenders who had a penchant for gossiping. Most of the women inside Twist were transgender—in the process of adding and removing a few body parts like Bruce Jenner. They were still shocked to find out that Scar was fucking a man—a man who was in the process of becoming a woman.

It was ironic.

But they weren't there to criticize his sexual lifestyle. They were there to plot against him and kill him. The girls were keenly focused on his mistress, whose name they found out was Christy. Christy was a popular bitch inside the club, knowing lots of people and looking like the life of the party.

They followed Christy to the bathroom. Once inside, Cartier approached the mistress with some minor aggression, thrusting a small pistol into her side and demanding her attention.

"We need to talk, Christy," Cartier growled at her.

"How do you know my name?"

"Bitch, does that matter?"

"What do y'all want?"

Cartier had rehearsed a different approach. With brute force she was supposed to strong arm Christy into helping them. But for some reason her gut told her otherwise. "We need to talk about the nigga you're fucking," Cartier said, making eye contact with Kola.

"Scar?"

"Bingo, bitch!"

"So you're Citi."

"So you know about me?"

Christy exhaled. Here comes the drama. And at her second job too. It was messy, and Christy hated messy. She never set out to be a mistress but, somehow, she always was. The list of girlfriends and wives that showed up at her doorstep was endless. Christy knew that Citi was dangerous and not just a female with a slick mouth. She had to tread carefully.

"Can we go somewhere quiet to talk? Please let me explain."

The four women exited the club through the back door into a small alley. To most, it would have been intimidating, but Apple, Cartier, and Kola weren't the least bit unnerved. Christy walked ahead. "There's a small café on the corner."

They followed her to the quaint café and took a corner booth. There Christy tried to explain that she didn't know Scar had a girl when they met, it wasn't her fault that he was cheating—all the shit other women spit when busted.

Cartier snapped, "I don't care 'bout all that."

Christy swallowed hard. "I understand. And I am sorry. I promise I won't see him anymore."

"Do you know what he did to my brother?"

Christy nodded.

"He can't get away wit' that shit."

"What do you mean?"

"You know what I mean."

Apple and Kola didn't interject. They liked where Cartier was going with this, and they could clearly see that Scar must have told Christy enough stories about Citi to spook her.

"What are you asking me to do? I don't understand."

"Scar has to answer for tryin' to assassinate my brother. He continually crosses the line wit' his fuckin' temper, and he has to be put down."

Christy looked at the pretty girl and couldn't imagine having to sleep next to the man who tried to kill your brother.

"Does he beat you?" Christy asked out of the blue.

Cartier didn't know how to answer. Apple did a slight head nod and Cartier replied, "All the time. The nigga is always laying hands on me. He hates strong women. Even after all I did for Scar—the car he drives, the money he tricks on bitches—that's all me."

"Well, he's not doing any tricking over here. I can promise you that."

"What?" All three girls said at once. And then they began laying on the compliments thick.

"A pretty woman like you?" Cartier asked.

"He should be making it rain on you," said Kola.

"His ugly ass should feel honored to be wit' a queen like you," stated Apple.

Christy drank in all the compliments and beamed. Her face lit up like Christmas lights. She expected the elephant in the room to be addressed. She expected all type of homophobic epithets and xenophobic slurs.

"He beats me too," Christy said, embarrassed. "I feel like I need to confess something."

"What's that?" asked Cartier.

"I'm transgender."

"You're what?" Cartier and the twins feigned shock. "Are you serious? I can't tell."

Again, she blushed. "I am. It's true. Scar didn't know at first. But when it was time for us to get intimate I had to tell him. He was down, but afterwards he got angry and severely beat on me, screaming that he wasn't a faggot. I wanted to call the cops, but he threatened my life."

"And then what?"

"And then I healed and he came back around for more."

"More pussy?" Cartier asked.

"More something. I haven't had my surgery. It's so expensive, but I'm saving up. That's why I'm working two jobs. Here at Twist and also Floss.

I'm going to be a full woman one day. There's nothing on this earth that I want more."

The girls could listen to Christy talk forever. Her voice was sultry and melodic. And she had a beauty queen face.

"How much does it cost?" Cartier asked.

"Well, my gender reassignment surgeon charges sixty-two thousand, and that includes three days in recovery. I've saved nearly seven."

"Great. At that rate it'll only take another five to ten years," Cartier said. "I could help with that."

Christy's interest was piqued. But she didn't want any blood spilled for her cause. She shook her head. "There's my surgery and then there's murder. It's not an even exchange."

Well, damn. She got to the point.

"I don't want you to murder Scar, Christy. I need you to allow me to do what I do."

"And then?"

"And then you walk away with fifty thousand and never look back."

Christy was silent and then she spoke. "Could you ladies give me a day or two to think this through?"

Apple was about to object when Cartier spoke first, "Yes! Absolutely. But, Christy. I promise if you tell Scar about this meeting he will kill you. He will do you just as he did Cane. His paranoia will tell him that you're no longer trustworthy and he'll empty his clip in your beautiful face."

Christy's eyes widened.

"Don't look shocked. You know what I've said is true. He's a maniac."

Satisfied that their plot to assassinate Scar was coming along, the girls exited the café separately. They moved from the area to the car in stealth. There was no telling who was watching them. It was a dangerous game they were playing.

***

With their scheme to go after Scar in motion, the girls now wanted to try and open the safe from Nikki's shop. Kola suspected that the contents would be rewarding once it was opened. The girls tried everything to get it open, from renting a blowtorch to Googling, *how to open a safe*, and watching a string of YouTube videos on safe cracking. They even bought a stethoscope and tried to listen for the right clicks—but to no benefit. It was becoming infuriating.

Finally, Cartier came up with the idea to hire a professional—someone from Craigslist. A day later, they met a Tyrone Kenny in a parking lot of a local supermarket. He was a mild looking and thin man wearing spectacles. He met with Cartier and Apple, and they made him leave his phone in his car just in case he had a tracking device for a setup.

Tyrone climbed into the backseat of the girls' car, while Kola followed them in a separate car for backup.

The girls took Tyrone to a storage facility on the outskirts of the city, where they kept the safe. Inside, they quietly watched the man remove the tools he needed to operate from his bag, and then he went to work like a skilled surgeon in the operating room. He talked a lot, though, and he asked a lot of questions—questions that sometimes made the girls uncomfortable.

"So, where are y'all girls from?" he asked. And, "This is a really nice safe. Where did it come from? What do you think is inside?"

"Just do your damn job," Apple scoffed.

He took no offense to her bluntness. He focused on his job, and within fifteen minutes, it was open. The girls hurriedly looked inside, and they weren't disappointed. There were bundles of cash stacked over each other—about ninety thousand dollars, Apple believed. Not bad. Even Tyrone was taken aback by the contents.

"Damn," he uttered.

Cartier tossed him five grand for his services, but the money came with a warning. "You didn't see shit, right?"

He winked. "What is there to see?"

She smiled.

Loading the cash into a bag, they exited the storage unit and climbed back into their car, dropping Tyrone back off where they'd picked him up. They were glad that they didn't have to kill him.

Back at their hotel, the girls divided the cash and sparked up some weed and drank champagne. They had a reason to celebrate. They were winning. They killed Nikki and stole ninety grand from her. They connected with Christy and she agreed to think about setting Scar up, and they had robbed numerous trap houses in Miami that belonged to Citi and stolen a heap of cash and drugs from her.

They blasted music, they smoked, drank, and sang, making their place like their own private nightclub. The only thing missing from their personal party was niggas—some good dick. The girls had been so busy robbing, killing, and plotting, that they didn't have time for men or sex.

It was good times tonight, and then Cartier's burner phone rang. It was Christy calling her.

"Hey, turn that shit down. This is her," she told Apple and Kola.

"What's up, Christy?"

"Hello, Citi. This is Christy."

"Yes, I know. What's up?"

"I've been thinking about our conversation—"

"Not over the phone. Do you want to meet?"

"Yes."

"Will it be worth my time?"

"Yes, I think so."

***

Cartier and Christy met for lunch at The Zodiac in Bel Harbour. It was located in Neiman Marcus and chosen because the area was densely populated and cameras were everywhere. Apple and Kola hung back, taking a table toward the back of the restaurant—far enough to be out of sight, but close enough should anything pop off.

Cartier got straight to the point. "So will you help us?"

"Maybe . . ."

Cartier shifted in her seat. She was desperately trying to keep her cool. "What's it gonna take to change that into a definitely?"

"Some reassurances," said Christy. "I don't want to move forward in my life only to have detectives knock on my front door two years later."

"That won't happen."

Christy nodded. "So you can see into the future?"

"No, but I can make a conclusion based on my past track record."

"That doesn't do much for me."

The waitress came and took their orders. Both women ordered garden salads and sparkling water.

Christy continued, "What's your plan to get away with murder?"

Is she serious? "You tell us when Scar is at your crib, we come in, kill him, and we all live happily ever after."

"Will you remove his body?"

No, bitch. Because you're going to be dead right next to him. "Of course we will. We're professionals."

"And what about clean-up? Blood splatter? DNA? I can't actually hire someone for that."

Cartier cut her eyes. "We'll make sure he's on a tarp. It won't be messy at all."

Christy locked eyes with Cartier and said, "Yeah, you can go through all that trouble, or we can do it my way."

"Your way?"

Christy nodded. "I've given this a lot of thought, and if Scar has to die, then I want him to die for a cause."

Cartier was perplexed. She took a large gulp of her sparkling water and just said, "You have sixty seconds to get the point, or I'm walkin' out of this bitch. You've tried my patience long enough. This is murder. We're not studying for the fuckin' bar exam."

Christy saw Cartier's dark side, and she didn't like it. She began, "Florida is a tricky state, lots of controversial laws, legislation that are on and not on the books yet. When Scar comes to my home, I think he should be killed at my front doorstep, not inside—therefore, no blood seeping through my newly installed hardwood flooring. He should be shot with my registered pistol, and you and your friends should immediately exit my place while I call the police to report the incident."

"Are you stupid?"

"I assure you, Citi, I am anything but. I have an MBA and plan to return to the corporate world as a full woman once my reassignment operation is complete."

"So what's this about?"

"It's about getting a discrimination law passed in Florida for the LGBTQ community. We're still not represented as equals in this state, and I feel that this shooting, coupled with the controversial Stand Your Ground law, will shed light on phobias, hate, bigotry—everything my community experiences. Scar beat the shit out of me when he found out that I was a man. Each time we would have sex he would verbally and physically be abusive, yet he liked what I had to offer. There is a lot of shame attached to people who look like me—who are different, who don't fit societal norms. Scar will be someone who committed a hate crime against a transgender woman. If the ADA tries me for his murder—which I can assure you the grand jury will never allow, then I will be acquitted."

"Hold up." Cartier couldn't believe her ears. "You *want* to get caught?"

"I want to get caught for a cause. National news will certainly pick up this story because all involved; police, ADA, DA, and legal counsel will want their five seconds of fame. The spotlight will be on me to make a statement, and when I do, I will be ready."

Cartier shook her head. "This is too risky. What if you don't get off?"

"Sweetheart, this if Florida. We all get off."

"But what if you're the exception? We can't take the risk of this blowing back on us when you start snitching."

"What would I say? A shadowy female named Citi coerced me into killing the man we shared with my own gun? And then told me to use the Stand Your Ground law to my advantage and manipulate the public into thinking that this was a hate crime?"

"I see what you sayin'. It's a stretch, but it doesn't mean that someone won't believe you."

"Look, let me worry about that. I'm telling you I can pull this off as long as you keep up your end of the deal. You use my gun to kill Scar. I can't do it. I'm not a killer. I also get that money for my surgery, and I don't want to sound greedy or ungrateful, but could you throw in a little extra in case I have to hire an attorney? I give you my word if I don't have to then the money is yours to come back and get. I won't spend a dime."

"There's still one thing you didn't think of."

"What's that?" Christy asked.

"His goons. He rides two, three cars deep. We can't kill him outside or else we're all dead."

Christy smiled. "He only brings them on my block if he comes through during the day. When he comes for late night booty calls he comes alone. We have a neighborhood watch and they called the cops on more than one occasion on the unidentified vehicles and suspicious black males."

Cartier exhaled. She had to admit that Christy's convoluted plan was bold, risky, and took great courage. She would do all that for equality.

Cartier looked at the beauty and admired her. She was on board, but she had to clear this with Apple. It was her money. "I'll speak wit' my brother and if he's good then I'll have your back."

The two finalized the last details of the plan and hoped for the best.

Apple and Kola responded better than Cartier initially had. Immediately they got it. They read the news and knew all about the tribulations the LGBTQ community went through. Even the latest bathroom controversy was up for debate. If you're a transgender male fully reassigned you still had to use the men's room. What kind of fuckery was that?

There is one thing, though," Apple acknowledged. "I didn't plan on paying this bitch and we also said that we trust no one."

"What does she know about us? She thinks I'm Citi. And when this is over we'll be over a thousand miles away."

"And the money?"

"Apple, this is for Nick too. He left you a million dollars and if you have to give ten percent to get at the nigga who is the reason he's in the ground, then that's a no brainer."

Apple felt like being a stubborn bitch.

"And I'll chip in," said Cartier.

"Me too," said Kola. "I like her. You know, Apple, that I'm a feminist so let's bless her."

Apple grinned. "Today must be throwback Thursday because I'm feelin' like the old Apple who use to give a fuck 'bout people."

***

"He called. He's coming to see me late tonight," Christy informed Cartier.

"A'ight, what time?"

"After midnight," she said.

It was the golden opportunity that they needed.

"Okay, we'll be there soon. And, Christy, don't fuck this up or don't fuck with us. We're about our word and you better be about yours," Cartier sternly warned her.

"Believe me, I am. I'm ready," Christy said.

Cartier ended the call. It was time to take out Citi's most notorious killer, and the head of the muscle to her organization.

37

Though Miami was warm year-round, tonight it felt like the Devil was breathing on the southern city just for fun. But a heat wave wasn't going to stop the trio from executing their plan against Scar. He had gotten lucky far too many times, and tonight, they were confident that his winning streak would end.

The girls arrived at Christy's home hours before midnight to set a trap for Scar. A key was left in her mailbox for entry. As planned, Christy was at club Twist making an appearance. She needed as many patrons and transgender performers as possible to see her.

"Pattie, will you take my next slot? I'm going to head home early tonight."

Pattie was six-four, 210 pounds and, as no shock, loved to perform Patti LaBelle songs.

"Are you okay, pumpkin? You not feeling well?"

"I'm fine." Christy looked around and shook her head. "I think I've spotted someone in the audience. A real creepy looking male. I think he's been following me."

"What?" Pattie clutched imaginary pearls and continued, "Let's let security know and kick his ass out!"

"No, no. I would just rather go home. Not in the mood for any drama tonight. And I'm tired."

Pattie nodded. "Well let me walk you to your car."

"I'm good. Besides, I have this." Christy flashed her licensed pistol. "Go get ready for your set. I'll see you tomorrow."

Christy hurried back to her home, where Apple was inside waiting. She was taken aback, slightly, because she expected to see the other girl.

"Where's Citi?" she wanted to know.

"Don't worry, she's outside. I'm the one who's going to handle it from this end."

"You?" Christy wasn't sure she was a match against Scar. The other girl looked more intimidating. Apple noticed her reservation.

"Christy, I got this. Just relax."

"Have you done this before?"

Christy became visibly shaken. *What am I doing? Why did I trust them?* They switched up the plan, and when you do that things go wrong.

"Do you need a drink to calm ya fuckin' nerves? You makin' a bitch jumpy."

Christy made her way to the kitchen. "I could use one. You?"

"I'm on the job, remember?"

The hours went by and the night grew later. Apple was to remain hidden in Christy's home while Kola and Cartier would stand guard outside and keep an eye out for Scar's arrival. They had to be extremely careful to not alert the neighborhood watch. Midnight had come and gone. It was a nerve-wracking situation. Going after Scar was dangerous, and the tables could easily turn.

At a quarter to one, a car turned the corner onto the block and slowly approached the home. Kola and Cartier were crouched low inside a non-descript Toyota. They watched the headlights approach and come to a stop in front of Christy's house. A man other than Scar climbed out of the

Denali. He was alone. He looked around the area for a moment and then got back into the vehicle and drove away.

"You think he's a scout?" Cartier asked.

"I don't know . . . maybe. But that's new. She said Scar always came alone at night," Kola said. "You think she's trying to set us up?"

"If so, she's dead."

Cartier and Kola became extra cautious. Kola called Apple on her phone and informed her about the Denali. They had no idea who the person was and weren't sure if it was a coincidence or not.

"If we don't kill this dude tonight, then I'm convinced he's a fuckin' cockroach. He can't die," Kola said.

"We'll get him." Cartier was confident of that.

Ten minutes after one, Christy's cell phone rang. It was Scar calling. She answered. "Hey, sexy . . . where are you?"

"I'll be there soon," Scar said.

"I'm waiting for you."

"A'ight." He hung up.

Apple watched Christy's every move and kept her .45 close. She wouldn't hesitate to kill Scar and Christy too if the whole thing went against her. She was determined to leave that residence alive—no matter what. But she couldn't jump the gun. She didn't know what to expect when Scar came walking to that front door expecting a tryst with his transgender bitch.

At about 1:30, a black SUV slowly approached the house and came to a stop in the front. Kola and Cartier went on alert across the street. They watched Scar climb out of the driver's side door. Clad in all black, he was an imposing figure in the dark, and he was careful. They noticed the pistol in his hand, ready for action just in case something went wrong.

"Damn," Cartier muttered.

This was it—game time.

Kola got on the horn and contacted Apple. "He's outside and he's packing," she quickly said.

Apple jumped into action. She tucked her .45 and grabbed Christy's registered pistol.

"You ready?"

Christy exhaled. "I am."

"Remember, I got back-up outside," she reminded Christy.

She nodded.

Right after, the doorbell sounded, followed by hard knocking. It was time.

It took all of five seconds for Apple to swing open the front door, outstretch her arm, and train her pistol on Scar's forehead.

Scar and Apple locked eyes. He shouted, "Oh shit!" and he immediately sprung into action to try and defend himself. He lifted his pistol, but it was too late.

Bak! Bak!

Apple wanted to empty her clip into him, but she had to make it realistic. Scar's body dropped and she quickly handed the gun to Christy. "Shoot, bitch!"

Apple made her escape out the back door.

Christy shot wildly in the air so she could have the gunshot residue on her hands. She didn't want to look down but she did. Scar had fallen on his side. His body was twisted, and his eyes were closed, blood pooling around his head. The monster was dead.

✳✳✳

Back at the duplex the girls were feeling some kind of way. The murder of Scar was anticlimactic. Apple felt like he deserved a better kill.

"I feel you on that," Cartier agreed. "This nigga was one of the best that ever did it. He deserved to be captured, tortured, taunted, and gruesomely murdered."

"Facts!" Apple continued. "Yo, even though I got to get up close and squeeze off two to his fuckin' dome for my nigga, I still wanted more! I wanted him to know he got beat by bitches! Nick's bitch!"

Kola listened to Apple and Cartier go on and on before she finally spoke. "At first, I felt some kinda way too. Driving back I had this feeling I couldn't shake and I thought it had something to do with dude. What I'm feelin' don't got shit to do with him. This emptiness inside is because I lost my son. Whether we killed Scar slow or quick, at the end of the day he's still dead. So is it ego right now, Apple? You mad that Christy gets credit for your handiwork? You still need ya name ringing out? Still thinkin' you the baddest bitch?"

Apple was confused. What the fuck did she do?

"Bitch, I'm the baddest chick from South Beach to South America!"

"People only know ya name 'cause you my sister! There is no Apple without Kola!" Kola beat her chest for emphasis.

"Ladies, ladies . . . let's not do this tonight," said Cartier. "This shit ain't over yet. We still got two more targets and that's enough kills for everyone's ego. But, Kola, you right. I feel what you're saying. I lost my daughter some years back and nothin' will ever fill that hole. So perhaps that emptiness I feel is for my daughter. And, Apple, yours is for Nick."

Apple threw her hands up and said, "All this Dr. Phil shit is pissing me off! I'll see y'all bitches in the morning."

✳✳✳

The next morning, just as expected, the murder of Scar was broadcast on the local news stations. The journalists were cautious in reporting that this was an alleged hate crime. William Edmondson, who was known to many in the transgender community as Christy Valentine, was taken into police custody for questioning as police continued their investigation.

38

Liberty City's Pork 'n' Beans projects were infamous for gangs, drugs, murder, and violence. It was a warm day and the area was busy with residents, hustlers, thugs, and drug fiends—a typical day in the ghetto. A young hustler named Joc Man stood on the dangerous corner in a large white T-shirt, long shorts, and a black and white bandana tied around his head, indicating his gang ties to the Young Gotti Boys.

Joc Man smoked his square on the corner near a stop sign and in close proximity to one of the housing units that belonged to his cousin. He had a pocket full of crack vials to serve the traffic of fiends coming and going. He sold drugs from sunup to sundown. Hustling and the cruel streets of Miami was his life. All he knew was the Pork 'n' Beans projects—all he knew was how to make money and survive on the streets. He worked for his cousin, a shot-caller and dangerous man named Benjamin Knocks. Benjamin Knocks was under the umbrella of Scar's organization, and they received quality narcotics for a reasonable price and flooded the projects with the best. Scar and Citi had united with Benjamin Knocks and executed a business arrangement and a peace treaty with him. Everyone wanted to make some money.

But Scar's sudden death was shaking things up in Miami, and everything seemed to be falling apart for Citi. The streets were talking about a notorious crew at large who was robbing trap houses and getting away with hundreds of thousands of dollars. Drug crews became alert and stepped up security and their guns, not wanting to be next.

It was even rumored that it was a pack of bitches who were brazenly committing these robberies across Miami.

Bitches . . . unbelievable, many thought.

Joc Man took a few pulls from his cigarette and gazed at one of his associates approaching from his left. A man named Dipped greeted him with dap and joined him on the block.

"What's it lookin' like?" Dipped asked.

"It's quiet right now," Joc Man said.

"You got another cig?" he asked.

Joc Man reached into his shorts pockets, pulled out his dwindling pack of Newports, and handed one to Dipped. The man lit up and they stood there talking and selling crack.

As Joc Man talked, he looked across the street and noticed a young fiend approaching them. Felicia was grotesquely thin with her matted black hair in constant disarray. The streets and the hard drugs took away her beauty and her educated life long ago. She had become one of Joc Man's regulars. She eagerly marched toward the two men in a pair of stained and tattered basketball shorts, a frayed wife-beater, and worn flip-flops. It was the uniform of a ten-year addiction to crack and other hardcore drugs.

While approaching the two men, she displayed her toothless smile. Her main concern was getting high, all day and every day. Her fiendish black eyes were fixed on Joc Man and Dipped, and she clutched a wrinkly twenty dollar bill in her fist—money she made by prostituting herself to whoever would take her.

"Joc Man, I'm sick right now," she said.

"What you need?"

"Give me two."

He nodded. "Follow me."

He didn't want to sell on the open street. Too many eyes were around and probably watching. He led Felicia to the back of one of the project units in the cut and reached into his pockets and handed her what she needed. The transaction was speedy. Felicia had what she yearned for, and she pivoted in haste and marched away, ready to bless her day with her needed treatment.

Joc Man walked back to the area where Dipped was now chatting on his cell phone. The moment Joc Man reached him, a burgundy mini-van rounded the corner and came to a stop right where the two men stood. The back door quickly slid open, and Joc Man and Dipped found themselves staring down the barrel of a MAC-10. Two masked figures leaped from the vehicle, one gripping a baseball bat and the second a handgun. Joc Man and his friend stood there wide-eyed and frozen in fear. They had been caught off guard.

One of the attackers swung the baseball bat at Joc Man and struck him in the chest with it. Joc Man curled over from the hard blow that took the breath out of him. All of a sudden, he found himself immobile from the pain. The second masked figure attacked Dipped with the handgun, brutally pistol whipping him right there on the street corner. The attack on Dipped left him with a broken nose and a fractured eye-socket. He collapsed to the pavement while they grabbed Joc Man and tossed him into the mini-van.

The vehicle sped off with Joc Man inside and left Dipped lying barely conscious on the street.

While the driver raced away from the scene, Joc Man had a Glock 19 pushed into his face. He could damn near see the bullet in the chamber.

"Your cousin's stash house—we want the location," they said to him.

Joc Man scowled and remained stubborn. "Fuck you!" he cursed.

"You wanna play it like that, muthafucka!" cursed the person holding the gun.

The butt of the pistol immediately went smashing against his face several times, spewing blood and nearly knocking him out.

"Say 'fuck me' again, nigga, and see what happens," the gunman threatened him.

The van continued to drive in haste and Joc Man was angry.

"Your cousin's stash house—we want the fuckin' location," the man repeated.

Joc Man remained silent and stubborn. With his face coated with blood, he continued to stare at the person, fuming.

"Talk, muthafucka! You wanna die right now?" another figure uttered impatiently.

He remained silent.

"He ain't gonna talk," the driver exclaimed.

"Fuck yeah, he is," replied the gunman with the Glock.

Joc Man could barely see because of the thick blood coating his face. His entire face felt broken and on fire. He wanted to remain loyal to his cousin, Benjamin Knocks, but it was more out of fear than loyalty. He didn't want to be the one to give up the location for fear of what his cousin would do to him if he found out. But his hands were tied, and he found himself between a rock and a hard place.

The gunman was growing impatient. The dangerous figure thrust the Glock into Joc Man's crotch and made it clear to him what was about to come next.

"I'm gonna blow your fuckin' dick off in five . . . four . . . three . . . two—"

"Okay. I'll take you there," Joc Man screamed out.

It was what they wanted to hear. They restrained him with duct-tape around his wrists and ankles.

The driver hurried to the location in North Miami that Joc Man gave them. The area wasn't quite the suburbs, but it wasn't the ghetto either—

more in-between. The house was unassuming with a driveway that led to a carport, and a chain-link fence surrounded the property. The driver rolled by slowly, and everyone fixed their eyes on the home.

"We move in tonight," said the figure with the Glock.

For hours, they held Joc Man hostage. It was that time—go in and out, put on a show of extreme acts of violence, and beat down or kill everything inside. It was the way Apple, Kola, and Cartier did things—quick, violent, and careful—and always having each other's backs. They were putting a hurting on Citi's organization via intel and violence.

With Joc Man still bound and subdued inside the van, the trio knew that they needed to move quickly. Word had surely gotten out about his abduction at the Pork 'n' Beans projects, and their window of opportunity was closing.

The mini-van parked on the block, and the masked trio exited the van along with Floco. Floco had been up North for a beat to bury his cousin and console his family. The girls hardly missed him with everything that had been going on, but they were glad he rejoined the team because they could always use an additional shooter.

There were several surveillance cameras attached to the house, but no men outside. It was risky to charge in blind, but they were used to taking risks. Like so many times before, they were attacking Citi where it hurt the most, her money and product.

Floco charged toward the front door with a sawed-off shotgun in his hands. Apple and Kola clutched matching MAC-10's, and Cartier gripped a Desert Eagle. They had enough firepower to wipe out a block. Everyone was clad in Kevlar vests and all black.

Floco's shotgun was their key inside. Hurriedly, they ascended onto the property in the dark and Floco aimed at the weak points at the front door. Apple gave him the green light. They moved like they were the police—tight, organized, and fast. The plan was to fuck everyone up with sudden confusion and take them out.

Chk-Chk—Boom!

The front door blasted open and they stampeded inside with gunfire erupting. Right away, two men were gunned down in the living room by the MAC-10's. Cartier charged deeper into the house, and Floco went toward the kitchen with the sawed-off. More gunfire erupted as they spread through the house looking for victims.

One poor male had his face completely blown off by the sawed-off, and his blood pooled so deeply against the tile floor that someone could have drowned in it. Another victim was cut down by Cartier in the hallway, and the final target was found in the bedroom. He stood there wide-eyed at the terror happening around him. He was defenseless and he was immediately assaulted, and then he was asked by Floco, "Where it at?"

He breathed heavily. He was about to fly into a full-blown panic attack. His cronies were all dead. The masked man pointed the shotgun at his chest, threatening to put a basketball sized hole in him if he wanted to be naïve or stubborn.

He pointed to the closet and told them they could find more product and cash in the second bedroom, under the floor and behind the walls. Right away, the girls tore into the spots and found what they were looking for. The last man alive was no longer needed.

"Please don't kill me, man. I ain't gonna say shit! I promise you that!"

The nigga he begged and pleaded to wasn't listening. He was there to send a cruel message to Citi and her peoples on the trio's behalf—her time was up, and they were coming for her.

The shotgun exploded—*Boom!* The hot shells tore open his chest and sent his body flying across the room and slamming into the wall. His blood splattered everywhere. Floco smirked at his gory handiwork and uttered to the dead, "Yeah, I know you won't say shit now."

They got what they'd come for—kilos and cash—and they made a speedy exit from the stash house, leaving a horrific mess behind. They hurried into the van and sped away. There was one man still alive, Joc Man. He already knew what went down. He knew about their reputation and he knew his fate was coming.

A few miles away from the crime scene, Apple shot Joc Man point-blank in the head execution style, and they dumped his body on the side of the road. The message was sent. They weren't going to stop until Citi and everything she owned and loved was destroyed.

After Scar's murder, things began to quickly unravel for Citi. She was being attacked from everywhere. The trio continued their violent onslaught and then dissension between Citi's men started to ensue.

It was only a matter of time before it all fell apart for Citi and Cane. With Scar dead, many saw it as their opportunity for a come-up. Miami became a free-for-all of murder and violence. The streets were treacherous and it was becoming a vicious dog-eat-dog world out there.

***

The stolen RAV4 hybrid gripped the bumpy terrain effortlessly. Kola was at the wheel and Cartier and Apple rode with her in the creeping hours of the night, just past 4 a.m.

"We do this shit quick and then bounce," said Kola.

"Ever since you got down here you actin' like you runnin' shit," Apple replied.

Cartier was going to jump in and try to defuse the situation, but she was tired of playing referee. Since they were teenagers they'd always had this competition going. Both were competitive, and Cartier couldn't keep wasting her breath mediating.

"Bitch, you lucky I came!"

"Nobody asked you to, though."

"Keep talkin' shit and I'll head up 95 North tonight."

"Bye, bitch. You think I need you!"

"You gonna always need me!"

Finally the car came to a rolling stop. Cartier swung the door open before the vehicle was in park, which indicated that she was over their bullshit. She walked around to the trunk, which Kola popped.

Apple came around and helped Cartier pull out two heavy trash bags.

"Can we leave it here?" asked Cartier.

"I don't see why not. Ain't nobody diggin' graves. This ain't the movies."

Cartier nodded.

Both got back in the car and Kola drove them back to the duplex.

In the morning a golden retriever would find the corpses of Miranda Alvarez and Fred "Floco" Jackson. The trio was tying up loose ends.

39

Miami was a place Citi once called her paradise, but now it was becoming her personal hell. Every day she would receive some bad news—one of her men killed, another stash house robbed, a police raid here and there, and civil war inside her organization. All of her worst fears were coming true.

Many saw Citi as weak without Scar around. Many wanted to claim the throne for themselves. Day by day, the amount of soldiers and money was greatly dwindling. She was losing control, the flood gates had opened, and there was no containing the water rushing from the dam. The crack was widening and unfolding into chaos, and Citi saw no way of stopping it. She felt helpless. Her days felt numbered and it was inevitable that they would soon come for her.

Cane joined her on the terrace. He was finally released from the hospital and he wasn't in great shape. His body moved differently; wearily and broken. Citi continued to stare off in the distance, looking detached from the world around her. As her concentration was fixed on the moon and heavens, she uttered faintly, "How did this happen? What the fuck did we do? They're not gonna stop, Cane. They're gonna keep on coming for us."

"We need to leave this place, Citi. It ain't safe here for you or me."

She sighed heavily. She tried to stay strong, but she was gradually breaking within. She finally looked at her brother and said, "What would

Dad do? He was always strong. He taught us to survive and taught us to stay on top—to stay strong, because he was strong until the end. I feel we disappointed him, Cane. Look at us. We're running."

Cane frowned. He hated to run, but the walls were closing in around them. No matter where they turned, there was always going to be a threat gunning for them, either from within their own ranks or from outside.

And now the police were investigating their crumbling organization. The violence, the shootings, and murderous home invasions that the trio was committing across Miami had stirred up a hornets' nest, and the authorities were fed up. Politicians took to the media to lash out at the rising crime and the thugs. The mayor made a harsh statement to the public about fighting crime and executing justice—and he proclaimed that his city would no longer be torn apart by murderous thugs, drug cartels, and violent crimes. Their city was looking bad to the nation, and they refused to have Miami look like the violent 80's again. The sudden violence would scare away the tourists, and that was money lost—taxes and income gone. The city put together a task force to bring to justice those responsible for the sudden bloodshed, the drugs, and violent robberies.

Citi had to turn off the television. It felt like the mayor of Miami was talking to her. She had come down to Miami with an agenda—get money, get rich, survive, and live a life of luxury. But now there was no more life of luxury. There was no more power and glory. Every day was about her survival, moving carefully, and hoping to one day rebuild.

"Pops is dead, Citi, and he's been dead for a long time now," Cane replied.

"Do you think about him?"

"Why? Life moves on, dead or not."

Citi was upset to hear her brother say that. They were all once very close to their father. Curtis Byrne was once a man everybody respected. He had it all—money, good looks, beautiful kids, and respect. When his demise came, Citi and her brothers didn't have a choice but to continue where their father had left off. It was their way of keeping his memory alive. Now Citi felt she'd let him down—tarnished his legacy.

"This ain't gonna be the end of us, sis—best believe that shit," Cane said wholeheartedly.

She didn't respond to his statement. She just stood there and looked at the sky. She did her best to fight back the tears. It was hard. She didn't want to look weak, even though she was with her brother and they were alone.

"What next?" she finally said.

"Like I said, we need to leave here and go someplace else. And not New York. I have to fully recuperate," he uttered with disdain in his voice, thinking about how Scar fucked him up.

"But that's our fuckin' home, Cane."

She remembered not too long ago he was preaching a different sermon. Now it was "Fuck Miami" and "Fuck New York."

It was odd, she felt.

"I need a damn drink," said Citi.

She turned and went back into the penthouse. The place was too still and quiet. There was no one around—no goons to protect them, no muscle, no associates—just Cane and Citi, standing alone in a big penthouse on South Beach.

Citi poured herself a shot of Grey Goose and guzzled it. Another one was poured and that was guzzled too. She heaved a sigh. It still felt unreal to her; she'd lost so much in such a short period of time.

"We ain't got time for this, sis. The longer we stay here, the more we put our lives in danger," Cane warned her.

"I know," she quietly replied.

For good measure, Cane carried three pistols, each one loaded and cocked back. He would do anything to protect his baby sister.

"Let's get the fuck outta here," he said impatiently.

"And go where? Huh? We can't stay here. You don't wanna go back home!"

"I don't have time for this. Let's go to the bungalow and we can figure things out. Our next move."

She followed him out the door. She would never look back. That place would quickly be forgotten. The siblings took the elevator down to the lobby, and the entire time, Cane kept a .45 in his hand and by his side. Every step they took was a risky and dangerous one.

They moved through the underground garage and Cane hurried his sister into the passenger seat of the Tahoe and jumped into the driver's seat. Gun on his lap, he started the vehicle. To say that they were nervous was an understatement. Not only did they have to worry about Apple and her crew, but other rival crews too.

Cane steered the SUV out of the parking garage and onto the public street. His head was on a constant swivel. If anyone moved wrong, Cane was going to light them up. But so far, the coast was clear. He pushed his foot against the accelerator and drove off into the night. There would be no turning back, only moving forward.

As Cane drove away from the building, Citi took a deep breath and exhaled, and then a few tears trickled from her eyes. She tried to hold everything in for the longest, refusing to cry or show any weakness, but it was difficult. The pain of losing so much was heavy on her.

"We gonna be a'ight, sis. I promise you that," Cane said.

She wanted to believe him.

40

The Tahoe approached the ratty rented bungalow thirty minutes from the city. It was where Citi and Cane had been hiding out for several weeks. The place wasn't luxurious, but it was safe and it was comfortable. The bungalow was organized so that bedrooms were on one side and the kitchen and living and dining room were on the other side. There was an attached garage and a few neighbors, but the area was quiet and in the cut.

When given the chance, Cane would drive out for food and supplies. He did whatever he needed to do to keep them safe. Each room had a gun stashed, and they kept themselves isolated from neighbors. Their days spent at the bungalow were mundane and monastic. For Citi, it was like a nightmare. From riches to rags, from power and glory to feeling like she was on the run and a failure. They had no money and no men, no control or clout. Their fall from grace was fast and it was humiliating.

Citi barely left the place, choosing to spend most of her time either in the bedroom sulking or loitering out back, staring at plants and small animals. She sat there quiet and almost trance-like.

Cane stepped out onto the small porch and said, "I think tomorrow we should gas up the truck and head out—maybe Louisiana or Houston. My body ain't actin' right, Citi. I can't stand for long periods of time. A nigga feelin' weak. Whatever move we gonna make we need to make it now. Let's get a good night's rest and leave at first light."

"Shoulda never came down here," she uttered sadly.

"Did you hear me? Are you even listening? A nigga fucked up. We should have left weeks ago. Those bitches are still out there tearin' up the city. We ain't safe."

"You think I don't know this!"

"You act like you don't. You act like you can't snap outta whatever fog you're in," he hollered.

"So, what's the plan then?" she asked.

"There is no fuckin' plan," Cane proclaimed. "All we need to do is leave! That's it."

The plan sounded simple, but her life wasn't simple. Never had been.

Cane spun around and made his exit, leaving Citi alone. The next morning, to Cane's aggravation, his sister was gone. And so was their vehicle. Cane had a feeling that she could be one of two places, the penthouse or her favorite restaurant. He called a taxi and headed out.

✳✳✳

"I'm gonna fuckin' come!" Citi cried out. "Ugh . . . . Ugh!"

Citi tightly wrapped her legs around Irving, feeling his throbbing dick piston in and out of her like a jackhammer tearing up concrete. She huffed and puffed as Irving fucked her in the missionary position. He fucked her like he missed her, which he did. The two were entangled on her bed like magnets that couldn't be pulled apart—sucking lips and tongues connecting passionately. It was what she needed—great sex.

"I missed you," Irving announced.

"I know you did, baby . . . I'm gonna come!"

It was the one excitement Citi had experienced in weeks. Unbeknownst to Cane, she'd reached out to Irving and brought him back to their bungalow. It was somewhat risky, but she needed to see him. Besides, they were leaving today. Sex with him was uplifting and it was the distraction she needed from her hectic life. Irving agreed to see her eagerly and willingly. He thought that maybe she'd lost interest, but when she'd called him out the blue he was excited and relieved.

As they fucked, their minds became awash with waves of lust. They were losing themselves in each other. It was pure bliss—and maybe it was love.

"Aaaah . . . fuck me, Irving," she cooed.

His big dick was buried in her tight and soft pussy—the best he'd ever had. Citi's arms embraced his body, holding him close as his body twitched and his dick jerked in and out of her with the throbbing and milking motions of her inner walls. He began moaning and groaning—falling into perpetual bliss with his eyes closed and his mouth latched onto her dark, hard nipple.

"Ugh . . . damn . . . ugh," he whimpered like a child. "I'm gonna come, Citi . . ."

"Come in me."

But then his moaning and groaning shifted to a unexpected loud "Ouch! Ouch! What the fuck!"

Their pleasure was suddenly interrupted by Cane standing over them. He had knocked Irving in the back of his head with the pistol.

"What the fuck, Citi?" Cane shouted.

Irving immediately leaped out of the pussy and sprung from the bed in haste. Cane was all over him like flies on shit, trying to knock teeth out of his mouth and put him down violently. He wanted to kill the young boy. Only he couldn't. It was like a grandfather trying to beat down his grandson.

"Who the fuck is this nigga?" Cane screamed, angrily pointing his gun at Irving.

Citi leaped from the bed and threw herself in front of Irving to keep Cane from killing him.

"Stop it!" she screamed.

"What the fuck is you doing, Citi? Are you crazy bringing this nigga here?"

"I needed to see him," she protested.

"He's fuckin' trouble!"

"Cane, put the fuckin' gun down!" Citi shouted.

"I should kill this fool right now," Cane threatened.

Irving stood there bloody and panicking. This wasn't part of the program, and the look in Cane's eyes was menacing. He knew her brother wasn't bluffing.

"Look, I love your sister, man. I ain't come here for that kind of trouble," Irving pleaded.

"You got this fool in this fuckin' crib and in between your fuckin' legs? This clown-ass nigga? I should kill you, nigga."

Citi continued to stand between her brother and Irving. The gun was pointed at her, but she knew Cane wasn't going to shoot her. He would shoot Irving in a heartbeat, though, and she tried to prevent that.

"He could bring trouble back here, Citi."

"He won't, Cane. I promise you that. He won't."

"How you know that?"

She sighed. "I know. He's careful, and I trust him."

Cane still scowled. His arm was still outstretched with the pistol at the end of it. He was itching to blow Irving's brains against the wall behind him. Irving tried to keep his cool and not shit on himself, but staring down the barrel of a loaded .45 was terrifying. He'd never had a gun pointed at him. He wasn't about that life.

"Put the fuckin' gun down, Cane! Stop this shit! He's cool. He's with me and he's not a fuckin' threat!" she shouted.

Cane seethed, looking crazy and possessed. Citi grew concerned—maybe scared, believing his bi-polar disorder was setting in.

"Cane, please. He's cool. I trust him," she pleaded.

Cane stared at them for a moment. His presence was intense. He then exhaled and finally lowered the gun.

"We can't trust anybody," said Cane.

"I got lonely and I missed him."

"We can't fuck up like this, Citi. We got too much at stake for you to be making fuckin' booty calls."

"I know."

Irving felt somewhat relieved, but he knew that he wasn't out the fire yet. As long as Cane still gripped that gun, then he was still in harm's way.

"Get the fuck outta here, nigga!" Cane shouted.

"What? No!" Citi protested.

"You want me to blow his fuckin' head off right now?" Cane angrily countered.

"It's cool, Citi. I'll leave," Irving chimed.

"That's right. Leave, nigga, before I change my mind and take your fuckin' life right now," said Cane.

Irving hurriedly collected his things and got dressed. Cane had him shook. He didn't know that her brother was crazy—a maniac. He was in love with Citi, but he didn't want to lose his life over her.

Defeated, Irving accelerated toward the door with Citi marching right behind him. Cane kept his eyes on Irving, looking like he was still contemplating whether the man should live or die.

Outside, Citi repeatedly apologized to him for her brother's actions.

"I'm sorry, baby. I'm so sorry. We're just going through a lot right now and he's a bit paranoid," she said.

"A bit paranoid? Shit, I never had a gun pointed at me before," he said.

"And it won't happen again," she assured him.

He exhaled. "And we were having so much fun."

She smiled. "We were."

It was obvious that he didn't want to leave, and she didn't want him to go. But Cane was a crazy killer, and Citi didn't want to put Irving's life in danger with her brother being unpredictable. Seeing Irving again brought some normalcy into her world.

The two kissed and said their goodbyes, and Irving took off walking.

41

I t took them weeks to finally track Citi down, with the help of Christy. Two times a day, her face was splattered across the news as a victim of an apparent hate crime. Scar's mug shots along with his record were scrutinized and dissected. Soon, just as she said, Christy was able to start advocating for equal rights as the transgender community rallied behind her. Her beautiful face and sultry voice mesmerized everyone as she stood near her lawyer, strong and smart. She had the world eating out the palm of her hand.

Frantically, she called Cartier's phone. "We need to meet." Christy felt like someone was watching her, following her from Twist and Floss.

"Maybe it's five-oh. This ain't over until detectives decide whether you're being charged or not. You're still under investigation."

"She doesn't feel like the authorities. I can see her glaring from the driver's seat, and I'm a little worried. Does Scar have a sister or something I should be worried about?"

"I don't know. But listen, keep going about your business as usual, and we'll look out. You won't know we're there, but we will be."

"You'd do that for me?"

"I just said so, right?"

They hugged, and when Cartier left, the duffel bag she brought with her was transferred to Christy. It contained three times their original deal. Apple, Cartier, and Kola all contributed to the Christy Valentine fund.

Sure enough, what Cartier suspected was true. A distraught Citi would stalk Christy's place of employment. She couldn't believe that Scar would fuck a man. Citi wanted to see her in person, her movements, and then blow her fuckin' brains out. Seeing Christy in person was different than on television. She was tinier and even more feminine and ladylike than the cameras captured. Citi saw her beauty. She was beautiful, classy, and flawless. The trio followed her back to the penthouse and then finally to the bungalow. All they had to do was wait for the right opportunity to strike. The bungalow was the most ideal location because there was no security or surveillance cameras.

Apple, Citi, and Kola watched the property from a distance. When they saw Irving leave the bungalow that night and Citi following him out, observing the two hugging and kissing fervently, the biggest smile came across Apple's face. She grinned like a Cheshire cat.

"There that bitch is," said Apple.

"How you wanna play this?" Cartier asked.

"We go in and take that bitch out—put a fuckin' bullet in her head. There's no other way to do it," said Apple.

"And what about her brother?"

"He's one man. What the fuck he gonna do?" Apple replied.

"One man or not, we still need to be careful," Kola interjected.

Apple couldn't wait any longer. She was itching to strike and execute her revenge. Scar was put down, so she felt Nick could finally rest in peace. Now she couldn't wait to see Citi's face when she and her crew stormed into that house to finally kill her. Apple thought about torturing the bitch first—for hours and hours. Maybe it was too easy to kill her right away. She wanted that bitch to suffer.

The bungalow and the property surrounding it looked feeble and unprotected. There was nothing stopping the trio from charging into the place and creating bloodshed. But Kola advised them not to assume anything. They had to be extra cautious.

"There's nothing more dangerous than a trapped dog in the corner. That's when they get vicious and desperate, and they're gonna make every bite matter," Kola proclaimed.

"She's right," Cartier said.

"We wait another hour or two and continue to watch the place to make sure there aren't any surprises. We came this far. Let's not get sloppy now," Kola suggested.

Apple looked like she was growing impatient. Of the three, she fumed the most. She clenched her fists and gritted her teeth. Her opportunity was only a few feet away, yet, she still had to wait, knowing her sister and Cartier were right. Citi might have one final trick up her sleeve to use against them.

Apple sighed. "This bitch is gonna die slow, I swear," she grumbled.

Each lady had played her role in tearing Miami apart with murder and mayhem. They had become the grim reapers of the city. They were on a mission and so many lives were violently taken because of Citi's act of betrayal against them. The girls had stolen so much money from trap houses and stash houses that they couldn't spend it fast enough.

The plan was to commit this one final murder and then leave the city of Miami—hopefully for good. Things were too hot there. The task force was kicking in doors, making arrests, and trying to bring order back to a city that was spiraling with anarchy. There were rivals crews warring with each other and trying to take control over the drug trade in the city. They desperately wanted to fill the void that was left behind when Lynch was killed. What the trio created was a vacuum effect of mayhem, dystopia, and carnage.

The ladies continued to watch the house. There was no other traffic, only Irving's coming and going. Citi was completely alone besides Cane.

It was after midnight when they decided to make their move against Citi. Each girl wore all black, jeans, and a sweatshirt. Apple cocked back the Smith & Wesson .457, Kola gripped a SW99, and Cartier held onto a 9mm Berretta. They scowled as they climbed out of the car and approached the bungalow like trained soldiers. Their guns were drawn and their awareness was on high. They descended onto the property, moving in the shadows to employ their deadly style of justice.

The house was dark and silent, but that didn't mean everything was going to be simple. The girls moved like they were a tactical assassination team—crouched low, their heads on a constant swivel, and in tight formation, ready to have each other's back.

Reaching the back door, the girls didn't see a threat. There weren't any signs of security and it looked like there would be nothing for them to steal inside. The house was modest and needed some work. The backyard was somewhat disheveled with overgrown grass and shrubs and trees.

Apple took the lead. She grew antsy and lifted her foot and kicked in the feeble looking back door. Her strength came from pure anger and hatred. But the moment the door was forced open, an alarm sounded, breaking the silence of the night. They didn't see that coming. But that didn't stop the girls from charging inside. Their element of surprise was gone. Cane was on to them right away.

"Citi, run!" Cane shouted, and then he fired at them—*Boom! Boom! Boom! Boom!*

The girls immediately returned fire. He continued to strike back, releasing a barrage of bullets at the trio, keeping them trapped in the kitchen. Citi refused to leave her brother and she joined in on the gunfight as bullets were exchanged between the two groups.

Bullets whizzed by Apple's head, splintering the wood behind her and missing her by inches. It was a tight shot, and it was keeping Apple and her girls from moving forward.

Pop! Pop! Pop!

"Fuck!" Apple shouted, crouching behind the partition that separated the kitchen from the living room.

As their guns blazed in the night, the phone rang and the machine picked up. The alarm had alerted the security company and without anyone there to deactivate it, the police were being sent. The trio had no idea this raggedy place had a system. They were clever enough to not have signs. Fuck!

"You fuckin' bitches!" Citi screamed. "Get the fuck out my house!"

"Not before I blow your fuckin' head off, bitch," Apple retorted.

There was more gunfire, and Citi and Cane knew they couldn't hold them off for too long. Apple spun rapidly from her hiding position and took aim with Kola covering her and she released a hail of bullets at the siblings.

Bak! Bak! Bak! Bak! Bak! Bak!

Citi was hit in her leg and she stumbled to the floor, crying out from the pain. Cane saw his sister's injury and went berserk. He lifted sharply to his feet and fired away, but then he suddenly went down with two shots.

What Cane didn't know was that those shots came from his sister. Citi thought that this shootout was confirmation that her brother had been working with the enemy all along. Scar was right! How else did they find her? If she was going to die today, she was taking her brother with her.

"Citi, I'm hit. I'm hit!" he shouted. "Get the fuck outta here, Citi!"

When the trio thought they had their opportunity to end this, Cane wasn't down and out yet, and though he had been shot twice, he still had some fight in him. He maneuvered to his right and continued to shoot wildly at the girls, able to back them into a corner.

Sirens blared in the distance, racing toward the alarm ringing out and the loud gunshots that echoed from the bungalow. The 911 calls were flooding in, and the group was about to have some serious company.

But that didn't stop them from trying to kill each other. They continued to exchange gunfire and Citi was hit again. She held her waist, feeling crippled from the bullets that slammed into her.

"Go! Get out!" Cane continued to shout at his sister.

They were in a losing battle, and the police sirens were growing closer. The girls' window to escape was closing. And though Citi had been shot twice, she was still alive. Apple wanted to put a bullet in between her eyes, but Citi had managed to flee the scene, leaving her brother behind, who continued to defend her until his end. Cartier sprung toward him and ended him, firing four bullets his chest. He collapsed facedown. He was gone.

"We gotta go!" Cartier shouted.

She and Kola were trying to drag Apple out of the residence, but Apple put up some resistance. No way was she going to allow Citi to escape. But the heat was on and more trouble was coming their way—the police.

Apple broke free from their grip and dashed through the house in frantic search for Citi. She saw her blood trail and followed it. Citi had escaped through a bedroom window and Apple climbed out of the same window only to see nothing.

Once outside the house, the girls got separated. Cartier jumped into their getaway vehicle and went looking for the twins. A few blocks from the house, she saw Apple. Apple hurried into the car and then they sped off looking for Kola, who was nowhere to be found.

Immediately, several police cars converged onto the property. Uniformed officers sprung from their cars with their guns drawn. The alarm still sounded and they covered the property in haste, rushing into the house searching for suspects or victims. They only found Cane's body sprawled in the living room with multiple shots.

Apple and Cartier were cautious and afraid. Police were everywhere, they were riding dirty, and Kola was still missing.

"Where the fuck is she?" Apple cursed, becoming worried.

She refused to leave without her twin. The ladies did their best to look inconspicuous. The police kept coming, heavily flooding the area, and with Kola missing, they hoped that she didn't get herself arrested.

"Leave the guns in the car. We need to walk around and find my sister," Apple said.

***

Kola carefully crept into the abandoned house three blocks away from the crime scene. She had caught a glimpse of Citi in the distance and followed her. Not too far away, it was pandemonium with police activity. But that didn't stop her from going after Citi with her pistol in hand.

The side door to the house was ajar, and Kola slowly entered the dark quarters, with the wood floors squeaking as she took steps farther inside. That worried her, because it could indicate to Citi that someone else was inside the abandoned house. But Kola continued to search for her, gun in hand and carefully looking everywhere.

Citi had been shot twice, once in the leg and the other bullet went through her side. Both injuries were through-and-through, but she was losing a lot of blood. She cowered in a shabby bedroom, her breathing shallow and fear written on her face. She tried to use a torn shirt to make a tourniquet to tie around her thigh and waist to try and stop the bleeding, but she was doing a poor job at it. She was extremely weak, and she started to feel faint.

A sudden noise from the next room, a floorboard squeaking, alerted Citi that she wasn't alone. Then Kola loomed into her view, startling her. Citi's gun was on the floor, not too far from her reach, but Kola already had the drop on her. She pointed her large cannon at a weakened and bleeding Citi—aiming for her head. Kola had her dead to rights.

"So this is it, huh?" Citi uttered faintly. "Would saying I'm sorry squash this beef?"

Kola stepped closer, the barrel of the gun in Citi's face. She was ready to shoot her point-blank in the head. But then Citi uttered, "Please, Apple. Don't do this. I'm pregnant."

Kola hesitated.

Noticing the uncertainty, Citi knew she had her ear. She started to cry and beg for her life, believing that Kola was Apple. "I want my baby to live, Apple," she said. "I'm sorry for everything. I'm truly fuckin' sorry for being a foul bitch and betraying you and Cartier. But I'm going to be a mother, Apple. You hold my baby's fate in your hands and I am begging you to spare us. Let us live . . ."

Kola started to think about her own miscarriage and unexpectedly started to feel some pity for the young and stupid bitch. The two of them stared at each other. Things were tense. And then Kola sighed, making her choice.

Kola picked up Citi's gun. "Go!" she said. "But you better get ghost and never be seen in Miami or New York again."

Citi nodded. "Really? I can leave?"

"Now! Before I change my mind. If you're lying—if you go underground and try to resurface with a new team—let's just say that I'll murder you cartel style. You'll beg for mercy but won't get it."

"I promise you, I'll never be seen again."

"Go!"

Citi knew it was over. By a miracle, she was still breathing.

EPILOGUE

She's gone, Apple. Most likely, she's dead. Besides, Citi had nothing left. We took everything from her, even her dignity," Kola proclaimed to her sister.

"You don't know that for certain, Kola," Apple griped.

"That bitch was barely breathing and was bleeding heavily. She took a lot of lead. Most likely she ended up somewhere and died slow," Kola lied.

"That bitch didn't die. Her heart still beats. I can feel that shit."

"And? Who the fuck cares? She has nothing. Cane's dead. Scar's dead. She's finished."

"I still care, Kola! I wanted her dead!" Apple fumed.

"OK, let's just say by some miracle she's alive. What is it that you want?" Kola asked.

Apple didn't reply right away. "I want the throne."

Cartier knew that Citi was just a placeholder for Apple's chronic thirst for chaos. If not Citi, then it would have been someone else. It wasn't the player; it was the game that Apple craved. She had a restless spirit, whereas Cartier needed a time-out from everything.

"Head will be home in forty-eight hours," she informed Apple. "So in two days I'm officially retiring."

Apple looked at her with skepticism. "You? Bitch, please. You'll get a taste for the old life again. I guarantee you can't just walk away from it."

"Watch me," Cartier replied.

"I'll give you six months before you and I cross paths again, and all I'm saying is keep your cartel from crossing over the Brooklyn Bridge into my territory," said Apple.

"Or what, bitch?"

"Or you got a problem," Apple joked—maybe.

"No shook hands in Brook-land," Cartier sang.

The two of them then embraced. Cartier kissed the side of Apple's face and Apple did the same.

Cartier climbed into her new Bugatti Chiron and Apple and Kola climbed into Apple's brand new Maserati and both flashy cars headed north on I-95, going back home to their respective stomping grounds.

***

Amir was in the TV room watching *The Four*. He liked the battle concept and how the best person won. The room was somewhat crowded until inmates began to slowly disperse. As Amir chuckled, he was oblivious to the looming threat and his impending doom. The three guards on duty all decided to take their breaks at precisely the same time.

Finally, Amir noticed he was almost alone. He stopped chuckling and looked up to see Corey, flanked by three of the deadliest killers inside Clinton. Corey, an impenetrable figure with his salt-and-pepper beard and cold eyes, felt betrayed.

"You thought I wouldn't find out that you were helping the bitch who murdered my son?"

"Nah, Corey, it ain't even like that."

"How is it then, nigga?"

"I-I-I-I-I-I had it all w-w-w-w-worked out. That bitch was gonna die for what s-s-s-she did to Nick. You know he's my brother. I'd do anything for him." Amir was stuttering like he had a speech impediment.

"You was gonna take his bitch and spend his bread, nigga. That's what the fuck you were gonna do!"

"Corey, don't do me like this," Amir pleaded. "You know you like a father to me."

"Kill this fool," Corey commanded.

"You owe me!" Amir screamed. "If it weren't for me it would be Nick in here! Not me! I saved your son's life, and you gonna take mine!"

Amir was surrounded, and his muscular body was rapidly penetrated by homemade shanks over three hundred times. His body had so many holes in it, it looked like Swiss cheese.

Corey stood over the body of someone he loved. It had to be done. It was the game.

**

Citi and Irving arrived in the small town of New London, Connecticut just before dusk. Citi's long brown hair with blond highlights was dyed black and pulled into a ponytail. She had nothing left—but maybe a simple future with Irving. And Irving had nothing but a promise of employment at his father's auto body shop.

Irving would become their skilled mechanic and Citi agreed to take in humble work at the front desk as a receptionist. The pay would be lousy, but she had a second chance at life and she'd prayed to God that if he allowed her to live, then she would make it work with Irving, and most importantly, she would never complain again. She'd lost her entire family, and she didn't want to be alone. She didn't want to lose Irving too. So they left Miami right away to start a new life hundreds of miles away in Connecticut.

They had arrived in town via Greyhound bus. It was a long, tiresome trip on the smelly and loud bus. When they arrived, they weren't met with any fanfare. There was no one at the bus depot to pick them up. They had to take a train and two buses before they finally got to their new home—a newly vacated, furnished one-bedroom rental over the body shop.

Citi sighed. This was it—her new life.

They entered the building, climbed the stairs one flight up, and entered their residence. Irving clicked on the lights and escorted the love of his life inside. But as soon as the light came on, the roaches started to scatter.

"Shit!" he cursed, stomping around repeatedly, trying to kill as many possible.

Citi was disgusted, but she didn't fuss.

"I'll get some roach spray and some roach baits first thing in the morning," he said.

She nodded.

He then walked her around the worn looking apartment with the shabby and smelly furniture.

"A little paint, some new sheets, and a new sofa cover, and we'll have this place looking really nice—maybe get some throw pillows, too." He smiled.

Citi stood there deadpan.

"Look, baby, as soon as I get my first paycheck, I promise I'll do whatever it takes to make you love it . . . and love me," he promised her.

But she began to weep. She was a long way from South Beach.

"Please, just give me a chance" he pleaded.

She sighed and replied, "I will, and I do." She took his hand and placed it on her stomach. "I will give you a chance because I do love you. And our baby will need both its parents."

Irving was overjoyed hearing the news that he was going to be a father. He immediately embraced Citi and hugged her and kissed her. To him, it was still a wonder how he got with a phenomenal and beautiful woman like her. If it was a dream, despite their appalling living quarters, he didn't want to wake up.

"If we're going to make this work, Irving, I need to know that we're on the same page. I need some reassurances from you."

"Anything."

"With me by your side, you will own your own body shop in three years. In five years, you will own your own fleet," she said.

"I will?" he replied with skepticism.

"Yes, you will. Now say it."

"With you by my side, I can do anything," he said.

It wasn't verbatim, but it was enough. Irving knew behind every great man was an exceptional woman.

He wrapped his arms around her and whispered in her ear, "What day is it?"

She squealed, "It's Black Love Monday."

BROOKLYN Bombshells

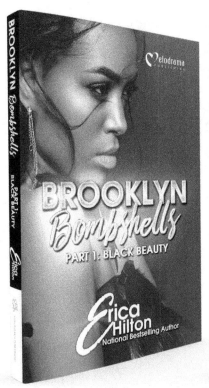

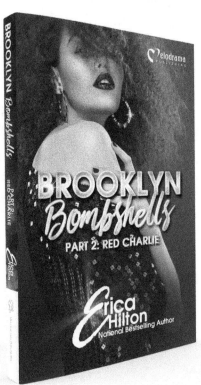

THE SERIES BY

EXCERPT FROM
BROOKLYN BOMBSHELLS
PART 1: BLACK BEAUTY

BY ERICA HILTON

Bacardi was coming unhinged. The weeks following the killing of the cop, she sunk into a deep depression and started to drink more with her husband. Now the girls would come home and find both of their parents drunk. But the drinking wasn't the only thing the girls had to worry about with Bacardi. Sometimes after downing a half bottle of Hennessy, Bacardi 151, E&J, or Jack Daniels, Bacardi found herself worked up and angry. She would sloppily get dressed and march toward the front door with a knife in hand. When either Charlie or Claire would confront her, she would curse them out and shout, "Get the fuck out my way, bitch! I'm gonna fuck that bitch up! She cost me my fuckin' job and that bitch still owes me five hundred dollars!"

"No, you can't go over there, Ma! You need to fuckin' chill out!" Charlie would shout at her.

Charlie would sometimes have to wrestle her mother away from the front door. They couldn't afford to make things worse for themselves, especially with a criminal case still pending in the courts. With Bacardi unable to take out her anger and frustration on Keisha, she went to the next best thing, Chanel. The more depressed Bacardi got, the more she took it out on Chanel. She would burst into her youngest daughter's room at random and throw venomous threats and insults at Chanel. But it didn't stop with words. Sometimes she came at Chanel with a belt, a stick, or whatever she could get her hands on and tried to beat the black off her. She would call her daughter black and ugly even though they were the same complexion.

Today was a day that Chanel decided to take Landy's advice and defend herself against Bacardi's unrelenting foul mouth. It all started over a Twinkie.

"Who drank the last of my Pepsi?" Bacardi asked as she stared into the almost empty refrigerator.

From the living room Chanel rolled her eyes. "I did."

Bacardi snorted and slammed the refrigerator shut before sauntering over to the cupboard looking for something sweet. She reached for the Twinkies only to grab an empty box. She looked inside, shook it, and then turned the box over as if it was a magic trick and a Twinkie would magically drop to the floor. The rage began as a slow, simmering emotion slowing coursing through her body. Just as Chanel placed the last Twinkie bite into her mouth, Bacardi appeared. Chanel could see her mother looming over her from her peripheral vision.

"You ate my muthafuckin' Twinkie?" Her voice was an unwavering, accusatory growl.

Wide-eyed and frightened, Chanel stopped licking the cream from her fingers. She swallowed hard and simply said, "Yes."

Bacardi's rage was still on pause. She knew that if she pressed play she might kill her daughter in there. She continued with, "What . . . the . . . fuck…I tell your greedy ass 'bout touching my personal shit?"

"You didn't even buy the Twinkies; Charlie did. So, technically, the food belongs to my sister."

"Oh, so you Claire now? You think you're a smart bitch?"

"I'm only playing the game you started."

Bacardi placed the palm of her hand to her forehead and simply breathed in and out to calm her nerves. There was always one child that gave each parent hell, and Chanel was it.

"Chanel, tread muthafuckin' lightly. I'm tryin' to be nice here, bitch, 'cause I'm on my menstrual. But if you ever eat my fuckin' Twinkies I will break ya fuckin' neck. Do your ugly li'l black ass—"

"You black and ugly too!" Chanel hollered. "Look in the mirror, bitch! We're twins!"

That remark stopped Bacardi dead in her tracks. Her? Ugly? In her day she had her choice of the biggest ballers in Brooklyn. Everyone lusted after Bernice. And she was hardly black. In Bacardi's eyes she was 'brown-skinned'—imaginary shades lighter than her daughter.

Bacardi let out an egotistical snicker. "Chanel, I'm gonna keep it one-hundred wit' you 'cause you too stupid to see the truth wit' your own eyes. I don't know where you came from. I think you got switched at birth like that other li'l black child on the news. You don't look like me, and you damn sure don't look like your father. There's some other family out there missing a troll 'cause my pussy only pushes out dime pieces and that, you're not!"

"My black is beautiful, Bacardi, and if you don't think so then your mind is still stuck on a plantation! You Uncle Tom turd!" Chanel had been doing her homework. She was ready.

When Bacardi heard 'Uncle Tom', she finally lost it. Her strong fists beat mercilessly across Chanel's arms, head, and back. The punches were solid, quick, and unforgiving. She pulled globs of hair from her daughter's head—just ripped out bundles of hair from the roots. Chanel refused to cry out and got some slaps and punches in too.

"Eat my Twinkie again, bitch!" Bacardi continued to yell as she wailed on her third-born. She needed to make this about the Twinkie then skin color.

Chanel broke free and ran into the kitchen with Bacardi right on her heels. The butter knife was the only weapon she could grab. She missed the serrated steak knife by an inch.

Wildly Chanel swung the knife at her mother as Bacardi blocked each blow with her forearms. The dull butter knife only left scratches and long welts, but the message was sent. Chanel was no longer easy prey.

A drunken Butch was able to pull the two apart. But things were growing so ugly in the Brown household, Chanel thought there were only two ways for her to escape it—run away or commit suicide.

SHATTERED ILLUSIONS

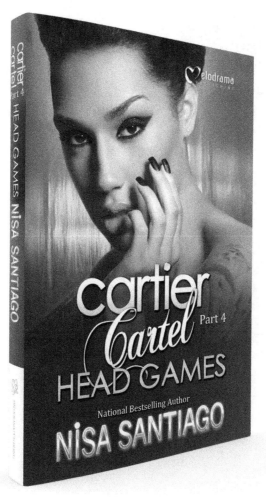

Cartier is back from South Beach and anxious to begin the next chapter of her life with Head. She soon awakens from her love fantasy, however, and realizes that her dark knight isn't all he seems.

With her love life on the rocks yet again, Cartier has a nightmare case of déjà vu that she must snap out of. Vowing to harden her heart for good this time, she redirects her energy to forming a new Cartier Cartel.

OFF WITH HER HEAD

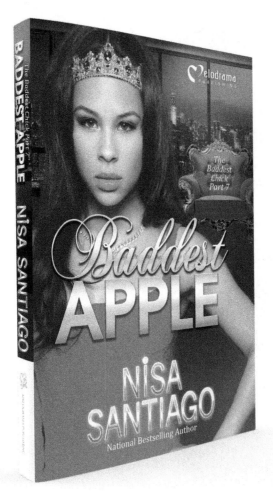

Even with South Beach in her rearview, Apple is still unable to settle down and focus on being a mom. Not when the streets keep talking about Queenie, an enigmatic sista who is calling herself the Queen of New York.

Queenie, a hardcore former drug mule, has seen and done it all in her young life. She doesn't scare easily, if at all. When it's time for her to step up to her newfound adversary, Apple, her heart skips no beats.

Apple refuses to give up her title after just reclaiming it. She's determined to snatch the crown from Queenie and see her bow down to the real queen.

CPSIA information can be obtained
at www.ICGtesting.com
Printed in the USA
LVHW032041201218
601223LV00018B/622/P